tempting promises

WHITLOCK
FARMS

Forbidden Hearts

Broken Dreams

Tempting Promises

Forgotten Desires

tempting promises

NEW YORK TIMES BESTSELLING AUTHOR
CORINNE MICHAELS

Tempting Promises

Cover Design: Sommer Stein, Perfect Pear Creative
Editing: Nancy Smay
Proofreading: Ashley Williams, Julia Griffis & Michele Ficht
Cover Art drawing: Samaiya Beaumont

dedication

To Stephanie Hubenak, because you manage to change them all to say
your name anyway. Might as well give you one ...

Dear Reader,

It is always my goal to write a beautiful love story that will capture your heart and leave a lasting impression. However, I want all readers to be comfortable. Therefore, if you want to be aware of any possible CW please click the link below to take you to the book page where there is a link that will dropdown. If you do not need this, please go forth and I hope you love this book filled with all the pieces of my heart.

https://corinnemichaels.com/books/tempting-promises/

author's note

Thank you for purchasing Tempting Promises. I truly hope you enjoy this book as much as I enjoyed writing it.

Tempting Promises utilizes American Sign Language through the story. For better ease of reading, it is not written in proper ASL format. ASL is different from written English with it's own rules and structure. Most of the time, my characters will speak aloud at the same time as they sign. There are no clear rules on how to format sign language and I went back and forth with how to do it. In the end, I chose quote marks and italic.

ASL has its own dialect, which is called glossing. You may notice words not contracted, this is because there is not a contraction form for each word. This is mostly done when we are signing.

As always, I do my best to write situations and characters the best possible. Any discrepancies are mine alone and based on my experiences or those who I consulted with.

I want to address the d/Deaf writing in regards to Olivia specifically. The D/DHH community is so diverse and it is honestly a spectrum - no deaf/hard of hearing individual is the same. Everyone has a different experience, whether it's the medical diagnosis/aspect or the community aspect. I consulted with many people and there was diversity among those people to which I used my best judgment in writing. Olivia was born deaf, therefore, she would identify as Deaf (capitalized). I use this several times even though we are not in her point of view. Some members of the D/DHH do not choose to capitalize the word, some do. I am always striving to learn and do better, and hope that the Deaf representation is seen with compassion and understanding as well as bringing awareness to what some may experience.

one

ROWAN

"**D**o *not tell your parents I brought you here*," I sign to my niece, Olivia. She may be ten, but her father doesn't think she needs to frequent the livestock auctions or anything that might get him into hot water with Liv's mother. It's better for everyone if we keep this our little secret.

Olivia grins as we're looking for seats. "*Brought me where? You would never take me somewhere I am not allowed, Uncle Rowan.*"

I love this kid. And much to my brother's dismay, she likes me best. I wink at her and point to two open seats.

Olivia is seriously the best kid in the world. She's so much like me at her age in a lot of ways. We fish together at least once a month, and she enjoys working on the farm with me. What I love most is that she lets nothing stand in her way. She never lets being deaf define her—it's just a part of who she is, and we don't treat her any different than other kids her age.

"*Can I hold the paddle?*" she asks with bright eyes.

"*No.*"

Her brows furrow. "*Why?*"

"*Because you will cost me a fortune.*"

Olivia shakes her head and then opens the auction booklet.

I seriously hope Asher or Olivia's overprotective mother doesn't

1

have some tracking device on her phone because he really will kick my ass—well, try to—if he finds out we're here. While the auction isn't a bad place necessarily, there have been a few fights when things got heated, and since he's a cop, he's had to break them up.

Plus, some of the ranch hands who attend drink too much and the rancher's daughters . . . well, they like ranch hands and dress for that—if you know what I mean. It can get rowdy.

Speaking of one of those daughters, there's one across the way who's smiling rather alluringly at me.

She waves.

I wave back, aware that I have my niece with me because I would definitely like to take her home tonight.

Olivia nudges me to get my attention. *"Are you bidding on anything?"*

"Maybe."

Honestly, I only came to the auction because my ranch manager, Micah, said the last two auctions had great bull options and I needed to see what the competition was buying. With the capital I just put up to buy a couple of extra pastures, I'm a little tight on cash. However, opportunity is priceless and my goal is to grow my farm and replenish my coffers, so to speak.

"You need a better bull," she signs.

"There is nothing wrong with the bull I have now."

Olivia shakes her head. *"He is old, and Micah said he is not as good as he was."*

"Are you a cow expert now?" I ask her with a smirk.

She shrugs and then goes back to reading the list of animals to be auctioned off. Then she taps my leg and points to one that'll be coming up.

It could be a good one, but it also could end up as a dud, but that's part of owning a farm, I guess.

Olivia glances down at her phone for the hundredth time, and I nudge her. *"Your dad and Phoebe are fine."*

Asher and Phoebe had to go to the doctor and needed someone to stay with Olivia. Normally, my sister would have the honor, since the two of them are "besties" or whatever crap they say. If not her, then the next logical choice is Grady, but since he's flying today, that went out the window, which leaves me. I'm always the last choice, but I'm Liv's favorite.

"*I know.*"

She doesn't, but it's okay.

"*If you say so,*" I sign back to her.

Olivia goes back to reading, circling another bull. Clearly, she's not going to give this up or she just really wants to use the paddle.

I turn my attention back to the group of beautiful women over in the corner who keep looking my way. I wink at one, who smiles and then dips her head a little.

From behind me, I hear a voice that instantly makes me want to leave. "If it isn't the bane of my existence."

I turn, coming face to face with the one woman in Sugarloaf I can't stand. "If it isn't Charlotte Sullivan. My favorite person in the whole world."

Olivia shifts as well, smiling and waving energetically at her.

Charlotte waves back. "Will you interpret for me?"

I nod. "Can't promise I won't ad-lib."

The sigh that comes from her says she expects that from me. I am the villain in her story. At least she knows that Olivia can read lips and, if I do sign something mean, she has a chance of knowing the truth. "Hi, Olivia, are you having fun?" Charlotte asks.

I translate. Olivia nods.

"She said yes," I say to Charlotte, who rolls her eyes.

"Tell her I really love her hair."

I translate incorrectly. "*She said you took her chair.*"

Olivia jerks back. "*I'm sorry.*"

This is really fucking fun. I look to Charlotte. "She said she's sorry."

Now it's time to see the confusion on her face. "Oh. Okay."

I fill her in. "I might have told her you said something else. Might."

Charlotte's green eyes narrow and she lets out a heavy breath through her nose. "God, you're so immature."

I lift my hands to sign to Olivia. *"God, I love the smell of manure."*

Liv looks to Charlotte, then to me, and then back to Charlotte before shrugging.

"She's not sure she agrees," I tell Charlotte.

"Thanks, genius."

I turn to Liv. *"She thinks I'm a genius."*

Olivia's shoulders shake with laughter. *"She does not."*

"She does."

"She didn't mean it. We all know Charlotte doesn't like you."

"What did she say?" Charlotte asks.

I sign and speak aloud so they both know my answer. *"Olivia said she doesn't like you because you are mean to me."*

Olivia shakes her head quickly. *"That's not what I said."*

"Fine," I say to them both. *"She didn't say that. She said that she knows you don't like me."*

"She would be correct," Charlotte says slowly.

Olivia taps my leg. *"Why don't you tell her how great you are?"*

"Because she's stupid and hates me for no reason."

My niece side eyes me with a smirk. *"I heard it's because you cheated on her sister."*

"What is she saying?" Charlotte butts in again, but I ignore her.

"Where did you hear that?"

Olivia shrugs. *"Everyone knows."*

Everyone knows, my ass. No one knows because it's not fucking true. Sure, two years ago I was sleeping with Aurora. We had a fling. One where I made it crystal fucking clear that it was just that—a fling. There were no feelings, no dating. I couldn't have cheated on her because we weren't even together. However, I didn't sleep with anyone else when we were having our sexfest, so it's bullshit, regardless.

"It's a lie," I tell Olivia.

"I know, the Whitlocks don't like cheaters."

No, we do not. And there's a sound reason for it. All of us

watched our mother's husband number three destroy her world when he cheated on her. It was me, the youngest son, who picked up her pieces and tried to be there for her as she cried at night. I remember how broken she was, devastated that he could do that to her when she gave up everything for him.

I would never, ever cheat on a woman.

However, Aurora didn't like it when I told her I didn't want more and so she spread her rumors far and wide.

Charlotte groans. "Do you know how rude you're being?"

I turn to her, my brows raised. "Coming from you who spends hours doing nothing but talking shit about me? Get over it, sweetheart."

"Don't call me sweetheart."

"Sour-heart? How about no-heart? Or maybe blackheart? I think that's the most appropriate."

Charlotte chuckles and lets out a deep sigh. "Please, we all know who the blackheart is here. Spoiler alert." She leans in. "It ain't me."

I turn to Liv and sign. *"See? There's nothing good at the auction."*

Olivia laughs silently and points a finger at me. *"Tell her the truth about what I sign."*

I nod.

"Promise?"

"Yes, I promise," I assure her.

Charlotte groans. "Why are you such an ass? I swear, if you weren't with your niece, I wouldn't be this nice to you."

"Yeah, you're a ray of sunshine now." I lift my hands to sign. *"Olivia wants to tell you something, and I was promising her that I wouldn't . . . interpret the words differently. That's what we just said. The stuff before is between us Whitlocks."*

My niece looks to the she-devil behind me, and I speak as Olivia signs. *"I understand sometimes why you think Uncle Rowan is stupid. Sometimes he is, but he is not a bad guy. If he was, I wouldn't love him so much."*

Charlotte gives her a soft smile. "He really is stupid."

I roll my eyes but sign it correctly.

Olivia's grin grows. *"Aunt Brynn says all boys are."*

I'm going to have to talk to my sister about that comment. I sign to Olivia and say it so Charlotte isn't excluded. See, I can be nice. *"All boys your age are idiots. Don't ever talk to them."*

There. I can impart my unclely advice where needed. Olivia is too young to even think about boys, let alone date. Not that I think Asher would ever let her near a boy, sometimes a father needs backup, which is where I can come in.

The auctioneer announces that they are calling forward the bull we were interested in. I nudge Olivia and point to the bull she has circled eleven times. She pulls out the paddle and I sigh. Looks like I'm buying a cow today.

Charlotte clears her throat. "You're looking at that bull?"

I turn my head to see hers right there, reading over my shoulder. Great. "Maybe, why?"

She shakes her head and shifts back in her seat. "No reason."

The hair on the back of my neck stands. She wants that bull. She wants it, and I want nothing else but to thwart whatever she wants. Like buying the land I just did. While I wanted to expand the farm, I wasn't planning on moving on it right now.

When that plot came up for sale, I went back and forth, until I heard Charlotte put an offer in as it's between both our farms. Another plot like that wouldn't come up until who knows when. My farm is smaller than most in Sugarloaf. I do all right, but we're not a major operation at this point.

I brought Micah on as manager last year, and since then, we've increased revenue month over month and he convinced me I should start thinking of adding more land so we can increase our cattle.

"Are you planning to bid on that bull?" I ask.

"Not sure."

Yeah she is.

Olivia looks to me with curiosity on her face.

"You can make the first bid when I tell you, then I need the paddle."

"Why?"

I smile. *"Because Uncle Rowan is going to kick Charlotte's ass. Don't tell your dad I said ass—twice."*

Olivia nods and then holds on to the paddle like a lifeline. Even if I don't win, which I will, it's fun seeing Liv happy.

The bidding begins as paddles are lifted and Olivia is watching me, waiting. I've learned that, when it comes to the auction, patience is key. I need to see who else is bidding and use a strategy to not let the bidding get out of control.

I turn back to Charlotte, who is sitting with her back straight. Her hand lifts and then drops. She's totally going after this bull.

I go to give Liv the signal, but Charlotte bids before me. As soon as the auctioneer goes around again, I give Liv the thumbs-up.

She throws the paddle up in the air with a lot of enthusiasm and beams when he points to her.

Charlotte groans, and I turn to see her green eyes filled with frustration. "Ugh, you."

God, this is fun. I lift my baseball hat in a howdy gesture, knowing it'll further irritate her.

She raises her paddle, taking the high bid again. Charlotte is the opposite of her sister in every way. You'd never know they were related based on their looks. Aurora is tall, skinny, blonde with brown eyes. She's pretty, but she's got nothing on Charlotte.

Charlotte is stunning, arresting, fucking breathtaking. Until she opens her mouth and the hate for me falls from those pouty lips.

She's short—maybe comes up to my pecs—and is dark haired with green eyes. She's a spitfire and no one can banter like her.

Another person enters the bidding, probably because the two of us are bidding, so they either want to drive up the price for fun or they think that, since we're both going after it, this bull is worth something.

I lift the paddle, feeling something in my gut that there's something special about this bull.

And then Charlotte does.

Of course she's going to make this painful. Even if she doesn't want this bull, she'll enjoy making me pay higher than he's probably worth.

I bid again.

She does too.

Back and forth we go until I'm at the point where I'm not going any higher.

Olivia's eyes are wide as she watches this go on, bouncing in her seat.

I'm holding as the winner, the announcer says going once, twice, and I wait for her to take her shot, but she doesn't, and it's over.

I turn to Olivia. "*We won.*"

"*Good job.*"

I nod, not really agreeing since I'm paying about three hundred dollars more than it's worth, but I won.

Charlotte stands and I turn to face her, and the normal hostility when she looks at me seems muted. Then she gives me a slow, evil smile. "I didn't want him anyway, congrats on spending way more than he's worth." She looks to Liv. "Bye, Olivia."

Then I watch her walk away, wanting to scream.

two

CHARLOTTE

"I understand that, sir, I really do, but I'm asking for two weeks. I swear, we'll have the money by then."

At least I hope so. I plan to sell off a few more calves that were just born. While I need them, I need to pay my mortgage more. I feel like I'm robbing Peter to pay Paul, but Peter is about out of cash.

"I understand your issue, Ms. Sullivan, and I want to help."

"Then, please . . . give me two more weeks. If I don't have the money by then, I'll . . . I'll have to sell."

And that makes me want to die just thinking about, but I won't have a choice.

"Two weeks."

I exhale deeply. "Two weeks."

Yeah, I have no idea how I'm going to keep doing this. My farm is in trouble, and it has been in my family for six generations. I can't be the one to let it fall apart.

I sit back in the kitchen chair, not wanting to look at the ever-mounting pile of bills. "Think, Charlotte."

Aurora and I both got ownership of this place when my grandparents died. I'd been basically running it when Pop got sick, though. Aurora never worked on the farm, just owned it. I love this place. It's rich with memories of running around the fields and catching fireflies, and then, as we got older, drinking and cow tipping.

Pop asked me to keep this farm alive. To do whatever necessary to not let it fail.

Little did I know that a month after that conversation, we'd lose them both only five days apart.

And with that came the farm and the bills. All the dreams I had of going to college, seeing the world, or finding love were ripped away from me, especially when my sister asked me to buy her out.

My phone rings, snapping me out of my thoughts, and I see my sister's face pop on the screen.

"Hey!"

"Hey yourself! How are you?"

Falling apart. "I'm great! I'm just getting ready to make dinner."

Which consists of Ramen because it's all I can afford.

"Awesome! I'm heading out to dinner with Ryan, he's taking me to some steakhouse he loves and then a rooftop bar somewhere in midtown," Aurora says all dreamily.

My sister is living her best life in New York, refusing to come back to Sugarloaf, even if just to visit.

All thanks to the asshole whose farm butts up to mine.

"Wow, that sounds so fun."

"Are you doing anything tonight?"

I sigh, hating the answer. "Does nursing a newborn calf sound fun?"

I can only imagine Aurora's face at that. "Not even a little."

"You're sure you don't want to come home and visit? Help out a bit?"

She goes silent and I know what's coming. "You know that's not a good idea."

My sister is a lot of things, beautiful, funny, smart, and a great cook, but brave is not one. If Rowan Whitlock had humiliated me like he did her, I would've kicked him in the balls. I wouldn't have just cried to my friends and family. Hell no. He would've been the one in tears.

No matter how many pep talks and solidarity sister speeches I gave, she just thought it was best to leave town.

So, she sold her land to me, and left for a better life.

Which left me in debt.

"You're happy now, Aurora. You have a great job and an amazing boyfriend, but you really can't handle coming home for just a few days?"

"No, I can't. You don't get it, Char, I saw him with her. I was there and it wasn't just my heart he broke, it was my spirit too."

I love my sister, I really do, but dear God, is she dramatic. "He didn't break your spirit! Look at you now. I really hate him and hate the power you give him."

"I wish I was like you, but I'm not. I blame it on my daddy issues." She laughs at the end, and I do as well.

"I have them too."

She acts as though she's the only one who lost her parents. I was there when he died too. I've felt the pain of being an orphan, but that doesn't mean I use that as an excuse for every bad decision I make.

"Not nearly as bad as me." She's not wrong there. "Although, maybe you have them bad but in another way. When is the last time you had a date?"

I can't go back that far. "I don't need dates. I need to work."

And to save the farm.

"Granny would want you to be happy, not to work yourself old and lonely." I open my mouth to tell her that Granny would also want me to save the farm. I swear, it's there, on the tip of my tongue, but she gasps and then squeals. "I have to go, that's Ryan."

Right. "Have fun. I love you."

"I love you too. Come see me this weekend. I know you're busy, but you can take a day or two. I think you'd fall in love with New York, Char. It's . . . a world of its own and one far better than cow pastures."

I say the exact thing I say each time she tries to convince me of this. "I'll think about it."

"Yeah, yeah. Love you."

And with that, my sister is off to live her life, and I'm trying to figure out how to save mine.

⚷

"Why won't you come with us, Charlotte?" my best friend Faye says as she rifles through my closet for a shirt.

"I don't want to go this time."

Which is a lie. It's more that I can't afford to go.

"You love the mountain cabin."

"Yes, but I'm busy on the farm, and it's really not a good idea to go away right now." I try because it's partially true. I had to let go of one of my last ranch hands this morning. I can't afford him. I was able to keep one, because he agreed to do whatever tasks I needed as long as he could stay in the back house rent free. So, while I'm losing the rental income that was helping me pay my mortgage, my only paying ranch hand more than makes up for it.

Basically, I can pay the electric this month and worry about the next one later.

"Please, we know that the boys can handle it. Come on, Char, you haven't come the last two years, and each time, when we get back, you bitch about how you wish you went. You deserve a little fun."

Faye doesn't really understand what it means to work and have responsibilities. She's grown up with a silver spoon in her perfect lips, even if she doesn't act like it. Her father is a sought-after plastic surgeon who makes ridiculous money. She goes and does as she wants and no one says a word. However, she's one of the kindest and most selfless people I know. One who is constantly supporting the charities and foundations that need her.

She's like a fairy princess, sprinkling her happiness all over.

"Fun and running a business don't really go hand in hand. Since becoming certified organic, it's a ton of work. Like, a ton," I remind her.

She pulls out a shirt. "Ha! I knew I left it here."

Looking at it, I'm incredibly confused. "In what, eighth grade?"

"Tenth, but it's still cute. We'll call it vintage." Faye sits on the bed next to me, flopping back so we're both staring up at the ceiling. "Do you remember when we used to do this as kids? Wish on the stars on your ceiling."

I turn my head to face her. "You always wished for a boy."

"And you always wished for a horse. I'm wondering if that wasn't the first sign of your issues."

"Yeah, wanting a horse instead of a boy, totally an issue," I say with a laugh.

Faye sighs. "I worry about you."

"I'm fine."

"Are you? You seem out of it the last few months. You know you can talk to me, right?"

I do know she thinks that, but I can't. Faye would jump in and fix it, no questions asked. She'd pay all my bills, and I would forever owe her. I can't do that. Through the years of our friendship, I've seen so many people use her for her money or connections. Her father is a plastic surgeon for A-list celebrities. She lives a pretty amazing life thanks to his funds, and everyone wants to be in Faye's life just for a chance to be at a party with her. I'll never give her a reason to think I'm like them.

So, I give her what truth I can. "I miss my grandparents. I miss my sister. I miss the way life was easier when they were all around."

She kisses the tip of my nose and then taps it. "You still have me."

"I do."

"But I get it. Aurora isn't far, though. She can come home and visit, can't she?"

I sit up, groaning as I do. "She could, but she won't because of Rowan."

"It's been like, two years already, why is she still letting him bother her?" Faye asks the million-dollar question.

"No idea, he's not even that hot."

15

My friend laughs. "And that's a lie too. He's ridiculously hot. We all know that, but he's a player. No one wants to date him, but we all want to fuck him."

I roll my eyes. "Gross."

"Tell me you don't."

"I don't," I say immediately.

"Oh, please! I am so not buying that. If Rowan Whitlock wasn't your sister's ex, and you didn't think he was a total douchebag, you wouldn't want to bang him?"

I really hate the direction this conversation is taking. "Sure, if he was a totally different guy inside his body, I guess."

Faye sighs dreamily. "I'd totally let him rock my world."

Seriously, my friends are all in need of help. I nudge her and stand. "Thanks for the invite and the break, but I need to get back to work."

There are cows to feed, and I have two expecting that I need to check on again. Not to mention, I need to try to patch the roof area on the barn before it snows this weekend. Lord knows it'll cave if I don't figure something out.

She stands and grabs the shirt she found. "I'm serious about the mountain trip. It'll be, like, six of us. Joey is inviting his friends, and it'll be fun. Maybe you'll even meet a guy. Who knows? I want you to come with us."

"I really can't, Faye."

"Don't say no. It's in a month and a half, and who knows, by then you may have the cows or whatever in a place so you can go for a *weekend*. I repeat, a weekend. Not a week. Not ten days. Just three whole days of relaxing, drinking, and laughing. I'm sure the guys are going to hike because they always do, and we know you like that. It's a win-win."

She's freaking relentless. It's better if I placate her a little. "I'll think about it."

Her eyes brighten as she bounces. "That's almost a yes!"

"It's also almost a no."

"You're so pessimistic. Slap that frown upside down and smile a little, boys like that."

"Yes, I'm so worried about the boys," I say as we link arms, walking out of my room. "Go do whatever it is you do all day. I am going to tend to the cows."

Her nose scrunches. "I don't know how we are friends sometimes. You're all . . . country, and I'm . . . not."

That's true. "It's by design."

"I guess so. All right, I'll be sure to annoy you in the next few days, and seriously, dig out those boots or whatever it is you need because no matter what you say, you're going. I love you, bye."

"Love you back. Bye."

She shakes her head and heads out to her car. Her very new, very ridiculous SUV that looks more like a tank, but with the way she drives, it's the people around her who need the armored vehicle. Faye waves from the window, puts the car in gear, heads toward my house, which is not the way she should be going, slams on the brakes and then smiles.

Dear God.

"Reverse is the R, Faye!" I yell out the door.

Her window lowers. "Sorry! I'm glad I caught that."

"Yeah, me too, otherwise I'd be homeless!"

Which is still a possibility if I don't find a way through these bills.

three

ROWAN

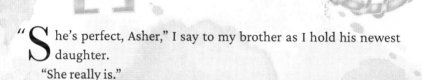

"S he's perfect, Asher," I say to my brother as I hold his newest daughter.

"She really is."

"She's already spoiled by her daddy," Phoebe says as she smiles up at him.

God, these two are so grossly in love it's nauseating. Honestly, both of my siblings are. Grady making his kissy faces at Addison. They both need an intervention.

"Well, of course she is because that's my damn job."

I scoff. "Your job is to fight off the assholes like us when they come sniffing around your girls."

"That won't be an issue," Asher says with a half laugh. "No one is getting near my daughters."

So he thinks. "Oh, Brynn reminded me that yesterday was also your birthday. So, happy belated birthday. I didn't get you anything."

Apparently, he went out to dinner with Phoebe and Olivia to celebrate, and her water broke before they even ordered. She had a pretty easy labor, and Sienna Whitlock is now here to be adored and doted on.

"I got the best gift from Phoebe." Asher's eyes are all mushy as he looks at his daughter.

"You know, you've become someone else since you fell in love. You're all . . . I don't know, weird."

He shrugs. "Love does that."

Whatever.

"How are you going to handle this much estrogen in this house?" I joke. My brother went from basically living alone, except for when Olivia came to visit, to having a fiancée and now another daughter. Yeah, that sounds like the eighth circle of hell if you ask me.

"That, I'm not sure of."

Phoebe giggles. "A lot of patience."

He laughs, and I hand him back Sienna. She wiggles a little and then settles in his arms. "You did good, Ash. You got a wonderful woman and two amazing daughters. As much as I joke about your home full of girls, I'm happy for you."

"This could be you, Rowan, you just have to put the past where it belongs and realize we're not Mom when it comes to relationships."

Asher and I are similar in how we view—or I should say he *viewed*—relationships. I'm the only one who hasn't abandoned the belief that love is a weakness. How many times do people do the dumbest shit in the name of love? All the fucking time. They convince themselves that it's okay someone did a horrible thing because they love you. No thank you. I'm perfectly fine being single and only worrying about my damn self. I watched my mother fall for it time after time. I fell for it once, in high school, and decided that was a road I was never going down again.

"The past is where it belongs, thank you very much. Anyway, I'm happy for you, and maybe someday you'll get your balls back." I shrug.

"I like his balls right where they are," Phoebe jokes.

I bet she does.

"Speaking of balls, I heard you got yours handed to you recently." Asher grins, and I have no idea what he's talking about.

"When?"

"When Charlotte got you to, *once again*, pay more for something you thought she wanted at the auction. The auction you tried to keep Olivia from telling me about, I might add."

I shake my head, hating my brother and my traitorous niece. "I didn't tell her to lie, just to omit our location, and I didn't pay too much. Micah is happy with the purchase, he said it was a great move."

"How are you funding all this?"

By dying a little inside each day.

"Don't worry about it," I tell him. "You didn't want the family farm, if I remember correctly."

Asher raises his hands. "I'm sure you've got it figured out."

Yeah, I don't, but it's fine. I have a possible contract that will give the farm more than enough funding.

Maybe.

If I don't keep spending like it's my damn life's mission.

However, my farm is now producing a steady income, which is keeping us from falling into any kind of debt.

There's a knock on the door, and Brynn tiptoes inside. Her face looks as if it's ready to crack from her smile as she walks over to Asher and Phoebe. "Sienna, you beautiful thing. I am your auntie, and I will spoil you rotten for the rest of your life and love you the most."

"You were here after me, so I think you lost that one."

Brynn glares at me for a second before fussing over the baby. "Oh you're so tiny and so perfect."

Asher walks over, pulling Sienna closer and kissing her forehead before handing her to Brynn.

She coos over the baby while Asher sits beside Phoebe, his arm wrapped around her. Phoebe stares at him, and a part of me—a very small part—is jealous. My brother deserves happiness, and he's found it in a woman who is looking at him as though he is her reason to breathe.

But she isn't who makes my chest ache just a bit—it's Asher. He's finally found someone worth putting himself out there for. He loves Phoebe beyond measure and is building a perfect family.

At one point, I really wanted this, but I'll never have it.

I step out into the hallway, feeling shit I really would rather not feel, and shake my head.

What the hell is wrong with me?

I don't want or need love or some woman who is going to make me crazy more often than not.

No, I need someone who isn't going to give me shit when I need to work, or fight because she woke up after the me in her dream did something stupid.

"Rowan?" Brynlee's soft voice calls my name as her hand rests on my shoulder.

"Hey."

"You okay?"

Always the worrier, this one.

"I'm fine, why?"

"Because I happen to know you fairly well and something bothered you enough to make you leave the room."

"Too much affection makes me itch." I give her a half-truth.

Brynlee, being the annoying and overly observant sister she is, narrows her eyes. "Or makes you wonder what's wrong with you?"

"There's not a damn thing wrong with me."

She scoffs. "Oh, dear brother, how wrong you are about that. You sleep with these random girls and don't even bother to know more than their first names. You work like a lunatic, trying to prove whatever it is you need to prove, and you pretend that what Asher and Grady have doesn't bother you."

"Only one of those was correct, and that's the first—which, I might add, I'm totally fine with. Thank you for the psychoanalysis, though, it was adorable." I tap her nose, and she tries to bite my finger, but I pull back before she can.

"Stop deflecting, jackass."

I sigh, knowing this is going to be one of those scabs she picks until I bleed. "I'm not deflecting. Look, I don't have some deep emotional wound that I need healed. I'm happy with my life, Brynn. I like being single, not worrying about any of the bullshit. The farm is growing and thriving, I don't have a spare minute for dating."

"If you don't think what you saw go down with Mom fucked you up, you're out of your damn mind."

Lord deliver me from sisters. "I appreciate," I say the words through my teeth, "your help, but I came out to the hall to call Micah."

Her arms cross over her chest, and she grins. "Micah?"

"Yes, Micah. You know, my ranch manager."

"You're full of shit, but . . . I've learned that you three stubborn asses have to figure it out on your own. Just know I love you and that what Asher and Grady have right now could easily be yours too. You just have to let yourself."

"Thank you, Dr. Brynlee."

"Any time." She pushes up on her toes and kisses my cheek. "I love you."

"I love you, too, even if you're a pain in my freaking ass."

And it's true, my brothers and I are fiercely protective of Brynn, and I'm completely content with her being the only woman I'll ever love.

⚷

"This is a big commitment, Mr. Whitlock. Are you sure the farm can produce quality at this level?" asks Damon Knight, the co-owner of Knight Food Distribution.

"Absolutely. We've increased our production schedule along with expanding our farm to ensure we can continue to grow with contracts like this," I assure him.

This is the big account I need. It'll get me out of debt and fund various improvements that need to be made. Knight Food Distribution is the number one supplier for schools, and what do kids drink at lunch? Milk.

I caught wind about a year ago that their current distributor was having quality issues. I found out that Carson Knight, who co-owns and runs the company since his father is getting ready to retire, has hired Grady a few times for courier jobs.

My brother is brilliant and was able to get us a meeting.

However, we're a fraction of the size as their last supplier.

Micah clears his throat. "We also go through rigorous third-party testing to make sure we can catch and correct any issues. Though, they have yet to find anything, so we're clearly doing something right."

I nod. "Micah helps oversee the operations, and neither of us have any doubt that we'll be able to meet your needs."

"Well, all of this sounds good. I'd like to come out to the farm with my son and see the facilities. Carson likes the idea of having several smaller farms producing so we can add or drop without a shortage."

"There won't be issues from us," I say firmly, needing to reaffirm my confidence and commitment.

He steeples his fingers and bows his head. "Then we'll make arrangements to come out there for a day or two. We have another dairy farmer in Sugarloaf we plan to visit as well. My office will be in touch."

The three of us stand, shake hands, and Micah and I walk out as my mind reels. Who else could he be meeting in Sugarloaf? The other farms are smaller than us, and already have contracts that they're barely meeting.

When we exit the building and are standing on the busy New York sidewalk, I turn to Micah. "Who?"

"I was going to ask you the same thing. The Mitchell's farm is way too small to take on the volume we will. The Arrowoods aren't even farming, really. They have a few cows probably for a tax break. The only other farm that might want to grow is . . ."

"Charlotte," I say her name as a curse. That damn woman is

going to drive me to drink. How the hell she found out about this group is beyond me. She doesn't have the connections I did with Grady. Beyond that, she can't possibly produce that much milk. Not what this group wants to see, at least.

"She's ambitious, I gotta give her that," Micah says with admiration.

"She's an idiot. She can't do it."

He tilts his head. "I wouldn't put anything past her. She's driven, smart, and she could do a lot if she was able to expand. It's a good thing you got the land she wanted. If she'd gotten it, it would be her getting this contract before we even walked in."

The sad part is he's right. Charlotte isn't stupid, not by any means. When she took her farm organic, it opened a few doors that I can't get entrance into. She's one of only two in our county that actually got the certification, which means she can sell at a much higher price point.

Even though my farm operates almost the same way.

"They would want to bring organic milk in? That seems like a pretty high price to pay when most schools can't afford it," I say as we're walking back toward the truck.

Micah pulls off his tie and shoves it into his pocket. "We have no idea. With the rise of consumers going to purely organic, it could be her. Parents are way more concerned than when we were young, that's for damn sure. I don't see it being affordable, but who the hell knows?"

"Maybe, but cost matters too. I can't imagine any company being willing to pay a higher price just to get the stamp when they can get the same product from us for a fraction of the cost."

"Yeah, but that stamp also means they can charge more to the consumer."

He's right. I sigh. "Well, we can't worry about the other farms vying for it. We just have to keep our heads down and the plan in place. The more we're able to grow this year, the better the chances that we'll be able to pull off what we just promised."

Micah gives me a flat smile. "We just have to wait until they're born."

"And get the next group pregnant."

"All of what we planned out is working, Rowan. We just have to be patient."

Micah, for all his faults, is actually brilliant. The two of us realized there were opportunities that most farmers were missing out on and planned how to fill that gap. However, if Charlotte Sullivan sees the same thing, I might just lose out and then I'll really be fucked.

"I've never been very good at being patient."

He laughs. "Me either. Hey, are you going on the mountain trip in New Hampshire?"

"Hiking, drunk girls, and hot tubs? Fuck yeah I am."

"I guess that means I'm not."

I smile and slap his shoulder. "Nope. Welcome to being the manager."

There's not a chance in hell I'm missing that trip.

four
CHARLOTTE

"Hello there, Charlotte," Mrs. Cooke, the owner of the small grocery store, says as I bring my basket up to the register.

"Hello. How are you and Mr. Cooke doing?"

She smiles warmly at me. "Very good, dear. How are you?"

Broke, tired, and barely hanging on. "Great! I'm just getting a few things and then heading back to the farm."

"That's nice. Your grandpa would've been so proud. You know we dated once, right?"

Ah, yes, the story that never seems to die, even though both of my grandparents are gone. Mrs. Cooke had a crush on my pop when she was in high school and I swear, she loves to tell me.

Every time I see her.

"I do. I know he was very fond of you."

She scoffs. "Please, he dumped me for your grandma."

I laugh softly. "And you found your true love."

Her gaze moves to her husband, who is stacking boxes on the end cap. "Yes, I did, even if the old fool can't hear worth a damn." She raises her voice. "And won't wear the damn hearing aids!"

"Huh?" Jimmy says, having heard his wife yelling but not what she yelled. "What did you say?" I fight back the wince at his near screaming.

"I said, you need to wear the damn hearing aids!" Mrs. Cooke rivals his volume.

"I don't need them. Quit your nagging, woman."

She huffs, and her eyes meet mine. "Don't get married, dear, there's a reason they say only fools fall in love."

"I'll take that under advisement."

The door pings and in walks the man who can cure any woman of wanting to marry. "Rowan!" Mrs. Cooke clasps her hands together. "I have your bag here for you."

"Thanks, Mrs. C."

His eyes move to mine, and the light blue that mingles with dark seems to brighten. "Well, well, if it isn't Charlotte Sullivan. Did you know I come here every Tuesday at this time? Did you miss me? Needed to see me? Were you dying to try to catch me on the sly in order to hit on me?"

"You know, you'll find this super hard to believe, but I don't, in fact, keep up with the daily rituals of baboons. I'm actually running a farm, working hard, and doing it without a staff so no, I don't care or know that you go to the store every Tuesday."

Rowan grins. "And yet . . . here you are, in the store on Tuesday and not on your very important farm."

I turn to Mrs. Cooke. "Thank you, Mrs. C. I appreciate you pulling these for me."

"Of course, dear."

I walk out into the abnormally freezing cold in early March, heading to my very old, very loved pickup truck I call Frankie, and open the passenger side. I do this because the driver's side door doesn't open. It's been stuck since 1989, and I definitely don't have the funds to fix it. I put the groceries on the floorboard and haul myself up.

"We drive on the left side here in America," Rowan says as my ass is still hanging out of the door.

I get all the way in and turn to him. "And people say you're the smart one?"

"They also say I'm the hot one."

"Let's not forget, the lying, cheating bastard one. I know I've heard that one too."

Rowan grins. "Only your friends, darling, and that's because you and your delusional sister spread the bullshit far and wide."

I get into my seat, glare at him, and turn the key. "Whatever you say, asshole."

I turn the key again since the engine didn't turn over the first time. The truck sputters, but it doesn't start.

I do it again.

Come on, Frankie, don't fail me. Start.

My truck doesn't do as I ask.

"Having truck issues?" he asks as he rests his arms on the window frame. "Need some help?"

"Not from you," I grumble. God only knows what it is this time. Frankie has been around for a long time. He's old, cranky, and paid off, which is what my grams said about Pop.

Frankie also has been temperamental as of late and clearly the universe is trying to make a point that he's ready to retire.

I scoot back over to the passenger side, where Rowan is still leaning, and push the door open, not caring if it hits him.

It doesn't move an inch. He is like a brick wall. "Can you move?"

"If you ask nicely."

I'm so not in the mood for this. "Move."

He tsks and shakes his head. "Manners, Sullivan."

"Move, Whitlock," I say again.

Rowan doesn't because, why would he? "The word you're searching for is 'please.'"

"No, the word I'm searching for is '*move*'!"

He steps back, and I push again, the door opening this time. I jump down, stomp around to the front, and lift the hood. I'm not sure what I'm looking for, but where there's a will, there's a way.

The cables all look good, nothing appears to be leaking—not that I can see much over the pillows of steam from my breath. Still, I go over the things my grandpa always did. He was a master at keeping things running, and I wish, more than anything, that he was here now.

"Looks like your battery cable is loose." Rowan's voice startles me. "Right there, tighten that one."

I look to where he's pointing, which is the same area I just checked. Thankfully, I am smart enough not to make some snarky comment because, when I touch it? Sure enough, it's loose. After twisting it back into place, I step back. "Thank you."

"How did that taste?"

"Like battery acid," I reply.

Rowan's laugh is almost infectious. Almost.

"Go try it, I'll stand here to adjust if it needs it."

Accepting help from Rowan goes against every instinct, but I have no choice. I hop back into the cab and try again.

Still dead.

"Try again!" he yells back to me.

So I do, and Frankie fails me again.

He comes around the passenger side. "I think you need to call the shop."

"Again with the helpful advice. I'll call. Thank you for the help that didn't help."

"The guys are probably at Sugarlips," Rowan informs me as if I hadn't already known. Donny is the only mechanic in this town, and he works the most bizarre hours—probably because he's drunk most of the day—and closes for three hours during lunch. Three. Who does that?

Of course, my truck breaks down during that timeframe.

"Well, I'll wait until they're done," I say, waiting for him to leave.

There's no reason for him to wait around.

"I know you need to get back to the farm. Why don't you let me drop you off, and you can have Donny come look at it once he's eaten enough bread to sober up."

"I can walk," I say, feeling defiant.

"I know you can, Charlotte, but it's freezing out, and it's at least eight miles. I'd rather not be accused of allowing you to *die* on the road. Get in my truck, I'll take you home, and you can tell everyone that I browbeat you into going," Rowan says before letting out a heavy sigh.

It's really annoying that it had to be *him* who not only witnessed this but also has to help now. While my defiant nature wants to rebuke his offer, I'd like to keep all my fingers and toes, which probably wouldn't happen if I walked home in this weather.

"Okay. I'll let you do something nice for a change."

"I knew your grandparents, and I know they taught you manners. You should be saying, 'Thank you, Rowan, you're such a great guy. I know I've been a raging—'" He pauses. "Insert adjective of your choice, 'but I was wrong all along and accept and appreciate your help.'"

Oh dear God. "That's never going to happen. A thank you is about all you'll get."

He opens the passenger door for me, grabs my bag of groceries, and walks over to his—very new and very large—truck.

"Overcompensating?" I ask, literally hanging on to the handrails and jump to get in.

I start to teeter back and his hand moves to my ass, pushing me up. "Get in the truck and be nice."

I try to turn so I can kick him for touching my ass, but he is already walking around the truck. Rowan doesn't have to jump or climb. He just puts his foot on the running boards and steps in as though it's not an almost four-foot leap.

Show-off.

I buckle my seatbelt and cross my arms over my chest, feeling a mix of several things. I'm appreciative that he offered to take me home because I'm not sure I would've been as nice to someone who has continually been nasty. But Rowan didn't hold that against me. I'm a little irritated that I need his help because I really hate the idea of not being able to do everything myself. However, I didn't ask. He offered, and I took it. That's *totally* different. I also hate this because I used to like Rowan before he broke my sister's heart. He was funny, nice, and freaking hot. Aurora is only sixteen months older than I am, and we always had the same taste in men.

Which is pretty much the guy next to me. Tall, scruff on his chiseled jaw, dark brown hair, and the most beautiful blue eyes a girl could stare at for days.

And that part sucks because I'm bound by sisterly duty to hate him forever.

"Are you cold?" he asks as I rub my arms.

"A little."

He pushes a button on the console, and a minute later, my butt is warming. "You have heated seats?"

"Brynn calls them hiney heaters. They also have a cooling option, and she calls those cheek chillers."

I laugh. "I guess business is good then? You're driving this insane beast of a truck with your fancy gadgets and you bought all that land that I wanted—I might add."

"Things are good. The land wasn't in my immediate plans, but once it went up for sale, I knew I wouldn't get this chance again. No hard feelings."

Getting that land would've been incredibly hard and I would've had to beg my sister for money, but I could've expanded so much. It would've helped to dig out of the hole, just like the fucking bull the asshole won would have done.

It's another reason why I can't stand him. He cuts me at my knees every chance he gets.

"Yeah, no. Definitely. We're on our way to being best friends," I say in a sugary-sweet voice.

Rowan looks over with a smirk. "I can't wait. I've always wanted a porcupine as a best friend."

"Porcupine?"

"Yeah, you like to stab things when you're mad or scared."

"I'd like to stab you," I mutter. His low chuckle irritates me further. "Can we just finish this drive without speaking?"

It's another ten minutes, and I can only imagine what else he'll say to piss me off.

Instead of speaking, he starts whistling and tapping his thumbs on the steering wheel. I try ignoring it and then singing in my head to drown out the sound. I shift, looking out the window, counting fence posts. I try it all, and every second I hear that tapping and the high-pitched whistle, I feel my anger rising.

Please stop. Please stop. I don't want to kill you. Orange is really not my color.

But he doesn't. He starts humming.

"Rowan!" I screech after another minute. "My God!"

"What?"

"Please stop with the tapping and whistling. You're driving me insane."

"You said you didn't want to talk."

"I take it back. Let's talk," I say, feeling my nerves start to splinter. "Let's talk about the weather or Olivia or your truck. I don't care, but the whistling is killing me."

He grins. "Humming is okay then?"

I should've held it in. Now he's going to do it just to annoy me more. I need to keep him talking. "How is Olivia? Does she love her baby sister?"

"That girl is obsessed with her. It's crazy how fast she's growing too."

Safer ground here. "Did she have fun at the auction?"

"She did. She liked talking to you and wanted me to tell you that you're very pretty. I tried to reason with her, stating that the Devil usually disguises himself to make people *think* he's not a hideous beast, at least that's what my mother said when we were kids. However, she couldn't be swayed and said you weren't evil. I think she hasn't spent enough time around you."

Seriously. He's the most annoying human on this planet. "For the life of me, I can't understand what the hell my sister ever saw in you."

"I'm adorable."

"Stupid is more like it."

Rowan snorts. "They say that girls who are mean to boys do it because they like them. I can't help thinking all this anger and frustration is just an attempt at covering your undying love and hunger for me and my body."

I make a gagging noise. No one can argue that Rowan Whitlock isn't really freaking hot, but the minute he opens that big mouth, he's not so attractive anymore. "You figured me out. I'm dying for you, salivating at every possible chance to be around you. I want you so much. Oh baby, oh baby," I say with zero emotion.

"I knew it."

He turns onto my little dirt road, and I thank God for small miracles. This horrific car ride is almost done.

Rowan stops at the end of the driveway, and I open the door and reach to grab my groceries, but he grabs my wrist. "Call me if you need a ride back to your car. Don't walk."

I look down at his hand, to his eyes, and then pull my arm back. "I'll get a ride."

"I mean it, Charlotte. You may hate me, and I may think you're a pain in the ass, but don't let your pride stop you from asking for help."

"I don't need help, but thank you."

And with that, I exit the car, ignoring the way my skin tingles where he touched me.

five

ROWAN

"*I want to go hiking, but Mom won't let me,*" Olivia signs as she's sitting on the seat of the quad.

"*I'll take you,*" I promise her, and she practically bounces. "*Just not on this trip.*"

She rolls her eyes and sighs dramatically. "*I don't think you're going on this trip since you can't find your gear.*"

This is true. We've been in the storage barn at Asher's house for the last hour. I know I put it here because I didn't want to clutter my barn. It's much better to dump my shit at my brother's.

"*I think you moved my box.*" I purse my lips as I sign.

"*I did not.*"

"*I don't believe you.*"

Olivia looks affronted. "*I do not lie.*"

I walk over to her and smile. "*I know. Can you help look?*"

My niece's eyes fill with mischief, and I know that look well. "*I could, but it will cost you.*"

Of course it will. The women in my life are maddening, even the young ones. "*How much?*"

"*A fishing trip.*"

I shake my head. "*You get your mother and father to agree, and I'll take you.*"

39

"That will never happen." Olivia huffs.

"Never say never." I tap her nose.

I go back to searching for my hiking gear, and not five minutes later I hear my brother's voice from behind. "What the hell are you doing out here?"

"Looking for my stuff!" I reply, moving another box.

"In my barn?"

"Yup."

Olivia must tell him something because he replies aloud. "No, you can't go fishing with Uncle Rowan." My brother laughs at whatever she says. "You're right, he doesn't look like he's going hiking on this trip either."

"Fuck you, Asher. Have you seen my poles?" I turn to look at him.

"No."

He's so goddamn helpful. I swear.

"Go inside and help Phoebe make that horrendous soup she loves," he signs to Olivia. Once she's gone, I go back to my search and then he clears his throat. "So, how did your meeting in New York go?"

I pop my head around the stack of boxes. "Fine."

"That's all I get?"

"Yup."

My brother sighs. "I think the box is in the loft. Did you look up there?"

I'm going to kill him. "You knew where they were?"

"I said I *think*."

Asher attaches the wooden ladder as I navigate my way through the mess I've made. Once I get there, he's already halfway up to the loft, but he doesn't fully go up. "Yup, they're here."

"I really hate you."

"Sure you don't."

"I need the poles, boots, backpack," I tell him. "And the tent. Oh, and can you get the box with all the other gear for emergencies?"

He looks down at me. "Anything else, princess?"

"No, that should be good."

Asher tosses down all the stuff I asked for and a lot of shit I didn't ask for, but I can't really complain since he did find it all. Although, the asshole moved it to begin with. Once my pile is complete, he heads down and detaches the ladder.

"You're going camping in the freezing cold?"

Camping was something that Asher and I did every year. We'd get our gear, head to the mountains, and just get lost. It was fun and my brother was always up for an adventure, until he got himself shackled.

"I am, wish you could go?"

His gaze moves toward his home, and he shakes his head. "I'm good here."

"Pussy."

"I get it on the regular," Asher quips back.

"I'm happy for you, you got what? Two more weeks of celibacy coming your way?"

Asher's face falls slightly. "Your point?"

"Just that . . . you must be awfully familiar with your hand again."

"As are you. By the way, what was the outcome of the meeting?"

Deciding to stop our normal bickering, I fill him in on what happened with Damon Knight and how they want to come out here to see the place. However, it's been a few weeks, and I haven't heard shit. They said they'd be in touch for the visit, and I assumed it would've happened already, but I have no idea.

"I'm proud of you."

Asher is the oldest of us, and even though there are only five years between us, he's always been more of a father than anything else. When our father took off, he stepped in. When we had shitty stepfathers, Asher protected us.

"Thanks. I couldn't have done any of this if it weren't for you," I say in a moment of honesty. "Well, all of you really."

When Mom died, Asher inherited the farm. Instead of taking the land for himself, he immediately divided it up between each of us. I took a larger portion of the land because my siblings knew I had plans to actually farm on it. And when I asked if they'd be willing to sell me some of their acreage, they'd said they wouldn't be. Instead, they gifted it to me.

"You did what Grandpa would've wanted. He loved this land as a farm."

"He wanted us all to raise families here. And you're the only one doing it so far since Grady lives with Addison now."

Asher laughs. "Let's be real, none of us thought he'd ever come back here."

"No shit."

Grady wasn't like us. He wanted to see the world, live outside the confines of a small town, and he definitely didn't want to come here after he joined the military. Asher and I came—for Brynn. He came first and I followed shortly after. She needed her family after Mom got sick, and we needed to be there for her.

"When is the trip?" Asher asks as we leave the storage barn, heading back toward his house.

"Two weeks."

"Who's going? The normal crew?"

I nod. "It's three guys and three girls. I don't know all the girls who are going, but the guys are me, Joey McNair, and Sawyer. I know Faye and her friends are going, but that's just what Sawyer said."

"Is Sawyer going on the hike with you?"

"No, I'm going alone. Those guys like to stick to the partying, and I can do that shit here."

I can see the concern flash in his eyes. "Rowan . . ."

"I'll be fine. I know what I'm doing. I've been to that area before. Don't get your panties all twisted, okay?"

He shakes his head. "I swear, one day your luck is going to run out."

"I'm like a cat with nine lives."

"Yeah, and how many have you used up?"

Too many, but I'm not going to admit to that.

"Do you come around here often?" a voluptuous blonde asks as she rims the glass with her finger.

"You could say that. I live here, which makes it a very convenient option." Peakness is the only bar in Sugarloaf, so we're all here a lot.

She nods slowly. "It's my first time in Sugarloaf. My brother is annoying and demanded I come out here for a few days to see the area."

"Your brother *demanded*?" I ask before taking a pull from my beer. "My sister would kick my ass if I ever tried that."

Brynlee would do more than that if I'm being honest. She's feisty as hell when it comes to me, Asher, and Grady. There's not a chance in hell she'd put up with us demanding anything. Although, it might be fun to try and see what happened.

The blonde snorts. "To be fair, he's my boss as well, so I guess I should say my employer demanded it."

I laugh once. "Sounds like a fun time. I could never work with my siblings."

"Oh, the family business is super fun, and we don't really have a choice. I'm Kimberly." She extends her hand to me.

"Rowan."

"Nice to meet you, Rowan. So, since you live here, what is there to do?"

I chuckle. "Not much. Hence, why this place is packed."

"This is packed?" she asks, looking around.

I do the same, see Charlotte, Faye, and some other girl doing shots, and roll my eyes. I came here to get away from people I don't like, only to run into the one I hate the most. Fantastic.

I turn back to the hot blonde and force a smile. "Well, for Sugarloaf it is."

Her eyes widen. "Wow."

Yeah, it's not a lot, but this place is pretty full tonight. "Where are you from?"

Kimberly smiles. "New York City."

"I was just there about two weeks ago," I say, leaning back. "I had a good time." I guess.

"Really? You don't seem like a guy who likes the city."

She has no idea. I fucking hate it. I've lived in small towns my whole life and after spending a day in New York, I wanted to lock myself in a quiet room for days. However, Kimberly seems like she loves it.

"Maybe you can sell me on its merits," I offer her a chance.

Kimberly launches into all the reasons she loves it. The food. The smells and sounds. How you can turn in any direction and find something new. Her entire face lights up as she talks about the city.

While in no way am I sold on it, I can see why she loves it so much.

"Well, I think I'm just a country boy at heart."

She leans forward, running her tongue across her lips. "And what's different about a country boy?"

"Lots of things."

"Your turn to sell me on it." Kimberly grins.

I chuckle and, again, my eyes find Charlotte, who is sitting on the table, throwing back another shot.

Not my problem. Not my issue. Not my concern.

Instead of worrying about someone who I don't give a shit about, I turn to Kimberly and explain a bit of my life. I explain how there are no sounds at night other than the crickets or the creek. The food here is decent—for a small town. All the things I love and it's the total opposite of everything she explained.

"You know, even though we're opposite, we have a lot in common." Kimberly grins and pulls her lower lip between her teeth.

"We do?"

She nods. "We're passionate, and while I've never been into the country life, maybe I just haven't found the right guy to show me all the ... perks."

Seems I'm getting lucky tonight.

I grin. "There are a lot of perks."

"Really? Like what?"

I nod. "We have no problem doing whatever has to be done to make others happy."

Kimberly's eyes flash with heat. Yeah, I'm so getting laid.

"And what exactly has to be done that you're so willing to do?"

"Well," I say, moving toward her. "For one, we don't mind getting dirty."

"Dirty, you say?"

"Very."

I hear a loud female voice laugh and recognize it immediately. My eyes move to where Charlotte is standing against the wall and the guy who is caging her in.

Faye is dancing with the other friend, not paying attention. I look back to Kimberly, smiling, and then glance back at Charlotte for some stupid reason. This time, the guy is dipping his head into her neck. She tries to push him away, but he leans harder into her.

Not my circus. Not my monkey.

Kimberly's finger moves up and down my arm as she pulls her lip into her mouth for a second. "You know, I have this really big suite a town over at this fancy hotel."

There's only one of those in this area, and I happen to be very familiar with it.

"You do?"

She nods.

Thank God for city girls who want a little dirt left in their sheets.

I go to lean in, wanting to get the hell out of here and her out of her clothes when I hear something that causes me to stop.

My eyes move to where Charlotte is trying to move the immovable man in front of her.

Fucking hell.

I groan internally and turn to Kimberly. "Excuse me a minute, I have to take care of something."

I stand and walk over to where the guy is now pressing his groin into her. "Stop. Dude, let me go . . ."

This is so not my fucking job, but I'm not going to let any girl be disrespected. The fact there are five other guys not doing a damn thing is a whole other thing I'm going to address.

I grab his shoulder, pulling him back immediately. "What the fuck?" he yells as he stumbles back.

"Exactly. What the fuck is wrong with you? She said stop. Which means no, and you step the hell back."

He laughs. "Who the fuck are you?"

"A man who doesn't have to force a very drunk girl to fuck me. Now, say sorry to her and leave before I break both your legs."

He glares at me. "Fuck off."

"Please, say one more word other than 'sorry' so I can beat your ass."

The douchebag looks at Charlotte, clearly hearing I'm not dicking around, and speaks. "Sorry."

"Now, go run along." I turn to the other guys. "And you all watched? Didn't say a word as a woman was being shoved against the wall? Bunch of fucking assholes. Stay the hell out of here or I'll enjoy breaking all your legs."

Faye has Charlotte in her arms, and she starts to slip. I rush over, helping to lift her. "She's completely tanked."

Faye sighs. "I know, she started with the shots, and there was no stopping her. I need to get her to the car, but I can't carry her."

"I'll get her outside for you."

"Thank you!" Faye says with relief in her eyes. "I need to pay the tab."

I pull Charlotte to my side, and she bristles. "I can take care of myself."

"Really? Is that what you call this?"

She glares at me. "I like shots, okay? I like to forget it all."

"You're going to wish you forgot a lot more when you wake up with a hangover. Come on, I need to help you outside."

Charlotte pulls away but then stumbles, falls against my chest, and starts to laugh uncontrollably. "I'm so drunk."

"You are, now will you let me help you?" I ask, frustration mounting as I stand here.

She lifts her eyes, the flecks of yellow seeming to dance around the green. "I have no choice." Charlotte's voice drops to a whisper. "I can't feel my tongue."

Oh, for fuck's sake.

"Can you feel your legs?" I ask.

"A little bit." Her laugh is loud but trails off, and I worry she passed out. Thankfully, she's still with us, so I pull her closer to me and she wraps both of her arms around my waist.

I move us to the bar, where Kimberly is waiting with pursed lips that are also a sort of smile. "I guess this is another thing country boys do?"

"Take care of a kind-of friend? Yes."

"Kind of?" she asks with a brow raised.

"Long story and I need to get her to the car." I notice she has her purse in her hand. "Are you leaving?"

Kimberly smiles softly. "I have a big day tomorrow and it would be better if . . . well, I don't need to piss my boss off more than he already is."

And just like that, my very fun night disappears. "I get it. It was nice meeting you, Kimberly."

"You too, Rowan."

I watch as she walks off, her hips swaying, and I let out a groan of frustration.

Charlotte giggles and hiccups. "Sorry, Row-wan! No sex for you."

Unreal.

By the time Faye walks over, Charlotte is swaying back and forth, making a low moan. "Don't puke," I demand.

She snorts. "Bossy jerk."

"Bossy jerk who saved you from that asshole."

Charlotte groans again, her head resting on my shoulder.

Faye looks at her and then me. "I think something's really wrong with her."

"Yeah, she's fucking hammered."

"Well, there's that. Charlotte never gets this drunk, though.

She did shots and started crying. So, I got her up, and . . . well, she started talking to that guy, and we know where it went from there."

Charlotte snorts. "I'm sleepy and feel woozy. Do you feel woozy too? Like the ground is upside down."

Faye looks to me. "Can you help?"

"Of course."

She starts to slump, and my arms wrap around her. Her speech is so slurred I can barely make it out. "I can't feel my face."

"I'm going to carry her out," I tell Faye.

She nods. "Okay, let me get Margot and we'll leave with you."

I adjust Charlotte so I can lift her into my arms, and her arms fall limply as if she can't even hold on to me.

"Charlotte, open your eyes," I command.

Her lids flutter. "Rowan?"

"Yes, can you hold on to me?"

She lifts one arm around my neck. "You smell good."

If she wasn't drunk, she'd never say that out loud.

"Hold on, okay?"

"Okay." She breathes the word and then rests her head on my chest. "I wish you didn't smell so good and you weren't hot. That would be nice too. You could be ugly and smell bad."

I pull her tight to my chest as Faye and Margot follow behind. When I see the bartender approaching with concern, I stop. "Hey, Carmen," I say. "There were a group of guys, and one of them pinned Charlotte against the wall. I stepped in, threatened them, and told them to leave, but you may want to let Asher know."

"Of course," Carmen says quickly. "I'll keep a watch out for any other girls too."

"Thanks."

When we get to the parking lot, Charlotte shivers. "I'm c-c-cold."

"Just a minute," I reassure her.

Faye unlocks her tiny sports car and curses. "Shit, I should've brought my truck. I drove Charlotte here, but Margot is drunk too and she can't drive. This car is a two-seater and I can't bring them both. Damn it."

"Someone has to stay with her," I say, concerned she'll be getting sick and need help.

"I was planning to sleep at her house, but I need to drive Margot back to her place."

"I'll take Charlotte home and wait until you get there," I say without pause.

"Rowan . . . you shouldn't have to . . ."

I shift Charlotte higher. "Go drop her off, I'll stay with her."

"Okay."

Faye follows me to my truck and helps me get her in. Once buckled, she curves into the heated seat and snuggles into my coat.

"I'll meet you in an hour. Thank you," Faye says quickly.

"Not a problem."

I get in my truck, blare the heat since the temperature is dropping, and look over at Charlotte. She's shivering, so I turn the heat up a little more. Seeing her like this is not normal. While this quiet version of her is great, it's not what I enjoy. I like when she's spitting fire. She makes me crazy, and I push every button.

Whatever caused her to get this drunk must be bad. She's never been the party girl.

The drive to Charlotte's house takes fifteen minutes, and when we get there, everything is locked and she's passed out.

"Great."

I grab my phone and call Faye. "Her house is locked, and I have no idea where her keys are."

"Oh my God! I have her purse. I'm so sorry, Rowan. I'll be at least an hour. Can you wait there?"

This night is going great. "I'll bring her to my house."

"What?" Faye practically screams.

"I'm not waiting here for another hour until you get here. She needs to drink water and probably empty her stomach. I'll take her to my house, and you can come there."

There's a long pause, which I'm sure is shock, but regardless of my tumultuous relationship with her, I'm not the kind of guy to walk away from a woman in this condition.

"I'll be there as soon as I can."

I turn around and head to my house, calling Asher to tell him about the assholes at the bar who I've never seen before.

"So, you carried her out?" my brother asks with disbelief.

"What would you rather I have done?"

"Nothing, I'm glad you got her out of there, but now you're taking her to your house? Are you nuts?"

Most likely. "Faye will come there, I'll pack her ass in the car, and they can leave."

"Okay. Well, I'll stop by Peakness and make sure nothing is out of the ordinary," he promises.

"Good. I'll talk to you later."

Asher laughs softly. "Yeah, I'll definitely call tomorrow to find out the rest of this story."

We get to my house, I open my front door and go back to the truck to carry Charlotte in.

"Charlotte, wake up."

She moans a little. "Want to sleep."

"No, I need you to wake up, look at me." I try not to shake her but end up jerking her a little.

Her eyes open, and she sighs heavily. "What do you want?"

There she is. I fight smiling. "I need you to walk with me into the house. Then you're going to drink water."

"I don't want water."

"I'm sure you don't, but you're going to do it anyway," I inform her.

Charlotte makes a clicking noise with her mouth. "I'm thirsty."

And contrary. "The water is inside. Can you let me help you?"

"Sure."

I get her down carefully, and she holds on to me as we walk inside the house. I kick the door closed and bring her back to my bed. I have a one-bedroom house that isn't much to write home about, but it's just fine for me.

This was the old cabin my grandfather used when he had to move cattle out in the back pasture. It's got the bare essentials, and it's my favorite part of the Whitlock farmland.

"I'm going to get water, okay?"

She nods. I grab four bottles of water, and she drinks one without issues.

"I'm so dizzy."

"I know, it's the ridiculous amount of tequila you drank."

"Why are you being nice to me?" she asks.

"I'm not quite sure yet."

Charlotte lets out a heavy sigh and leans her head back against the headboard. "We're supposed to hate each other."

I laugh once. "We still do. Don't worry."

She grabs for a second water, drinks most of it, and I give her the next bottle. The more she can hydrate the better.

Her eyes flutter as she looks at me. "I don't hate you all the time."

"Good to know."

"Do you hate me?" she asks.

She's tanked, and I know she won't remember any of this. "No. I just wish you'd believe the truth."

She smiles softly. "Truth about what?"

"That I never cheated on Aurora. I'm not that man, regardless of what she's said and the lies she's spread about me."

Charlotte purses her lips. "You made her leave me to deal with this on my own."

"Deal with what?"

"Life."

Maybe she believes that, but it's not true. I didn't do anything to her other than be honest about how I felt. I didn't want Aurora to end up hurt, but she did anyway. Then she became a vengeful bitch and told everyone I cheated on her and that she walked in on it. Which never fucking happened.

She was relentless, and I became the asshole in this town. At first, I tried to deny it, and then, I just let it go because people believed what they wanted to anyway.

I hear a knock on my door. "Drink your water," I tell her as I get up. "I'm going to let Faye in."

"Bossy." She rolls her eyes and then drinks more water.

Faye smiles as I let her in. "How is she?"

"She's herself, only drunk. I've been trying to keep her up and drinking water. You can have my bedroom, I'll sleep on the couch."

She rests her hand on my chest. "Thank you, Rowan."

"Don't thank me."

"Well, I am. You're a good man, and you left the girl who was probably a sure thing without even looking back."

I shake my head and sigh. "I'm glad I was there to help."

She kisses my cheek. "Me too, and I know Charlotte will be as well."

six

CHARLOTTE

My head is pounding. I roll over and rub my face in the pillow, wanting to sleep because the pain is excruciating. God, how much did I drink?

I inhale, but it doesn't smell like my pillow. There's a woodsy scent that is definitely male.

Oh no. Oh Lord. I keep my eyes closed and try to think back through the haze of my brain to remember how I might've ended up in a man's bed.

I remember getting to the bar. Faye and Margot convinced me to go and I had no plans to drink, but then I got an email stating I needed to pay about four thousand dollars to fix my truck's engine issues.

I mean, why the hell not just keep piling on the bad news, right?

So, I did a shot. I figured one wouldn't kill me, but when one turned to six or seven . . .

Okay, Charlotte, time to face the music and see just how badly you fucked up.

First thing I notice is that I have pants on. So, that's a good sign.

Second thing is that there's someone next to me.

I open my eyes and, instead of finding a man, like I expect, I see my best friend.

"Faye?" I whisper, confused and head throbbing like a bitch.

She rolls toward me and smiles. "How shitty do you feel?"

"Is there a barometer for it?"

"No, but I assume it's pretty horrible."

I nod.

"There's Gatorade and Ibuprofen over there," Faye explains.

When I roll over, another fact strikes me. We're not in Faye's house. In fact, I don't know where the hell we are. I grab the Gatorade and sit up, holding my palm against my pounding temple.

"How much did I drink?"

The bed shifts, and she laughs softly. "Well, my friend, you went at least ten rounds with Jose Cuervo."

I chug some Gatorade, swallow the pills, and then put it back on the nightstand of someone I still don't know. The room is small, literally a bed, tall dresser, two nightstands, and a chair in the corner. A jacket is thrown over the arm of the chair, and it's not mine or Faye's.

"Where are we?" I ask, my voice filled with uncertainty.

"We are at a friend's."

"A friend? We don't have friends."

She smiles. "Well, you don't, but I do."

Fair point. "What friend?"

Faye's smile is a little sheepish, and that causes my already roiling stomach to churn more. "Faye . . ."

Her sigh is heavy as she lifts one shoulder. "We're at Rowan's."

My jaw drops, and I gasp. "What?"

"Rowan stepped in when you were being . . . manhandled a bit. He pushed the guy off you, and you were hammered. I mean, you couldn't walk straight. So, he carried you out and took you to your house, but I had your keys so he couldn't get in. That's how you ended up here, I drove over after I'd dropped Margot off. I know you hate him, but he was really, really great."

The worst part is that I don't hate him. I just hate what he did to my sister. I hate that he drove away the one person I had left to help me and now I'm alone.

And broke.

And going to lose everything.

"Why did it have to be him?" I ask her.

"I don't know, but thank God it was. He didn't have to do any of it, Char. He didn't even hesitate, though, and he took care of you until I got here. I've never seen him so protective."

I don't want to be in his debt.

"You really don't know him."

She tilts her head. "Or maybe it's you who doesn't. Anyway, he left early this morning, got us some coffee and bagels but then had to run. He said he'd be back after he checked in with Micah."

That was kind of nice. "So you're saying I need to thank him."

"That's exactly what I'm saying."

"Great."

Faye laughs. "Although you two communicate through bickering, so maybe you should just call him an asshole or something. That can be your new code word for thank you."

I roll my eyes and move out of Rowan's bed. God, just thinking those words makes me feel ill. Or maybe it's the tequila—whatever.

Something flashes back in my mind. "Wait, you said he carried me out?"

"Yes."

"I have a vague recollection of something, but there's no way." Her brows lift. "Oh?"

I should've kept my mouth shut. "I think I said something about his cologne or him smelling good."

"I can't wait to ask him."

"Do it, and you'll die," I warn her.

She laughs. "Yeah, like you scare me. Please."

My fears are completely different because I have no idea what else I might have said to Rowan Whitlock.

Before I can think too much, I hear a door open and bite back my groan. Great. Now I have to thank the man for taking care of me when I was clearly unable to do it myself. Just one more notch on my pole of awesomeness.

There's a soft knock on the door, and Faye nudges me. I glare at her, but she just scowls back.

Fine.

"We're up, Rowan."

The door pushes open, and he's standing there in tight jeans, a brown jacket, and baseball hat. I really wish he was ugly, but of course, he's not. He's always been hot, and he's like a wine that only gets better with age.

I hate that.

"I bet you feel like ass," he says, making all those nice thoughts evaporate.

"Better to feel like one than to be one, which you know . . ."

Faye clears her throat. "You're like children. Now, what did you want to say to Rowan?"

I look at her for a beat, and she gives me a stern look, clearly thinking I need to be treated like a child.

Whatever my feelings are about him, he was really nice and I do owe him my gratitude. "Thank you, Rowan. For taking care of me and getting me home safe and away from the sleezy guy. Also for the medicine and electrolytes that will allow me not want to bury my head."

He smirks. "You're welcome."

Yeah, we all know what that smirk means. That he won and I have to eat the crow I so bitterly dislike.

"Yes, well," I say, not sure of where I go from here. I do know it's out of his room though. "Do you know where my boots are?"

"I do actually."

I swear. "I'm way too hungover for you to be cute."

"You think I'm cute?"

Faye snorts and then lifts her shoulders when I give her a look that would shrivel a man.

I turn back to Rowan. "No. Where are the boots?"

"They're here somewhere. Are you worried I might steal them?"

"If your feet are small enough to fit them, I can understand why my sister isn't in a hurry to see you again. You know, small feet, small . . . you know . . ." I make the colossal mistake of glancing down to where his dick is.

"Charlotte, if you want to see my cock, you just have to ask."

"And on that note." Faye gets up and walks over to Rowan. "Thank you again. You took care of her, and I appreciate you letting us stay here instead of making me drive the drunk ass back to my place and risking her puking in my car. We'll get out of your home now." She pushes up onto her toes, kisses his cheek, and then points to me. "You, let's go. You really need to learn how to say thank you."

I sigh heavily, hating how he riles me up so damn easily. "I wanted to leave five minutes ago, but I don't know where my damn boots are."

"They're by the front door because after I settled you in *my* bed, I went and slept on the couch, which *I* don't fit comfortably on, and I put your shoes and jacket there because I tripped on them after you tossed them while I was helping you. Anything else, princess?" Rowan asks with sarcasm and a bit of anger under that.

I deserve that. I'm being a bit of a bitch. "I apologize. I'm being ungrateful and rude."

His head jerks back. "Can you say that again?"

"No."

Rowan laughs. "Fair enough. Apology accepted."

I give him a soft smile. "Thank you."

He nods and steps aside as Faye and I walk out of the room.

We get to the door, and I grab my coat and slip into my boots as he leans against the doorjamb, arms crossed over his big chest.

Faye turns to him first. "You're the best, Rowan. I mean it."

"Thanks."

I jerk my head his way. Ugh. "You aren't the worst anymore."

"Wow, that's a step up."

"It is," I toss back with a grin. "Maybe you have *some* redeeming quality buried under all that . . . mess."

He pushes off the door and comes to me, dipping his head. "I

59

guess we'll find out, but until then"—Rowan pushes my hair off my shoulder—"at least I know I smell good."

Then the asshat walks into his kitchen, and I can't get out of this house quick enough.

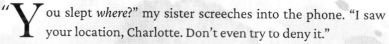

seven

CHARLOTTE

"Y̲ou slept *where?*" my sister screeches into the phone. "I saw your location, Charlotte. Don't even try to deny it."

I'm lying on my couch with an ice pack to my head as the throbbing continues. The last thing I need is to be yelled at by my sister. "I'm not denying anything because you won't shut up long enough for me to reply."

"There's no response you can even give! You slept at the Whitlock farm. I saw it."

"Then you're calling to, what? Yell at me? Tell me all the reasons I shouldn't have slept at Rowan's?" I ask rhetorically since she's already doing those.

Aurora groans. "God, I knew he would do something like this. But my *sister?* Of all the people in the world you could have . . . I can't even believe you, Char!"

That's it. I'm not in the damn mood for this. I sit up, which intensifies the pounding, and let out a heavy sigh, prepared for my tirade. "First of all, you're not fucking *here* and don't know what happened. Second of all, I'm not a damn child, Aurora. I'm running this farm, handling all the things *you* walked away from, and trying to keep my goddamn head afloat. I didn't sleep *with* Rowan. I slept at his house. I got blackout drunk, some guy was hitting on me, pushing me, trying to get me to leave with him, and Rowan stepped in. He didn't do anything but make sure I was safe. He brought me to my house, but I didn't have my keys, which is why he took me to his place where Faye came and spent the night. So, stop fucking yelling at me!"

There, that should shut her up.

Only it doesn't. "You should've never gotten in a car with him! What if he took advantage of you?"

"Did you hear anything I said? Is that really what you think?"

The world has officially flipped on its axis. I am defending Rowan Whitlock to my sister. I don't know what kind of alternate reality I just woke up in.

"Yes! It's exactly what I think. You don't know him like I do. He's a liar and a cheater who broke my heart."

"Two years ago! You're in New York now. You left! You left me, and you don't get to call me after I had a horrible night, when my head feels like it's in a vise, and scream at me for allowing someone to take care of me. If you want that job, Aurora, come home and do it yourself!"

That shuts her up, though. I can hear the silence driving the wedge deeper through our relationship.

Aurora was my best friend. My only friend. When our parents died, it was her I clung to. Then our grandparents took us in, raised us here, and we lost them.

She left me just like all of them did.

I know it's not fair or right to feel that way, but it's the truth.

In my heart, I feel her abandonment even worse than if she'd died. My parents didn't choose to leave. They drove home one night after a parent-teacher conference and were hit head-on by a drunk driver. There was no goodbye. No time to prepare for what it would mean, we were just . . . orphans.

But I had her.

We both dealt with the loss of our parents differently, I guess. I learned to love people, but with a bit of distance, where Aurora clung to everyone. Which is why I think when things don't work out with a guy, she's left angry and hurt.

"I didn't leave you," she says after a minute of absolute silence.

"You did."

"I had to go." Her voice is shaky and cracks at the end.

"I know."

And I do. She was never a farm girl. The dust and chores and never-ending home repairs were never her thing. All Aurora wanted was to go back to New York City where we were born and lived until our parents died.

She loves it there.

I love it here.

But she would've stayed if Rowan hadn't broken her heart.

"But I didn't leave you, Charlotte. I just . . . staying there wasn't where I belonged."

I nod even though she can't see it. "I don't begrudge you because you left. All the two of us have ever wanted for the other was to be happy. I know that Rowan hurt you, and you decided to leave because of it."

"Not because of it, but it was what drove me to go and do what we both know I always wanted," she corrects.

"I understand all of it, which is why I never asked you to stay, but don't you dare question my loyalty to you. I did nothing wrong. I was simply lucky enough that he kept that guy from forcing himself on me. I don't remember all of it, but I know I kept saying no, and he didn't take the hint."

She sucks in a breath. "Oh my God."

"It wasn't like that. We were in the bar still, but it could've gone that way fast. Rowan made sure it didn't."

"Then I guess that's . . . well, it's good he was there."

The one thing that weighs heavy on my mind is how he remains adamant he didn't cheat on Aurora. "You know he says he never cheated on you."

"Well, I saw it with my own eyes. I don't want to talk about it. It hurts too much still."

"Okay." I roll my eyes. It's been two fucking years.

She clears her throat. "Will you come visit? I miss you."

"I can't come to New York. I have so much going on here with the farm." I don't tell her it's because I had to let go of one of the farm hands because I couldn't afford to pay him. "Faye is trying to convince me to go to the cabin so if I can get help, I can't do both."

"You should go with Faye! You love going up there, and you never do anything for yourself anymore."

I can't because I have no money. However, Faye isn't hearing it. She told me it's already paid for thanks to her parents and none of us have to worry about anything. It's her present to herself, and it would be rude of me not to go.

"I might. She's really good at guilting me."

Aurora sighs. "Maybe that'll be my route to get you here then."

I stay quiet, hating her because she doesn't seem to care what's going on here. "I have a killer headache and really need some sleep. Can we talk tomorrow or something?"

"Of course, I hope you feel better. I love you."

"Love you too."

And again, I face this alone.

However, about all I can face right now is getting rid of this headache. I vow to never drink again if it would just ease up a little.

Knock, knock.

Great, now my headache is literally pounding. I shift the ice pack over my eyes.

Knock, knock, knock.

You have got to be kidding me. It's someone at the door? Why? Because I am having to repent?

"Ugh," I groan. "Who the hell is here?" Not that I'm expecting an answer since I whisper it to myself.

I roll off the couch, clasping my head as I get upright. Shuffling my feet to the door as the knocking starts again. "I'm coming, keep your pants on!"

I swear to God, if Rowan is on the other side of this door, I'm going to slam my head against it and hope to be knocked out.

When I open the door, it is not, in fact, Rowan Whitlock. It's a very pretty blonde I've never seen before. "Um. Hi?"

She smiles. "Hi, are you Charlotte?"

"Are you lost?" I ask, not answering the question.

"I am if you're not Charlotte Sullivan."

"Then you're not lost." The sun is freaking blinding. I squint before continuing. "Who are you, and why are you looking for me?"

Do they send debt collectors to your house now on a Sunday? Is that a thing? I really hope not because it's going to make it much more difficult to hide from them.

"Well, my name is—"

I don't have time for this, I cut her off to save us both time. "Whatever you're selling, I'm not buying. We don't want solar panels or pest control. I'm all stocked up on meat and whatever else people are going around town to sell. I had the worst night of my life, my head is pounding, and while normally I am much nicer, today . . . I don't have it in me."

I start to close the door, but her hand shoots out. "Kimberly Knight, with Knight Food Distribution."

No. No, no, no. This can't be happening. Oh my God. They said they'd be coming out in a few weeks to see the farm. Not today. Not after a bender from hell. My jaw opens and closes and then does it again as I scramble for words. "I . . . I didn't . . ."

She smiles sympathetically. "Expect me?"

"Yes. I didn't expect you."

"We like to surprise our potential new clients prior to bringing them on."

"Consider me surprised." I force a smile. "Would you like to come in? I need to go upstairs and change, but you're welcome to wait, if that's okay?"

Kimberly, who looks like she stepped out of a fashion magazine, enters the house. She's stunning—blond, skinny, with big blue eyes and a perfect nose. She's probably about five or six years older than I am, but there aren't any bags under her eyes.

I get her settled in the living room, rush up the stairs, and head to the bathroom.

Oh for the love of . . .

My hair is nothing like Kimberly's. It looks like absolute shit. My straight hair has more kinks and creases than if I'd actually crimped it. My eyeliner from last night is smudged and there is the stamp from the bar partially on my cheek.

"Shit!" I whisper.

Okay, I can do this. I have got this.

First, I brush my teeth because . . . gross. After that, I grab the makeup wipe, clean my eye area, and then scrub off as much of the stamp as I can.

"What did they use, permanent marker?"

"Charlotte?" I hear Kimberly calling up.

"Just a minute!"

This is the best I got. I toss my hair up in a messy bun and rush into my bedroom to search for a pair of jeans that does not smell like the bar. I find some and toss on a sports bra and a sweatshirt to go over it. If she wants to tour the property, none of that is going to matter anyway.

I am so not ready for this.

"Charlotte? Someone is at the door."

What in the fuck is happening? Two in one day. I swear, if this is the bank people, I really am going to lose it.

"Okay! I'll be right there!"

I rush down the stairs, forcing a smile and pretending I don't have the world's worst hangover.

"Let me just see who it is. I'm sure it'll be just a minute."

"No problem," Kimberly says with a bright smile.

It's definitely a problem—this whole weekend is, but I need to keep that piece of information to myself.

When I open the door, there is the man I didn't want on the other side.

"Hi, it's really not a good time."

His deep voice echoes in my head as I keep the door open just wide enough to see my face. "You forgot something at my house last night."

Can just one thing in my life go according to plan? Just one. "Do you have it, or do I need to come and get it?"

He lifts up my maxed-out credit card. "It must've fallen out of your pants last night, I found it in my bed."

I extend my hand so he can give it to me and get out of my life. "Thanks."

"Can we talk?" Rowan asks.

"No."

"No?"

I shake my head. "Really, it's not a good time." I look back at Kimberly, who is definitely listening to my conversation, and we both smile. "I'm sure we'll see each other around."

"Is someone here?" he asks.

"Yes, and I really don't want to be rude."

"Who is it?"

"Goodbye, Rowan."

Kimberly clears her throat. "Rowan?"

I turn to her. "Yeah, umm, he's an old friend . . . kind of . . . and—"

Kimberly steps closer to me and I have no choice but to open the door. She lets out a laugh when she sees him, and he looks as though he's been punched in the face.

"Well, this is interesting," Kimberly says as she looks at us. "You . . . him? You're the girl he carried out?"

I feel like I'm missing something.

Then Rowan speaks. "Kimberly, I apologize," he says her name, and I swear I'm in an alternate reality. Apologize? What the hell did he do? And how does she know he carried me out of the bar?

I gasp. Oh Jesus. I remember, he was talking to a blonde at the bar last night. It's official, I don't have bad luck, I have no luck.

"Rowan, nice to see you."

He smiles with a soft laugh. "You too. Sorry I bailed last night."

"Seems you found what you were looking for anyway." Kimberly's smile never fades as she says it and then looks to me. "If now isn't a good time . . ."

"No, it's perfectly fine. Mr. Whitlock was just leaving," I say pointedly.

"Wait, Whitlock? As in Whitlock Farms?" Kimberly asks, looking at the two of us.

"Yes, the same." Rowan's brows furrow.

"Well, this makes things easier. As I said to Ms. Sullivan, my name is Kimberly Knight, with Knight Food Distribution. I'm in town to visit both of your farms since you're up for the same contract."

Unreal. And here I thought this day couldn't get any worse.

eight
ROWAN

This could've gone really wrong if I'd ended up fucking Kimberly last night. I guess saving Charlotte wasn't such a bad move.

"It's nice to meet you, Ms. Knight," I say smoothly.

She laughs. "We can dispense with the formalities. I promise this isn't a formal meeting. I usually come out, look at the property, see your setup, and let my brother Carson know whether I see any red flags. Whatever last night was or wasn't isn't my business."

Charlotte nearly chokes as she quickly corrects her. "Oh, no! We didn't . . . we aren't that way."

Kimberly raises her hands. "I promise, it doesn't matter. All I care about is the farm and your product."

"I understand that, I really do, but I need you to know there is nothing between us. We don't even like each other."

"I understand," Kimberly assures her, but her smile says otherwise.

I do nothing to back Charlotte up and her eyes narrow, lips pursed as she nudges her head toward Kimberly. Nope, not saying a word. "Okay, well, I'm happy to show you around and go over things here. Rowan, thanks for bringing my credit card back, I'll see you around. Bye."

Seems I've been dismissed. Only, if Charlotte is vying for this contract as well, there's not a chance in hell I'm going to walk away easily.

I smile my most charming smile. The one that gets the girls willing. "Why don't we take our tours together? I think it would probably be easiest since our farmlands connect in the back acreage, if you toured hers first and then we just went right into mine from that field. I can walk with you guys, and then Charlotte can come with us to mine."

Charlotte's eyes are saucers. "That's not going to happen. You should go back to your farm and wait."

Kimberly looks to Charlotte, then to me, and then back again. "I think it's probably best to do these separately. I'm sure you both have things you'd rather the other not see."

"Exactly," Charlotte says.

"Not at all," I say at exactly the same time.

"I'm completely fine with Charlotte touring my facility. Is there a reason you're not comfortable?" I challenge her, knowing this woman will not back down, which means I get my way.

"Absolutely not." Charlotte's voice has a sharp edge to it.

God, I love pissing her off.

Kimberly looks between us again. "If you don't mind, I'll tour here and then come to you. I think it's really for the best I get one-on-one time with each of you."

I nod once. "Understood. I'll see you soon."

I head back to my house, shaking my head at the absolute shit-show this all could've been. If Kimberly had shown up at my house earlier this morning, I'd have opened the door with Charlotte literally in my bed.

Not that anything happened with Kimberly or Charlotte, but it would've been a hundred times more awkward.

When I arrive home, ready to clean up and do whatever I can to make the farm look better, I head out to the barn where my sister is apparently waiting for me.

Great, this is going to derail my day.

Brynlee looks up, already shaking her head. "You really know how to stir up the town, all of you do."

"It's a gift," I say with a smirk.

"You should return it."

"I would, but I like it too much."

Brynn huffs. "You carried Charlotte out of the bar?"

"She was drunk, really fucking drunk, and some guy was being aggressive with her. I had no plans for it to go down the way it did."

"But you defended her?" she asks, her eyes softening.

"Of course I did. I may not like the woman, but I'm not going to stand by when someone is being a fucking asshole to her. She was clearly shitfaced and didn't want the guy's attention. He wouldn't back off, so I backed him off."

My sister smiles warmly. "And people think you're an asshole. If they only knew that big mushy guy on the inside."

"That's Asher, not me."

"Oh? I don't think so big brother."

I sigh heavily, knowing that trying to fight with Brynlee is like running on a treadmill, thinking you're going to end up getting somewhere. "Okay, Brynn."

"You're all so hell-bent on being these big, tough guys."

"No, we *are* big, tough guys."

Why do I not listen to myself? I know better than to keep going.

She crosses her arms over her chest. "Yeah? Where was Asher's big, tough exterior with Phoebe, or Grady when it comes to Addison? It doesn't exist. Now you're finally piecing together that you might have a crack in your armor when it comes to Charlotte."

Oh, for the love of God. "I think there's a crack in your skull if you believe that shit."

"Whatever you say."

"Have I told you lately that you're a real pain in my ass?" I ask, grabbing my gloves so I can move a few tools.

"Only daily."

I lean in and kiss her cheek. "And I mean it every day."

She laughs. "But you love me."

75

"I have no idea why."

"Yes you do, but I'll let you keep your tough-guy persona with me."

"How kind of you." I shake my head and head out of the barn.

"You like her more than you think, Row!" Brynn yells, and I keep walking, not even entertaining that one.

<hr />

"You need me to do what?" Asher asks.

I shake my head at his ineptitude at having to care for the farm and turn to Olivia. *"You do whatever Micah says. You shouldn't ride Brutus if you have to go out to the pasture. Take Whisper instead."*

She nods. *"I will take care of Dad too."*

Asher huffs. *"I can manage for three days."*

Olivia raises a brow. *"Okay, Dad."*

I love this kid.

My brother is the absolute last choice when it comes to caring for the farm, but alas, here we are. Grady is in Florida with Addison and Brynlee is heading to some meeting in California. Which leaves . . . Asher.

I sign so that Olivia gets the directions while speaking to my brother. *"It's important that you come here every morning at seven to open this door."* I place my hand on the metal gate that allows the cows into the pen. *"Every morning. Micah will be moving them to this area, and they need to be able to get in."*

"Door open at seven, I can handle that."

"I will make sure, Uncle Rowan," Olivia assures me.

"You're the one I trust." I tap her nose after I finish signing.

"What time do you leave?" Asher asks.

"In a few. I just need to load the rest of my shit in the truck."

He places his hand on Olivia's shoulder, holding her in front of him so she can't read lips or hear what he says. "Don't be a fucking idiot with your camping and hiking shit. Your niece loves you and would be devastated if anything happened to you. For some reason, the women in this family love you. So, maybe don't go out trekking where you could get hurt."

I smile at him and sign because we do everything we can to include Olivia, which is why I'm surprised by what he did just now. *"Everything will work out."*

Asher's heavy sigh tells me he thinks I'm a damn fool, which I am, but he'll get over it.

Olivia lifts her hands. *"Have fun."*

"I will. Make sure your dad follows the rules."

She smiles. *"I will. I love you."*

"I love you more."

Asher huffs. "Lord knows she's the only girl who ever will."

I stand so she won't see my lips or understand this one. "At least I didn't steal her babysitter."

Asher's face falls. "Asshole."

God, he's so easy to rile up.

I shrug, lifting my bag to my shoulder. "I'll see you when I get back."

⚯

Joey and Sawyer toss their shit into the back of the truck and then climb in.

"You ready for a fuckload of alcohol and hopefully getting laid?" Sawyer jokes as he buckles his seatbelt.

"Well, you will have both of those since one of the girls going is your girlfriend," Joey says with a laugh from the backseat. "Rowan and I are on our own."

I scoff. "Please, we know you and Faye will end up in bed together, just like every year."

Joey and Faye have been on again off again for years. They do this dance, mostly because her parents think he has a dead-end job and their precious daughter should be elevated by marriage.

Joey is a deputy for the town sheriff's department. He's a good guy, but thinks he's leagues beneath her. No matter what she's said, he won't get it through his head, and one day, she's going to get tired of it and he'll really lose her.

Until that day, I'll keep being amused by how they pretend they're not in love when they so are.

"Not this year," Joey vows. "Plus, we all know Rowan always hooks up with the third girl she brings along."

Sawyer nods with a grin. "For real, I don't know what they see in you since you're fucking grumpy each time we go."

"I'm not grumpy, I just go up there for the hiking, not the girls." I try to say it with a straight face, but the three of us burst out laughing. "All right, all right, I go for both."

Joey leans between the two front seats. "I swear, Faye finds her hottest friend for these trips."

"And it's a tradition I appreciate."

The rest of the ride up, the three of us catch up on life. Joey does his best to complain about his job without mentioning the fact that my brother is one of his bosses who drives him insane. Which, I could give a fuck less about it since I know Asher is a pain in the ass. Sawyer is a ranch hand a few towns over, and he shares his concerns they're going under.

"I just see the signs. Things are breaking more often and not getting fixed. He's patching other things up the way he never would've before. I just think it's a matter of time." Sawyer's voice grows quieter at the end.

"I know you've been there a long fucking time, but if it happens, you know you have a place at Whitlock, right?" I extend the offer, meaning every word of it. Sawyer is a good worker and a friend. I would never let him go without.

He nods once. "I know. You're a good man, no matter what they say about you."

Joey laughs. "Poor Rowan, the town asshole, but still the girls flock to him."

"Girls love a bad boy."

"Not all girls," Sawyer snorts. "There's one who thinks he's the shit on her boots."

I huff. "Can we not talk about the She-witch?"

Joey starts to say something, but Sawyer lifts his hand. "The man doesn't want to talk about her, Joe, let's honor that."

"Thank you," I say, glad I have one friend who I don't want to toss out on the side of the road.

We turn onto the windy road that leads to the resort where the cabin Faye's family owns is located. After another twenty minutes and only one almost heart attack as we slide a little, we get there.

The three of us hop out. "Lights are on, which means the girls are here," Joey notes.

"Great, grab your shit out of the truck," I say as I'm reaching into the bed to get mine.

The front door flies open and Faye is there. "Hello, boys! Ready to get drunk?" I laugh, and she steps aside. "You're in the last bedroom on the left."

"Thanks."

"Put your gear in the garage!" Faye calls out, but I'm already headed that way.

I arrange my things so tomorrow I can easily hit the trails. There's a trail out on the back ridge I've always wanted to explore. I think that'll be my route. After I'm content with my gear, I grab my bag and head to the bedroom.

When I open the door to my room, I find someone already in it. First, I see a back—a naked back—then I see her ass. Long brown hair touches the middle of her back and I grin, waiting to see if the brunette Goldilocks is going to be just right.

She turns, screams, and I realize this woman is much too cold, and definitely not who I want in my bed.

Charlotte.

nine

CHARLOTTE

"**G**et out!" I scream, pulling the towel that I tossed on the bed around me.

"You get out. This is my room," Rowan says as he enters, kicking the door closed with his foot and tossing his bag down.

Seriously, I get dragged out here with promises of a weekend of no stress and fun. I haven't gone up to the mountain in freaking years, and now, I have to put up with this asshole?

No.

No way.

"What the hell do you mean this is your room? No it's not. Faye put me in here."

"Well, it's a three bedroom, so I guess that means we're stuck in here together."

My jaw opens, closes, and then I huff. "We're not sharing a room."

"Are you going to sleep between Joey and Faye or maybe Sawyer and Meagan? I'm sure they'll love that. Although," Rowan pauses, "I think Sawyer might really like that."

I scoff. "You're so gross."

"You can sleep on the couch."

Yeah, like that's going to happen. "The hell I will."

Rowan walks over to the bed and flops down, his hands behind his head. "Suit yourself."

I hate this man. To think I defended him and was trying to be nice. No more. I need to drive him out of this room and out of my damn life.

"You're not sleeping in here with me."

"Well, the last time we were together, I slept on the couch because I was being considerate. However, I'm turning over a new leaf and have decided that was a mistake."

"A mistake?" I ask, wanting to throw something at him.

He nods. "Yeah, you don't deserve my niceness. You're trying to steal my contract."

His contract? God, he's delusional. Kimberly was very clear that it is no one's contract yet. We still have to meet with her brother and go over business plans and finalize our bid prices for them to review. Only after that will it be someone's contract.

Which I need. Not want. Need.

"The only thing I'm stealing is my bed back. So, please leave."

Rowan shakes his head. "No thanks. You can go, though."

I grit my teeth and groan. "You're so annoying."

"I'm so not caring."

There's a knock on the door and I'm sure it's Faye. I step over, towel now wrapped completely around me, and throw it open.

My best friend stands there, a smile on her lips. "Hey there."

"You're dead to me," I say without even a moment of hesitation.

"Yes, well, I told you that you were going to be rooming with someone."

"*Someone* is not Rowan Whitlock."

Faye peeks around me, seeing him lying on the bed like an emperor waiting to be fed grapes. Such a freaking asshole. "Hey, Row."

"Sweet room, Faye. Thanks for putting me here," he says back to her. "I love this room so much. Bed is super comfortable. I can't wait to get some sleep."

I turn, glaring at him, hoping that maybe I'll discover I have some kind of superpower that causes lasers to shoot out of my eyes. That would be a nice gift from the gods.

However, nothing happens other than a lazy smile forming on his kissable lips.

Wait, kissable? Umm, no. I don't mean that. I mean slapable face.

Faye tries to cover up a laugh. "You're welcome . . . I think."

"I'm sleeping in your room. Joey can sleep in here with Rowan."

She pulls her lips between her teeth, and her brows shoot up. "About that . . . not going to happen. Joey is . . . uhhh . . . already . . . uhhh . . . yeah. We're totally going to spend a few days fucking all over that room."

I really want to gag at the images that creates.

Rowan claps though. "That's it, Faye. Have a good time, unlike some people we know who can't seem to do that."

I ignore that one because I know it's meant to piss me off. "Then move Rowan to the garage."

"You go to the garage if you want a room change," he unhelpfully says.

I look at him. "I didn't ask you. It's Faye's house."

She sighs heavily, bringing our attention to her. "Listen, you two are grown-ups. I figured that, after the other night, there was some kind of truce and understanding. Clearly, I was wrong thinking you'd be able to be mature about it. If you want to sleep on the couch or in the garage or in a vehicle, I don't care, but this trip is meant to be *fun*, damn it, so figure it out and please keep the bickering to a minimum."

There wouldn't be any bickering if she didn't invite him or basically force me to be here. I had to beg one of Rowan's ranch hands to take care of my farm for a few days, not tell Rowan, and lie to anyone who asked where I was. I couldn't pay him, but I promised him I'd make it up to him by introducing him to a friend he's had a crush on.

Before I can say anything back, Faye turns and walks down the hall, back to where I'm sure Joey is waiting for her so they can start their sexfest.

However, there will be no sexfest in this room. What there will be is rules.

I let out a heavy breath, pull my towel tighter again, and glare at him.

"I'm going to get dressed and then we're going to lay some ground rules," I inform him and head into the bathroom.

Once the door is locked behind me, I throw on my incredibly short shorts and crop tank with its built-in bra. At least I packed that. I run a brush through my hair and head out.

Rowan is pulling stuff out of his bag, and I wait for him to finish so we can have this out. When he sees me, he grins.

Ugh.

"So, what ground rules do you have, princess?"

"You can stay in my room if you promise to agree to the terms."

Rowan cocks his head to the side. "Your room?"

"Yes, I was here first, therefore if we go based on the rules of dibs, then it's mine."

He huffs a laugh. "Let's hear your rules, Charlotte."

Here we go. "Number one, you will be nice to me."

"I'm always nice to you."

Yeah right. Instead of fighting with him, I let it go and focus on getting the rules out. "Number two, no touching."

"Like that's going to ever happen."

I try not to be offended, but it stings a little. Not that I want him to want to touch me, but I mean, doesn't every girl want to be wanted?

I'll address those thoughts later.

"Number three," I soldier forth. "I get the shower first, no matter when. I plan on going hiking tomorrow and I'm going to want to shower as soon as I'm done. Since I was in the room first and didn't know I'd be sharing with *you*, I call permanent dibs."

Rowan rolls his eyes. "There are no permanent dibs. If I get back before you're done, I'm not sitting around to wait for you to shower first."

"Fine, then I get it first if we get here at the same time."

He walks to me, stopping when he's practically touching me. God, he's tall. I don't know why I never really noticed it. Maybe it's because I feel a little small right now, standing here in a skimpy outfit, hair dripping wet, and Rowan is . . . not.

I wait as he just stands here, looking down at me, his blue eyes never wavering. "Any other rules?" His deep voice sends a shiver down my spine.

"Yeah, you can never tell anyone about this."

The last thing I need is Aurora finding out we slept in the same bed. She'll have a coronary.

"Believe me, no one would ever believe it."

"Do you agree to the rules?"

"And if I don't?" he asks.

"Then you're sleeping in your truck."

He smirks. "I agree, but you have to agree to my one rule."

"And what's that?"

His face inches closer, so close that we're breathing one breath. "You have to be nice to me the whole weekend."

Yeah right. That's never going to happen. However, I'm exhausted and tomorrow is going to be a daunting day. I need sleep before I head out early in the morning. "I promise to try. We can do this for two nights and be adults."

He shakes his head and then steps back. "Okay then."

Rowan rips his shirt off so fast I stand here stunned for a second. "What are you doing?"

"Getting ready for bed," he explains before pulling his pants down.

"Oh my God!" I turn around, averting my eyes. "You could do that in the bathroom."

"Why?"

I huff, keeping my back to him as I walk to the other side of the bed. "Because I'm here and I really don't want to see you naked."

"I'm done," he says, and I turn to further scold him, but I find him standing there in just his underwear.

My mouth is open to start my tirade, but the words die in my throat. I have always thought Rowan was hot. Everyone does. However, I did not know this was what was hiding under his clothes.

No wonder my sister cried when she didn't get to see this anymore.

He's perfect.

His chest is solid muscle that tapers to his waist and clings to the ridges and valleys of his abs, and his legs are like tree trunks. Yeah, he's hauled a lot of hay and I am completely tongue tied.

"Like what you see?" Rowan asks, the cockiness pulling me out of my stupor. I roll my eyes, pull the comforter down, and then grab the extra pillows to put them in the middle. "Is this you being an adult?"

"Yes, I need boundaries."

"I have no intentions of encroaching during the night. I'm not attracted to porcupines."

I let out a long sigh. "This being nice thing is really going to be hard for you. I'm at least *trying* to be nice."

"You're right." Rowan pulls his side of the sheets back and climbs in. "I'll be nicer to you since you're going to try to do the same."

I pull the covers up, tucking them under my arms. "So a truce of sorts?"

"Of sorts."

I guess that's something. "Good night, Rowan."

"Good night, Charlotte."

I turn the lights off on my side, and he does the same. Cloaked in darkness, this feels a hundred times worse than it did in the light. I lie still, staring at the ceiling, doing my best to ignore that one of the hottest guys I've seen is basically naked in bed with me. However, he's not just some hot guy, he's my sister's ex. The guy who has made my life hell. The man who is currently my competition on the contract I need to save the farm.

All of this is what he is . . . not a very, very toned and chiseled man.

Rowan rolls over, I can feel the weight and heat of him on the pillow barrier, and I huff.

"I'm not touching."

"The barrier is supposed to keep you over there," I say, turning on my side to face him.

"It's neutral territory. I'm technically not breaking any rules. I thought we were going to be adults?"

I smile, grateful for the darkness keeping him from seeing it. "Give an inch, take a mile?" I ask with a hint of humor.

"Well, I'm practically falling off the bed so I need to take back what space I can. You weren't very generous in your barrier spacing," Rowan teases.

"You're so dramatic," I tell him with a playful lilt in my tone.

"If that's not the pot calling the kettle black, I don't know what is. Scoot over so I can have more room."

I don't move, enjoying our normal banter. "I'm on my side."

His arm moves closer to where I can feel his body heat. "Rowan," I warn.

"Still not touching. Now, close your eyes and be a good girl so I can sleep."

I bite my lower lip and close my eyes, hoping sleep takes me fast so my mind doesn't venture back into thinking about what it would be like to be that pillow.

ten

CHARLOTTE

This feels so good. The warmth of the blankets and the smell of cologne against my nose, it's the best freaking dream.

I move closer to it, wanting to drown in this scent. I freaking love these dreams. The ones where me and the hottest actor in the world, Noah Frazier, are in Florida together, and we're tangled up in the sheets again. It's always my favorite, and I'm really hoping I don't wake up before the good part.

I rub my nose against his chest, breathing him in and loving how he makes a rumbling sound as I press a kiss there.

My fingertips glide up his chest, and his hand moves down my back slowly. His skin is so smooth, and I move up, burying my face in his neck.

His hand runs up and down my spine before going to my ass, pulling me so I can feel his hard length against my leg.

His cock is so big.

So hard.

So fucking hot that I feel like I'm on fire.

I pray to whatever dream Gods there are that I never wake up. Seriously, this is the best one so far.

The scruff on his cheek moves against my temple then his hands that are on my ass lift me so my legs straddle him.

I moan softly, and he rocks me against his dick.

Oh. Oh yeah. This. I need this. It's been so long.

I move my hips, and his groan echoes around us. "Fuck."

His curse is low and pained. I'm totally going to make Noah Frazier lose his mind.

I move my hands to his chest, pressing up, but his arms cage me, tightening, holding me from moving, and then his voice is in my ear. "And here I thought you said no touching."

My eyes fly open, and I see that I am not, in fact, dreaming. No, it's a nightmare. I'm literally on top of Rowan Whitlock and dry humping him.

I don't move, trying to think of how the fuck I'm going to extricate myself from this.

"I-I . . . ummm," I stutter, and my heart pounds against my ribs. Seriously, I would like to just die right now. That would be really great and a much better outcome than what's going to come next. "Let me go."

His arms release me, and I move to the left, but he goes the same way, and what I thought was a very large penis in the dream is actually real. Holy shit.

"Rowan!" I yell.

"You were rubbing your cunt all over my cock, Charlotte. I'm not sure what you expect."

I expected to never have this happen.

"You had to know I was dreaming." I sit on my side of the bed, noting the pillows are no longer between us. One is down at the foot of the bed and the other is on my side. Oh God, I moved it.

Yeah, death please. I want it.

"No, I didn't, because sometime in the middle of the night you were plastered to my front, legs wrapped around mine, and I tried to move you twice, but you nestled closer," Rowan informs me.

I cover my face with my hands. "This can't be happening. We don't like each other."

"You seem to like me in your sleep."

I huff and glare at him. "No, I don't like you ever."

"That's a shame because you were moaning and seemed to really like my cock."

"I was dreaming about a man who is much bigger and hotter," I lie.

Rowan smirks. "I bet you were. Well, I gotta go take care of myself now, and don't worry, I'll be thinking of a woman much nicer than you as I come all over the walls."

He gets up out of the bed, heading to the bathroom, and I wrap my arms around my legs to keep myself from following him so I can see if everything I dreamed is real.

God, I am a mess.

"Are you sure you want to do this?" Faye asks as I'm putting my backpack together.

"Yes, I'm sure."

"But you've never gone hiking like this, have you?"

"No."

She laughs. "And you think now is a good time to try it? Are you insane?"

I have to go get lost in the woods for a little while to get my head on straight. After my very horrible morning, I went to the kitchen while he was jerking off and had breakfast and read more about the stunning views in this area. All the guides talk about how beautiful the mountain is off the trails. I've always wanted to go, and Faye's parents have all kinds of gear here to make it possible.

Once Rowan came out of the room, I went in to shower, and by the time I came out, he was already gone.

That was one less thing to worry about.

However, now Faye is acting like a mother hen. "I'll be fine. I work on a farm and I've dealt with all kinds of stuff. I'll pack everything I need, and I'll be back tomorrow morning."

She sighs heavily. "If you say so."

"I do. I need this. It'll be an adventure and I need some peace and tranquility, not staying in the room with a big jerk."

One brow rises. "Okay . . ."

I lean in and kiss her cheek. "I promise it'll be great."

"It might storm, Char. The clouds are forming, and they said the temperature will drop if it does roll in. Maybe wait until tomorrow. Joey might want to go or Sawyer or . . ."

I put my hand up. "We don't talk about that last one. He's dead to me."

He has to be, because if not, then I'll have to see him again and deal with the fact that I dry humped him this morning.

No, for now, we are going to do what gives me peace.

"I see you two are still being idiots."

She doesn't know the half of it. "Nope, just best not to speak his name. He's like Beetlejuice, say it three times and he'll appear. I'd rather not take my chances." Faye shakes her head and hands me a pack with a shovel. "What's that?"

"Avalanche gear. You have to be prepared, and you really shouldn't go alone."

"You worry too much, you sound like Aurora," I say, knowing it'll irritate her. Faye and Aurora aren't exactly each other's biggest fans. Faye thinks her leaving me was shitty, and that she's dramatic, which she is, but . . . she's my sister.

"The snow is practically melted, and if it rains, which the weatherman said it's less than a ten percent chance, it'll melt even more."

"Well, for the first time ever, I agree with your sister."

I place my hand on Faye's arm and smile. "I'm not going far up. I promise, I'll be fine."

She lets out a long breath through her nose. "If you say so."

"I know so. I'll be back in the morning without any issues. Watch."

What a lie that was.

Little did I know that four hours later I'd be eating those words and wishing I had just stayed in Sugarloaf.

I'm in the back country, however, I'm pretty sure I sprained my ankle. I was walking one of the trails and misstepped, and then suddenly, I was rolling down the mountain. Thankfully, I managed to grab onto a rock, stopping myself from slamming into a tree.

As wonderful as it was not to end up with broken ribs, my ankle is still swelling badly and throbbing even worse.

I'm a six-mile walk from the house, and the sun is already setting. I can't go back in the dark without possibly falling further, and I could injure myself worse trying to get down to where I know there was a cabin. The one thing I really can't do is stay here and hope for a miracle. I'll freeze to death and the storm is coming in. Thanks to the weather idiots who were wrong again.

I push myself up to standing, wincing as pain shoots up my leg.

"Why me? Seriously? What did I do in another life?" I ask the sky and then reach for two small branches. I put them on each side of my ankle and wrap it with the ace bandage I brought. Once that's done, I grab a large branch and test if it'll fit under my arm so I have a crutch of some kind.

"Like I'm going to be able to walk? No. I'm not. I'm going to die out here of hypothermia or starvation. Why? Because I'm an idiot and wanted to get away from the man I tried to maul. Way to go, Charlotte. Super smart."

There's a rustling noise behind me. I freeze, stop my tirade, and look around. The guidebooks did warn about wildlife, which would've been totally fine, but it's March and the bears are probably still in their comfy caves or whatever.

Relax, Charlotte. Bears don't like the cold, and it's freezing right now. It's probably a deer. Deer are cute-ish.

The tree leaves shake again, and then there is a *twacking* noise.

"Hello?" I say carefully. Bears are bad, deer are a little better, but another human would be either a blessing or could be here to kill me.

Never to find my body.

Lord, I have an overactive imagination.

"Hello?" a deep voice calls back.

Okay, not a bear, but maybe a murderer. "Hello?"

"Charlotte?" the voice says, and immediately, I know it's worse than a murderer.

I look up to the sky, telling God what I think of this turn of luck. "You must hate me." Then I sigh. "Yes, Rowan, it's me."

He pushes through the tree branches and comes to a stop beside me. "What are you doing?"

"Knitting a sweater," I say with sarcasm dripping from each syllable.

"I'm an extra large, if you're taking orders."

"I'm not."

He smirks. "Your leg." Rowan's entire demeanor shifts when he sees my makeshift brace. Gone is the arrogant smart-ass, replaced with a guy who has concern etched on his face. He crouches, his hand moving down my shin, barely ghosting over my swollen ankle before settling lightly on the top of my shoe. "What happened?"

"My pole hit a rock and I slid. I ended up rolling down a hill and hurting my back and shoulder, but my ankle got the worst of it."

Admitting all of that hurts more than the ankle.

He nods, pulling his backpack off. "We're pretty far from the house. If we start now, maybe we can make it before the"—thunder booms and lightning flashes across the sky—"storm."

"Seriously, just leave me here, I'm sure I'll get struck and I can just be done with this insanity."

Rowan rolls his eyes. "You're not going to stay out here and die from the cold and rain. We need to get to shelter."

"That's great, but I'm not really able to walk fast and we're miles away from anything."

I'm only going to slow him down and make this worse.

"We're going to try for the hunting cabin about a mile away. If we can't get there for whatever reason, we'll set up camp and wait for the storm to pass."

The sound of the rain hitting the trees is enough to make us both look up. It doesn't sound like normal rain, it's more like ice.

"We can't camp in an ice storm," I say what I'm sure he's thinking.

"No, we can't, so let's go before it covers the ground."

Rowan doesn't give me a chance to say anything, his arm hooks under mine and he pulls me up. I lean against him, hand on his chest, trying to steady myself. "I don't know how fast I can go," I admit.

"We'll go at the fastest pace that's safe. Do you have another jacket?"

I nod. "In my pack."

Thank God I was at least smart enough to pack that. Rowan fishes it out and helps me get it on, lifts the hood, and pulls the straps so I look like a freaking orange condom. "Really?"

"You need to stay dry, not cute."

He then goes into his own bag and does the same to himself before pulling out two ponchos—one for him and one for me.

"I didn't even think to grab those," I admit.

"I worried I'd need it for shelter, but this is more important. We have to get down to the cabin and the hill is steep. Use that branch as a crutch and hold on to me."

This really couldn't get any worse, but at the same time, I'm eternally grateful he found me. "How did you know where I was?"

"I didn't." Then he goes in his pocket and grabs a walkie-talkie. "Come in Moist Beard."

My brows scrunch. "Who the hell are you talking to?"

Then I hear Sawyer come through the line. "Skittle Titties, this is Moist Beard. Come in."

Oh, for fuck's sake.

"I have Angry Elf and we're heading to the hunting cabin we found earlier to wait out the storm and deal with her injury. Copy?"

"You're kidding me, right?" I say to him as he grins.

"I copy. Is she okay?"

"Angry Elf sprained her ankle. We'll need assistance getting her

95

back to the house. We'll check in once we arrive at the cabin."

Sawyer responds. "Ten-four, little buddy. Moist Beard out."

I don't care that the freezing rain is coming down a little harder, I look at him as though he's a freaking oddity, which he is. "What the hell is wrong with you two?"

"Not now, you can be your normal prickly self once we're in a dry location." He grabs my pack, helping me secure it to my front instead of my back. "This way I can hold on to you easier. Lean on the tree while I get my stuff."

"Why don't we leave my pack since it's so damn heavy?"

"Because we have no idea what this storm is going to dump, and we may need everything we both brought. Come on, hold on to me."

I loop my arm around his middle and he holds me to his side. Together, we walk slowly in zig-zag patterns. My legs are throbbing from only really having use of the one side. I want to curl into a hot bath and cry, but neither of those will happen.

"Keep going, Charlotte, you're doing great," Rowan encourages when I pull us to a stop for the tenth time.

My leg hurts. My ankle is throbbing so badly that the smallest movement sends shooting pain up my leg, and I am exhausted. "I can't keep going."

He faces me, his hands cupping my face. "We're almost there. You have to keep going, it's just about a quarter of a mile, then you can sit and rest, but the storm is getting worse, and we can't take a break now."

Normally, a mile or so walk would be less than fifteen minutes, at my pace, we're at almost an hour. My feet are drenched, and I'm pretty sure my toes are going to fall off, but Rowan hasn't said one thing. He's just held on to me, keeping me from falling when I slip and forcing me to keep going.

"I'm sorry," I say, my feelings starting to overwhelm me.

"You can apologize when we're inside and warm. Come on, Charlotte. Let's go."

I exhale deeply and nod, limping my way to the cabin in an ice storm.

eleven

ROWAN

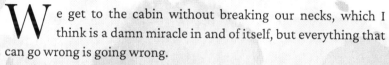

We get to the cabin without breaking our necks, which I think is a damn miracle in and of itself, but everything that can go wrong is going wrong.

There is no dry wood anywhere.

The ice storm has made what would normally be useable, absolute shit, so I am digging around to find anything to get us through. I need about five times as much tinder if I'm working with wet wood. Thankfully, the ice hasn't penetrated and covered everything completely yet. I've gathered a lot in the last forty minutes that was under a few big trees and am walking back for the third time to drop it off.

I have no idea what this storm is going to do, but I have a feeling it won't be good.

"Rowan?" Charlotte calls from inside.

I push the door open. "Yes?"

"It's freezing in here. We have to get the fire going."

"Hence the scavenger hunt I've been on the last hour."

"I'm just worried because there's ice coming in the fireplace." She tempers her voice.

I nod once. "I'll have it going soon. Did you find any food?"

"Yeah, the cabinet had some questionable items, but the dates are good. Plus, what we have in our packs will get us through at least five days."

"I pray to God we aren't here that long."

"Seriously, you'll be dead by then."

I laugh once. "I'll have killed you and buried the body."

Charlotte snorts. "Please, even injured I can kick your ass."

At least she still has her attitude.

"Anyway, go do whatever it is you can do while I take care of the important things." I close the door and head back out to get some more supplies as the freezing rain continues to fall.

Another twenty minutes, and the weather has only gotten worse. I can't be out here digging around much longer.

I just have to keep the fire going. If it burns out, we're fucked.

When I get back in the cabin, Charlotte is sitting at the table, her leg propped up on the other chair.

"I'm going to get the fire going."

"Okay, I can help."

I swear to God. "By the time you hobble over, I'll be done."

She huffs and stays put.

The walkie-talkie goes off. "Skittle Titties, this is Moist Beard. Come in."

"Can you answer him?" I ask since I have a lot of wood in my hands.

That's what she said.

"I'm not using your ridiculous names."

I smirk. "Then he probably won't respond."

At least, I hope he won't. Sawyer is as much of a smart-ass as I am, so I can imagine he's irritating Faye as well.

Charlotte picks it up and speaks. "Sawyer, it's Charlotte."

"Angry Elf, can you read me, Moist Beard, over?"

"Sawyer, I can hear you."

"This is Moist Beard, Angry Elf, I read you, can you confirm?"

I focus on the fire and not bursting out laughing.

Charlotte huffs. "I swear to God!"

Then Faye's voice comes through. "Idiots. All of you. Charlotte, are you okay?"

"I'm fine. We're in a cabin, and Rowan is getting a fire going."

You can hear Faye's relief when she responds. "Thank God, I've been so worried. Listen, the storm is going to be bad, they're saying we're going to be blanketed in ice for at least three days."

Charlotte's eyes meet mine. "Days?"

"We'll be fine," I assure her. I'm going to get this fire going and then get more wood because we definitely don't have enough for days.

She steadies herself, and then talks to Faye as though the worry she just showed me never existed. "It'll be fine. Rowan and I know what we're doing, and we have shelter, food, and I'm sure we'll both come out of this alive."

Faye laughs. "I'm not so sure about that last one. Lord knows I may kill Sawyer if he keeps up with his stupid names."

Yup. Totally pissing her off.

"You invited these tools," Charlotte reminds her.

"Next time it's just girls and no stupid hiking adventures on your own before an ice storm . . . and . . ."

Faye keeps going, lecturing her about the stupidity of her decision to go out hiking. Charlotte looks to me as she turns the volume down. "Can we shut this off to conserve batteries?"

I laugh and nod. "Toss it to me." She does, and I press the alarm button, which will stop her from being able to talk. "Fancy Princess, this is Skittle Titties, can you ensure that Moist Beard and Deputy Dewey move my truck off the hill?"

There's a pause. "Seriously, you're all annoying."

"Maybe, but you love us. Now, go let Moist Beard earn his name."

"What?" And then it dawns on her. "You're so gross! Take care of my girl."

"I will."

Sawyer comes on. "In all seriousness, you need to stay off the walkie-talkie in case we have an emergency. We'll have ours near and I'll get your truck off the incline."

"Ten-four, little buddy, keep it moist."

Charlotte gags. "You all need therapy."

"No more than you do, my Angry Elf."

She rolls her eyes. "I'm neither yours or angry, but you are definitely an idiot. Why the hell does he call you Skittle Titties?"

I pull my shirt tight and bounce my pecs. "Do your titties bounce, sweetheart?"

She groans. "So gross."

"You want to taste the rainbow?" I taunt.

Charlotte flips me off.

I go back to my task, getting everything arranged as best as I can. I elevated everything so there's air to breathe, crisscrossed the logs, and put in as much dry flammable shit as I could find. "Here goes nothing."

Charlotte hobbles over to the fireplace and settles a good two feet away from me.

I light the tinder, hoping it will start to burn the twigs and branches, willing it to start the fire.

Neither Charlotte nor I speak as we watch the smoke rise and the sparks start to work.

"Come on," she whispers to the fire. "Otherwise, we're going to freeze to death."

She's not completely wrong. We'll need to huddle together for warmth, which might end up being what kills us.

It's not that she's not fucking stunning, because she is, but she gets under my skin in a way that no man wants. Everything out of her damn mouth is a fight, and Lord knows we can't stand each other. She's maddening, beautiful, irritating, and I would like nothing more than to shut her up in other ways. Which will never happen.

Ever.

Charlotte leans forward, her hand touching mine just barely. "Please start," she begs.

"It'll light," I say, pulling my hand back.

The only reason I felt any type of spark was because I was thinking about how hot she is, that's all.

I feed the fire a little more tinder, and then it starts to crackle louder. Charlotte lets out a sigh of relief and leans back. "Oh, thank God. I was so worried we'd have to resort to other ways of keeping warm."

"Don't pretend you don't want to see me naked again and climb me like a ladder."

"I didn't want to climb you like a ladder."

"No? I seem to remember waking up with you wrapped around me, moaning and rubbing against my cock." I push her to recall the whole reason we started this day off with some action.

Doesn't matter that she tried to pretend otherwise.

We're stuck here now and we have nothing else to talk about.

"I was *sleeping*, thank you very much."

"You wanted me," I say with a smirk.

"I did not."

She did and still does. I can see it in her eyes. She may not *want* to want me, and heaven knows I don't want her.

Not like that.

Not that this morning wasn't fucking hot, because it was, but she's . . . Charlotte.

"Whatever you tell yourself to feel better."

She grunts and stands, hopping back to the other side of the room where our gear is. "I swear, it's a wonder any woman can stand you for more than three minutes."

"I last a lot longer than that."

Charlotte makes a gagging noise. "Gross."

I laugh because whatever she needs to tell herself is fine with me. She didn't think I was gross when she was grinding on my cock. However, we're stuck here, and I really don't feel like arguing the entire time.

She pulls out her sleeping bag and then tosses it. "Oh my God!"

I look over and she scoots back. "What?"

"It's got ... bugs ... in it."

I walk over and find a bunch of ants. Great. "It's going outside," I tell her as I walk over. "The last thing we need are bugs in here." I toss it out the door so it's still under the awning but not in the house. They'll die with the temp being this low.

"What the hell am I supposed to sleep in now?" Charlotte asks, looking longingly at the door.

"You'll have to sleep close to the fire."

She glares at me. "You'll just let me freeze?"

"Better than letting myself freeze," I say with a smirk. "But, no, you're not going to freeze, Charlotte. We have my sleeping bag and we're in a cabin the size of a tent with the fire going, it's going to be roasting soon enough."

Letting out a long breath through her nose, she grabs for the stick she used as a crutch and hobbles back to the fire that is now warming the small cabin. "Thank you for starting the fire."

"You're welcome. I'm going to take a piss, I'll be back. Don't get into trouble." I head out the back where there is an outhouse. It's definitely not my idea of a good time, but we're working with what we have. While walking, I look around for anything I may need to use. There's a small shed over to the left, which I already know doesn't have any firewood in it because I peeked into it earlier, but I plan to really go through it before going back to Charlotte.

I use the bathroom and walk over. The door sticks a bit, but a good tug knocks the ice off. Inside is like a shack of horrors. There's blood on the ground, chains hanging from the ceiling, knives all over the place, and jars of all kinds of shit. Yeah, this is clearly where they skinned and cleaned their kill.

Not going to mention this to Charlotte.

Or maybe I should.

I head back inside and find her sitting on the cot with my sleeping bag wrapped around her.

"What the hell?"

"What?" she asks quickly.

"My sleeping bag."

She shrugs. "I was cold."

"I'm cold."

She nudges her chin toward the fire. "Then warm up by the fire as you so sweetly suggested I should do."

I smirk. Smart-ass mouth on her does something to me. "Or you can give me my sleeping bag," I suggest.

Charlotte shifts, her lips quirking up into an adorable smile. No, not adorable. Nope. I refuse to think she's adorable at all. "I could, but I'm cold and you should be a gentleman and offer it to me."

I walk toward her. "I could, but I'm not." I lean down, grab the corner, and start to pull, but she holds on for dear life.

"I'm cold, Rowan. I'm freezing cold."

Her voice has a tinge of ache to it, but if she was so cold, she'd be by the damn fire.

"I don't buy it."

"Buy what?" Charlotte asks with surprise.

"That you're freezing cold. You've been inside by the fire while I've been in the damn freezing rain."

She huffs and pulls the sleeping bag tighter. "Well, I'm sorry you don't believe me, but it's true. Besides, I'm tired and injured, so I'm going to sleep."

"Not with my only heat source you're not."

"So, you want me to freeze to death?"

"It's not the worst idea. It'd be quiet at least," I toss back, and her jaw drops.

"You are seriously such an asshole."

I shrug. "You made that assumption about me a long time ago. Give me the sleeping bag. Also, that cot is mine."

"The hell it is!"

"Fine. Sleeping bag or the cot. You pick." I give her the option.

She stands, pulling the sleeping bag tighter, and grins. "Enjoy your cold cot, asshat."

I roll my eyes and extend my hand with a sigh. "Give me the bag." I plan to share it with her. The two of us don't need to die out here.

"No."

She steps back, and I move closer. "Charlotte, stop being so damn stubborn. Give me the sleeping bag."

"I'm not giving it to you."

"You're so fucking stubborn!"

"Of course I am! You want me to freeze on the dirty floor!"

I huff. "I don't! Jesus Christ!"

She takes the sleeping bag off, putting it behind her back. "If you want the sleeping bag, come and get it."

There's heat in her eyes, one that warms another part of me. I fucking hate this woman sometimes, but I hate myself even more right now with the want to kiss that attitude right out of her body.

"Don't push me," I warn.

Her eyes narrow. "If you want it, you can come get it."

I close the distance to her in two long strides, stopping when we're chest to chest. Her gaze is locked on mine, and there I see the same thing I feel in my chest. A tightness, an ache, a hatred that exists.

I lean down, my arms going around her as I grab for the sleeping bag. My only thought is to get it from her, set up the fucking cot close to the fire for her, and sleep in the damn kitchen where I can keep my distance.

However, that doesn't happen.

Instead, Charlotte lifts up, just a little, and whispers, almost as though it was a thought not meant to be shared. "Take it."

And I don't know if she means the sleeping bag or her, but I pull her to me and wait a second for her to tell me to let her go, but instead, her eyes close, and I crush my lips to hers.

twelve

CHARLOTTE

My arms move around his neck as he pulls me off the ground, his mouth against mine. I kiss him back, anger and heat swirling around him.

I don't like him. In fact, I hate him even more right now.

How dare he kiss me? How dare he make me kiss him back?

All of this is wrong, but I can't seem to stop myself.

I feel the wall against my back, his arms caging me in as I lift up on my toes.

Instead of pushing him away like I know I should, my fingers thread in his dark brown hair, pulling him closer.

Why am I doing that? I don't know, but I kiss him deeper.

The swirl of our tongues, the taste of mint from his mouth overwhelms me. He moans deeply as he grinds his dick against me, lifting me and supporting all my weight.

"Tell me to stop," he commands.

"Stop talking," I reply, kissing him again.

He shuts me up, his mouth ravishing mine, and his hands moving down my back, cupping my ass to adjust me again.

Rowan lifts his mouth from mine, staring into my eyes for a beat before kissing my neck and along the slope of my shoulder.

"Take your shirt off if you want me to touch you," he says, leaning back.

Now is when I should put a stop to this, but instead of shoving at his chest, I pull my shirt off, tossing it to the floor. "Now you."

He smirks. "I knew you liked what you saw."

"I didn't," I lie.

"Right."

Arrogant prick.

He tugs his shirt off, throwing it with mine. "Just like you don't want me to kiss you."

Before I can respond, his mouth is on mine again. I hate him. I hate that I want him. I hate that he's making me grind on his thick thigh, which causes his moan to vibrate through me.

"Fuck you," I say as I pull my mouth away, gasping for breath.

"I plan to fuck *you*."

He pushes my shoulder against the wood, my skin scraping against the rough wood panel, and I love it. "I never said I was going to let you."

He smiles at that, then runs his tongue along his perfect white teeth. "Your body is telling me you want my cock. Look at you rubbing against my leg, wanting to come like the dirty girl you are."

I push against his chest, but he doesn't budge. "You want me."

"I didn't say I didn't."

"I hate you."

"Good. Then we're both in agreement that this is a hate fuck and nothing else."

I can get with that. Anger and sex work just fine for me. "And tomorrow this never happened?"

He laughs once. "Oh, sweetheart, don't you worry, I'll never breathe a word about what happens here."

"Then shut up and kiss me."

Rowan does, he kisses me deep and hard then scoops me into his arms, carrying me toward the fire.

He places me down, and I do everything in my power not to think about what I'm doing right now. I don't let my mind ponder how fucked up it is that I'm about to fuck my sister's ex and arch-nemesis.

Nope.

Not thinking about it.

He lays out the sleeping bag in front of the fire before returning to me, scooping me up as though I weigh nothing.

"This is just sex," he tells me as he lays me down.

"Nothing more," I reiterate.

"Nothing more." Rowan pushes my hair back, tucking it behind my ear. Then sits back on his heels and moves to my ankle and carefully undoes the splint. "Be careful when this is off," he tells me.

"I know."

"I just mean when I'm fucking you, making you come apart, making you fall to pieces over and over, you need to remember you're hurt and it's not my fault."

I shake my head. "Or maybe when I'm bored because you're not as good as you think, I'll knit a sweater and think of all the other ways I could've been spending my time."

Rowan's eyes find mine and I see immediately that I made the wrong decision to challenge him.

Or maybe the right one because I am going to pay for that.

And I hope the price is in orgasms.

I could really use one that doesn't come from my vibrator in my bedside table.

His arms are on both sides of my head and he leans in so his nose is touching mine. "The last thing you'll be when I'm fucking you is bored."

"Promises, promises."

He huffs out a laugh. "You're going to see I make good on them. Be a good girl and take off your pants, Charlotte."

The defiant part of me wants to tell him to fuck off, but the heat in his gaze makes me keep my mouth shut and do it.

"That's it, you deserve a reward for listening." Rowan's voice is smooth as he stares down at me in nothing but my bra and underwear.

"A reward?"

He nods. "I think so, good girls get rewards, bad girls get spanked."

Yeah, so not going to admit that made my stomach—and other parts of me—clench.

"And what about you?" I ask, forcing my voice to stay even.

"What about me?"

"What if you're good? What do you get?"

He grins and runs his finger from my throat down to my core. "I get this." He pushes my underwear to the side. "I get to lick right here." His finger slides against my lips. "I get to taste this." Rowan touches my clit, and I moan. "I get to sink deep into here." I nearly scream when he pushes just knuckle deep and stops. "Do you want that, Charlotte?"

"Yes," I say, my head falling to the side. God, I hate that he made me admit that.

"I thought so." Then he pushes all the way in, fingering me and moving it slowly. "Look how wet you are. How much you want this."

I return my gaze to his and then look at his pants, which are seriously tented. "And by the looks of it, you want it too."

"I fucking hate that I do."

"Same."

"Then how about I find a way to shut us both up?"

I bite down on my lip as he pulls out of me. Then my underwear is gone and he moves to my bra, pulling that free and tossing it aside. I'm completely naked before him. Rowan doesn't wait, he stands, pulling his pants off, freeing his incredible erection.

Holy fucking hell.

He moves back toward me, kneeling off to the side, and takes my hand, wrapping it around his cock. "You shouldn't make me this hard. Not with your smart mouth and our mutual hate. But here I am, hard as stone for you."

"And I'm aching for you even though I hate you."

I move my hand up and down his dick and then push up onto my elbows.

"I think it's time for you to stop talking," Rowan says as his thumb brushes my lips.

"And how do you intend to make that happen?"

I'm really hoping it's the idea I have.

"Put my cock in your mouth and let's see if that works."

He pushes his hips forward, and I don't hesitate. I take him deep in my throat, his hands framing my face, holding me where he wants me. "That's it, baby, let me feel the back of your throat." His head falls back, and he thrusts, fucking my mouth, and I love it. I pump my hand with him, trying to make him lose his mind.

Not that we both haven't clearly gone stupid—the evidence being that I have my mouth full of Rowan Whitlock's cock and I have never been so turned on.

I lift my eyes, and he's staring down at me. "Touch yourself, Charlotte. Touch your clit." I move my hand down, circling it. "Good girl. Do you like that?"

I can't speak since my mouth is a little full, but I try to tell him yes with my eyes.

He smirks. "Do you wish it was my hand there? Do you want me to fuck your cunt with my tongue?"

I raise my brows a little, and he pulls out, pushing me to the makeshift pillow and spreading my legs.

Rowan's tongue slides against my clit and then he's feasting on me. There's no slow, soft building. It's straight savage. I raise my arms over my head to hold on to the stone on the fireplace. "Holy shit!" I yell as he moves his tongue in the most amazing direction. "Yes! Oh, right there!" I tell him, and my body starts to tremble. I have never gotten this close this fast. Normally, it takes a good ten to fifteen minutes and a lot of imaginative thinking on my part to push myself there.

But there's none of that now.

It's as though he's in my brain, knowing exactly what I like, how I like it, and how to deliver it.

"Rowan," I pant. "Please, don't stop."

The bastard doesn't listen. He lifts his head, his thumb just resting on my clit. "You said stop."

I lift my head, glaring at him. "I said don't stop!"

He pushes down, adding just a little more pressure. "You liked my head between your legs?"

I groan, dropping back down.

The pressure increases again, and he moves in a slow circle. "Answer me, Charlotte. Do you like me licking your pussy?"

"Yes," I mutter, shoving my hips up to get more friction.

"Do you want to come on my tongue, sweet girl?"

My nerves are shot. I'm climbing back up again, desperate for the pinnacle. "You know I do."

"Then beg. Tell me how much you want it, and it's yours."

Begging is so not my thing, but right now, there's not much I wouldn't do to get off. "Please, give me your mouth," I say, my body trembling. "Eat me out and get me off."

Rowan doesn't make me say more, he shoves my legs even farther apart, holding me wide open to the empty room with his strong hands. That tremble is more like full-on shaking now as I can't move my lower half because he has me immobilized.

"Rowan, yes! Fuck yes! You feel so good. God, I hate that you feel so damn good!" I start talking, my mind unable to control what comes out. "I hate that it's you, but God, it's you. Please, fuck, I'm going to come!"

He moans, his tongue moving even faster. I don't know if it's being pinned down or whatever magical skill he has. Maybe it's both.

I'm coming apart. I scream, my heart pounding as my orgasm crashes through me.

I swear the world around me goes dark for a moment, and then I'm gasping for breath.

As soon as I have control of myself, I shift, needing the upper hand.

"Get on your back," I tell him.

He smirks. "Ask nicely."

I shake my head. "I swear to God, you stupid, arrogant asshole, you either get on your back now or be prepared to need a very cold walk from some severe blue balls. You have two seconds to decide."

Rowan smirks, his arm darts out, grabbing me and tossing me on my back before I can even get to the count of one. He hovers above me. "Now, I told you to ask nicely." His hand squeezes my ass. "I think you need to be fucked into submission."

I laugh at that. "I will never submit."

"Challenge accepted."

I feel his dick slide against my clit, and I moan. The emotions inside me are at war. On one hand, I want to tell him no, to push him away and not let this happen. The other part of me is desperate to feel him inside me. For him to take me, to drown out all the noise and anger and pain from the last few months.

I'm tired of fighting.

I fight everything on my own, and God, I know it's insane and wrong on so many levels, but I don't want to fight anymore.

Rowan's eyes stay on mine. "I swear, Charlotte, you will submit, and when you do, I'll take it all from you."

As though he can read my damn thoughts. Why him? Why can't it be anyone else? Why does it have to be the one man in the world I could and should never let have control over me? The man who has driven away my support because he was a bastard. Rowan Whitlock, who I have sworn to hate but who has saved me multiple times, against my damn wishes and wants. Yet, here he is again, offering me a glimpse at a reprieve from all of the stress.

Even if it only lasts a brief time.

Don't I deserve it?

My jaw is so tight from trying to hold on. He rocks again, and his voice is soft like silk against my skin. "Let me take it from you."

The promise in those words hangs over my head like a gift.

I toss my head back and forth, wanting to keep some kind of control. Needing it because without it, I'll break. "I can't."

"You can."

I stare up at him as he rocks again. "Give in, Charlotte."

My hands cup his face, keeping our gazes locked. "I will never forgive you for this."

"I know."

"We don't have a condom," I say, as reality hits me.

"I've been tested."

"I have an IUD."

Rowan rocks his hips again. "It's just this once."

"And we never talk about it again."

"It never happened," Rowan says and a pained look crosses his face.

"Then fuck me, and it better be good."

Rowan impales me. And my mind goes blank with the pleasure and the pain of it all.

thirteen

ROWAN

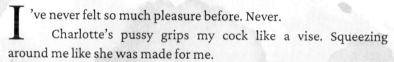

I've never felt so much pleasure before. Never.

Charlotte's pussy grips my cock like a vise. Squeezing around me like she was made for me.

This is a mistake.

A big one.

I don't know what I was expecting, but it wasn't this. She fits me perfectly, matches my thrusts in perfect rhythm. The only sounds in this small cabin are our heavy breathing, grunts, and the crackle of the fire.

Charlotte's fingernails scrape down my back as I slam my hips forward. "Yes, fuck, yes!"

"Damn right, yes. Say my name," I command her. Wanting her just as wrecked from this as I am.

"Rowan!" she answers immediately.

"Who is fucking you right now?"

"You are."

I moan, lifting her hips to a different angle. "Who owns you right now?"

"You!" Charlotte practically screams it as I feel her tighten again.

She's close. I want to make her come on my cock. Tasting her was fucking heaven, but this is going to send me to hell, which is where I belong for taking her.

"That's right, baby. Does it feel good?" I ask, unable to stop myself. If I'm going there, might as well enjoy the ride.

Her eyes find mine. "So good."

I slow my pace a little, watching my wet cock slide in and out of her. "You're so wet. So fucking perfect. Look at how drenched my cock is," I murmur. Charlotte's eyes find where the two of us are connected, and she tightens even more. "You like that. You like watching my cock inside of you." I move my hips, and she whimpers. "I do too, baby. I like that it's me fucking you," I admit—stupidly.

"You feel so good," Charlotte says, her words trailing off in a moan.

"We feel good together. So fucking good."

She adjusts her hips and then gasps. "Oh, God."

My fingers tighten around her hips, and I hit that same spot.

Charlotte shudders.

"Don't move. I'm going to make you come."

I do it again, her breath hitches and I know she's close. I press my thumb against her clit and hold the pressure there as my dick hits that spot inside of her.

Her entire body locks as she screams my name over and over, her cunt is milking me as her orgasm takes her. It's the most beautiful thing I've ever seen in my life.

I have to hold onto my control as my own release is looming. Watching her like this, seeing her in the throes of passion is too much.

I need to come. I need to mark her as she just did me and I can't hold back.

"I can't stop it."

"Don't stop!" she moans.

"Inside or out?" I ask, using the last bit of my sanity.

"Out."

"Fuck!" I scream, pulling out and painting her breasts and stomach with my seed, as I pump my cock, pulling every drop of pleasure I have, giving it to her.

I drop down on my forearms, struggling to catch my breath.

Charlotte takes my face in her hands, forcing me to look at her. "Now who lost control?"

Only she would try to gain back her power immediately. I smirk. "I think the question we really need to ask is: who lost it first?"

She glares, and I kiss her and tell myself it was to stop her from answering, but it's not, it's because I need to.

And isn't that a kick in the nuts?

***

The two of us pretty much passed out as soon as we cleaned up, which had been fucking fun with no running water. I had to get ice and melt it by the fire. Thankfully, the owners of the cabin had a few pots and supplies in the kitchen area.

She wiggles against my dick, still mostly asleep, and tightens her arm as she gets closer.

I know we don't like each other much, but she sure loves me in her sleep.

With as much as I'd like to let her stay snuggled against me, I need to add more wood to the fire before it burns out. The last thing I can have is that. I'll never find more tinder now.

The sleet hasn't let up, and the temperature has definitely dropped more, making the outside even more unbearable.

I doubt we'll even be able to use the outhouse now.

I brush her dark brown hair away from her face, tucking it behind her ear, and then trail my fingertips down her back. "Charlotte," I say softly.

She smiles in her sleep, and I fight back a laugh. She'd fucking die if she knew she did that.

"You need to wake up so I can take care of the fire," I tell her, rubbing my nose against hers.

Her lips part, and she moves closer. "Kiss me," she mutters.

I'm not sure if she's awake or dreaming, but before I can try to wake her again, she brings her mouth to mine.

Slowly, I part her lips, causing her to gasp as her arms tighten around me. I lick inside her mouth, toying with her tongue. This isn't like the kisses from last night, which were frantic and had a hint of anger.

This is deliberate and soft. I kiss her as though I have nothing else in the world to do, which is stupid because the whole reason I woke her was to get the fire going again.

But this ... fuck, this. This is everything.

I shift her so she's on top of me, her hair falling around us both, creating a curtain where only our mouths exist. Charlotte moans softly, and then her tongue moves against mine. I pull her face back just a little, nipping at her lower lip.

"Rowan," she breathes my name.

I don't know why it fucks with my head so much, but it does. I don't care if we freeze to death at this point.

Let the fire die.

There's enough warmth between us to set the cabin up in flames.

I move her so she's straddling my hips and I can feel how hot she is. Neither of us got fully dressed, so there's not much between us.

Just her tiny thong and my boxers.

I shift her a little, pulling myself free.

Fuck it.

Fuck all of it because I need to be inside her again.

"Again?" I ask the question, needing her agreement.

"Yes," she moans as she rocks again.

I pull her underwear to the side and push just the tip inside.

"If you want me, Charlotte, take it."

She doesn't hesitate, she sinks down on my cock and I'm buried deep inside of her. I pull her face to mine and kiss her hard. She pushes against my chest, breaking free of my hold and sits on my cock like a fucking queen.

"You had control before, now it's my turn."

I put my hands behind my head and grin. "Have it, sweetheart. My cock is your throne."

She pulls her lower lip between her teeth. "And I'm supposed to worship it?"

"Whatever you want, I'll hand the kingdom to you," I say, staring into those green eyes that I want to lose myself in.

Her hips move slowly, setting an easy, almost teasing pace. "What if I want to burn your kingdom to the ground? What if I want to leave nothing but ruins when I'm done?"

"Do your worst, Charlotte. I'll take whatever you think you can dish out. But you have ten minutes before our fire is out, and we're in a different kind of trouble."

She smiles at that, moving a little faster. "Ten minutes to do my worst?"

I nod. "Better make it count, sweetheart."

"And what happens at the end?"

I move my hands to her breasts, pinching her nipples. "We'll see who is left standing."

For the first time in my life, I'm not sure it'll be me.

⚷

Much to my dismay, she fucks my entire world up in less than five minutes. I have never in my fucking life lost it that quickly.

When she took my balls in her hand, rolling them as she fucked me hard, I fought as hard as I could. The battle was lost when she started playing with herself as she rode me.

It was too much.

I did my best to slow her, do anything I could to control the sensations, but nothing worked, and I came with a ferocity I didn't know was possible.

When we finished, she smiled down at me with my cock inside

123

her and winked. "I guess we know who would win the war between us."

"I'd say that was just a battle, this war isn't over yet," I informed her as I rolled her onto her back, slid out, and went to work on the fire.

In the time that it took me, which has been two minutes, she has managed to sprawl out on the blanket and is snoring away.

The fire is roaring again, flames dancing high, and I continue to feed it. I don't want to have to wake up again because I'm fucking exhausted.

I stare at the orange and red colors, wondering what in the hell the two of us are doing. This is Charlotte Sullivan. The pain in my ass who has called me more names than anyone else. Her and her asshole sister worked incredibly hard to smear my name, and now we're both fighting for the same contract with Knight Food Distribution.

This is a bad idea. A stupid one, but I'm growing hard again, thinking about how fantastic the sex was.

I hear the rustling of the sleeping bag and look over to see her sound asleep. She looks soft and sweet right now.

Then again, her mouth is shut and she's not spewing her hate.

I let out a deep breath through my nose and settle in behind her, wrapping my arm around her middle. Not allowing myself to think about why, I pull her closer and bury my face in her neck, inhaling deeply and allowing sleep to take me to a place where this won't be complicated when we wake up in the morning.

"I have to pee so bad," Charlotte complains as she's standing at the door and staring at the half inch of ice on the ground outside.

"So go pee."

She looks at me like she wants to kill me, which is basically her normal look when we're not naked. "I can't get there, Rowan. I'll break both my ankles if I try."

"I had no issues," I remind her.

Which isn't true. I just pissed off the side of the porch.

"Well, not all of us have a hose that can aim our pee."

"Sucks for you, huh?"

She flips me off. "Can you maybe be a gentleman and help me to the outhouse?"

I raise my brows and laugh. "Charlotte, it's literally a sheet of ice. There's no way to walk there on two good legs."

"What am I supposed to do?" she asks, throwing her arms up. "I'm going to pee my pants!"

"Come on," I say, not wanting her to pee herself.

"Come on what?"

"Do you want to piss your only pair of pants or are you going to let me help?

I grab the blanket off the ground and wait with my hand extended. Charlotte, not being a complete idiot, sighs and takes my hand. I help her over to the side of the porch. "Look, it's going to be cold, and it's not going to be dignified, but it is what it is, okay?"

Her face falls. "Nothing about this entire trip has gone the way I thought, so, whatever."

"Glad to see you're being mature. Now, slide through the top railing, and sit on the second rail," I instruct her.

"What?"

"You're going to use that lower one as a seat and piss off the side, but without the hose I come so generously equipped with."

"Kill me now," she mutters, but she does what I say.

Her arms are looped around the top wooden railing, keeping her upright, and I drop in front of her.

I pull her pants down past her knees. "Now pee," I tell her and move the blanket around the front of her to give her some privacy.

Her eyes meet mine and there's gratitude there, and she nods. "Please talk or sing so that you don't . . . hear this. I seriously want to die as it is, and I don't think I can take much more."

"Singing it is," I say, grinning because one thing I cannot do well is that. I belt out the lyrics to my favorite '90s rap song, and Charlotte shakes her head, laughing hysterically.

"Stop, stop! I take it back!" Her eyes are filled with tears. "I'm done. Did you bring a napkin?"

I extend it to her, and when she lets go of her one arm, she starts to fall, and I grab her, holding her steady.

"Seriously, this is the worst day of my life."

"You've had some pretty fantastic sex in the last twenty-four hours, I'd say it's been a good day," I offer her another perspective.

She rolls her eyes, drops the napkin into the bag I'm holding. "Can you pull my pants up please?"

I drape the blanket over her shoulders, help her get dressed, and then we carefully extract her from the railing before heading back into the cabin.

Less than five minutes outside and both of us are shivering. It's so fucking cold.

"How long are we going to have to stay here?" she asks, her teeth chattering.

I come around behind her, pulling her onto my lap, rubbing up and down her arms. "I don't know, but we have to stay here until we can manage more than five minutes outside."

Charlotte nods and shifts so she can curl into me as I pull the blanket around the two of us. Even in front of the fire, it's freaking cold.

"I swear it dropped another fifteen degrees. It's March! Why is Mother Nature so confused?"

"I don't know."

She looks up at me, head resting on my shoulder. "It seems she's not the only one confused. We're doing a pretty bang-up job too."

I smile and laugh once. "Our confusion will clear once we're back home."

"Before then, Rowan."

"What happened in the cabin stays in the cabin."

"We're having our own version of *Fight Club*?"

"Whatever you want to call it."

"Lapse of Judgment, that's what it needs to be called."

I nod once. "It won't happen again."

Charlotte sighs, shivering once again. "Good."

It is good because I don't need any complications in my damn life. Especially not from another Sullivan.

fourteen

CHARLOTTE

"Y ou cheater!" I yell at Rowan as his hand hits the deck of cards before mine, but there's no way he could've beaten me.

"That's not the first time you've accused me of doing that and not the first time you're wrong. I didn't cheat. You just lost."

I huff. "No, I didn't lose. You distracted me."

I never lose at slapjack. I'm like the best player in all the world.

"Clearly, you lost."

No, I refuse to accept defeat. "You did something because I never, ever lose."

"Until now," Rowan says with a shit-eating grin.

Such a cocky asshole.

He leans forward. "Lose the shirt, sweetheart."

Ugh, I hate that I agreed to this. "We never said the other gets to pick the clothing item."

"That's always how it goes."

"Maybe in your world, but not mine." I reach behind my back, unhooking my bra, and feed it through the armholes. "There, it's an item of clothing."

Rowan laughs. "That's fine because the next item you're

129

removing is your shirt, and I'm happy to stare at your beautiful tits for the day."

"That's not going to happen because I won't lose again."

At least I better not.

The walkie-talkie chirps a second before we hear Sawyer. "Skittle Titties, do you copy?"

I swear to God these two are the dumbest humans alive.

"I hear you loud and clear, Moist Beard. How is it up by you?"

"A fucking nightmare. The roads are completely covered and power keeps going in and out." Sawyer sounds frustrated. "I hoped we'd be able to get to your location and get you guys back, but there's no way with the ice."

His eyes find mine. "We're fine here. Playing cards right now. There's no electricity here, so we're making do with the lanterns and fire." He releases the button, staring at me as he says the last part. "And finding other ways to stay warm."

I feel the heat flame my cheeks. Rowan is shirtless, and I'd be lying if I said it wasn't making me hot. Seriously, his body should be illegal.

Then he makes his pecs bounce and I roll my eyes. Idiot.

Sawyer's laugh comes through the speaker, causing us both to flinch as we were lost in each other for a moment. "Cards? I figured Angry Elf would be digging a hole to bury your body by now."

He pulls the mic up to his lips. "She's found other things to do with my body—like ride my cock until she screams and comes all over it."

My eyes go wide, and I leap out of the chair, hopping and lunging for the walkie-talkie, but he's too fast. He stands, lifting it above his head.

I'm short, and there's no way I can reach. "You asshole! You did not just say that, did you? You can't tell him that! Tell him you were lying!" I yell, trying to reach for it while he laughs.

"Hello? Skittle Titties? Come in?" Sawyer says.

Please God, tell me he didn't hear what he said.

Rowan wraps his one arm around me, preventing me from

trying for the walkie-talkie, and his lips are at my ear. "I wasn't holding the button when I said it. Calm down."

Immediately, I feel myself semi relax. "That hole he was saying I'd be digging will happen if you're lying."

He chuckles and then licks the shell of my ear. "I'd much rather you do other things with your energy."

I really wish I didn't feel my muscles clench when I imagine what we could be doing.

Then he releases me, bringing the walkie-talkie to his mouth. "I copy. Check in tomorrow, and we'll see if it's safe to attempt to get back to you."

Instead of Sawyer's voice it's Faye who replies. "I swear, if you do anything to make Charlotte scream, I'll kill you myself, Rowan. Be nice to her, she's hurt and needs someone to make her feel better, not worse."

Oh, Faye, now you've gone and done it.

The mischief on his face tells me he's not going to pass this up. "Rowan, don't," I warn, but of course, he's going to do it.

"I promise, Faye, I'll be very nice to her and I'm doing everything I can to make her feel better."

"Good. We'll talk tomorrow. Save the batteries."

He releases me and I try to step back, but he comes with me. "Where are you going?" he asks.

"Back to my seat to finish the game." And to avoid what I'm pretty sure is coming next.

"In the end, we'll both be naked, and then what did you think would happen when you suggested this?" His voice is even, but the way his jaw ticks tells me he's not feeling so steady.

"We can't," I protest feebly as my ass hits the edge of the table and his arms cage me in. "We shouldn't."

He brushes his nose against mine. "I didn't ask that. What did you think would happen?"

This. I thought we'd end up doing this. Because I want to. Because I've already fucked up twice, might as well do it again, right? The harm is done, and we're stuck here, so . . .

My hands move to his stomach, the muscles tensing beneath my touch as I glide my fingertips down. "When in the cabin and all that?" I ask, my eyes finding his.

"No one will ever know," he says as our mouths come together, and we make another mistake on the table.

～

"I'm starving. Can't you go hunt a deer or something? A deer or a rabbit would be fine," I ask as my stomach rumbles.

It's been four days of us out here, freezing, with very little food. We had enough for about five days each, but we're not sure just how long we're going to be stuck here and the rations are dwindling.

Last night, we slept together with the fire crackling, racking up the sexy times we're never going to talk about.

It's like the dam has been broken, and I find myself naked more than dressed around him.

I still hate him. When we're not fucking each other's brains out, he makes me want to stab him, so that hasn't changed, but he's fantastic in bed.

Which really sucks because I'm bound to hate him for eternity.

"Yeah, Charlotte, let me go out in the goddamn ice storm with the wind blowing freezing rain at me and find you a deer. I'm right on top of that."

"Or a rabbit!" I say again.

"You're right, a rabbit would be so much easier. Why didn't I think of that? Hmm, I wonder though, do you think they'll just walk over to me as a sacrifice? Maybe I can do some kind of rabbit calling and explain you're starving and need it to just lie down so I can roast it on a spit."

"No need to be sarcastic," I say, crossing my arms over my chest.

He shakes his head. "I'm starving too, but according to Sawyer, if tomorrow warms up, he's going to see if he can take the ATV down the mountain and get us the fuck out of here."

Good. I can't spend another night like this. We've already crossed way too many lines, and none of them are the right ones.

I need to go back to my life, figure out how to get this contract, and get money to save my farm, not fuck around with Rowan out in this horrible cabin.

"I hope it warms up then," I say and make my way toward the window. The world outside is a shiny mess. The rain has finally stopped, but the cold weather hasn't done the ground any favors. Last night, a huge tree fell outside, causing both of us to jump. Rowan went out to make sure there was no damage to the cabin. After about ten minutes he came back, soaking wet because he'd fallen three times, and said the shack that was in the back is completely smashed.

"Was there anything in that shed thing out back?"

"You really don't even want to know what was inside," he explains.

"That bad?"

"It was a lot of weird jars of things. I saw a few mushrooms and other things, but a lot of fucking butchering equipment."

I shudder. "Great."

Super comforting thinking of the murder shack out back.

"I'll go rummage through it, see if there's anything we can use."

I nod. "I'd love some lotion."

His eyes cut to mine. "Lotion? You think there's going to be lotion in the shed where the owners probably strung up carcasses?"

My face scrunches at that image in my head. "Well, now I don't. But maybe there's some kind of provisions we can use."

Rowan shakes his head, clearly thinking that would be a bad idea.

Whatever. If we're stuck here, I need to make some provisions. So far, we're using a twig with the charcoal from the fire to brush our teeth. I, thankfully, brought a hairbrush in my pack, so at least my hair isn't a rat's nest.

For soap . . . that's been, a little tricky. We've been smashing together ash and leaves to make some kind of something we boil in water, rub ourselves down, and rinse it off the best we can. It's not perfect, but at least we're not smelly with bad breath.

My skin, though, is dying. I have a horrible burn from the wind and cold on my legs and a little on my cheeks. It's freaking freezing out there.

Still, we're surviving—mostly thanks to Rowan.

I look out the window, thinking about the many mistakes we've made in this place and how, if it ever got out, my world would be flipped on its side. My sister would never forgive me, that's for sure. Not to mention the incredible amount of gossip the town would have with this.

I've done some pretty dumb shit, but sleeping with him takes the cake.

We need to get out of here. That's all I know. Once I'm back in the real world, I won't feel some insane need to jump his bones.

It has to be this place because I have never once thought about him this way. Clearly, it's the weather or the woods.

My stomach rumbles loudly in the quiet space. God, I could go for a steak right now.

Rowan clears his throat. "Here," he says, handing me half a protein bar.

"I already had my half."

"I know, take mine. I'm fine and you're hungry."

"No," I say quickly. "You have to eat too."

"Charlotte, eat the bar, please. Your stomach is growling, you're hurt, and I promise, I'm fine. I need to go out and get more ice to melt so we have water, and I'm going to try to cut some more wood. We only had enough for today and I can't let the fire go out."

Him giving me his half makes me feel selfish and petulant. We're both hungry, and every time I've needed anything, Rowan has done or given it to me, so I didn't have to suffer. He's gotten wood, made the fire, and carried me out to the back wooded area so I could do my business not hanging off the side of the porch.

But him giving me his ration of the food makes me burst into tears.

This is too much, he shouldn't be nice to me.

"I'm so sorry!" I say as my sobs tear through my chest.

"What the hell?"

"I-I'm such a *bitch*! God, why am I such a bitch? You should h-hate me. I know you do, and you *should*!" I cry harder.

I seriously hate myself. My life is falling apart, and I just want to go home.

Rowan's eyes are wide, and he reaches for me, but I put my hand out. "What are you going off about? I don't hate you. Why are you so upset?"

"Because I hate me! I'm terrible to you! You've been so *nice*, and I've been a raging bitch! Take my food, all of it, I deserve to s-starve," I hiccup and wipe at my falling tears. "You've taken care of me this whole time, I can't-t eat your f-food."

Okay, it's official, I've lost my mind. Four and a half days in the woods, and I've cracked. That's got to be a record somewhere.

Even Tom Hanks lasted weeks before he lost it and he only had Wilson.

I have a living person and I didn't make it a whole week, but he was able to fish so he wasn't completely starving.

"Charlotte, easy, sweetheart, I don't hate you, and while you can be a bitch at times, you're not a bitch."

I shake my head. "That doesn't even make sense!"

He steps forward, pulling me against his chest. "It does. Listen, you don't deserve to starve or anything else. You're stuck out here, your ankle hurts, we're both hungry, and this went from being a one-night thing to being a bleak outlook. Don't cry, I can't handle it." He pulls my head back, holding it in his palms. "No tears."

I try to hold them back, but they keep falling. I want to go back to the house. I need a shower and a lobotomy after all the shit we've done. It's not just the hunger, pain, and inability to use the bathroom without risking my life. It's that all I want to do is strip him down and ride him like a pony again.

Which is fucking insane.

Maybe that's it. Maybe I've lost all of my mental faculties and

I'm sleeping with him because my sanity is frozen like the ground outside.

At least that would be a reason.

"I want to go home," I whine, and I know it's whiney and stupid, but I needed to say it.

"I do too."

"I want a shower and a meal and my bed."

As though he doesn't want the same thing.

"I know, sweetheart."

I'm not a sweetheart and when he calls me that, I feel that anger and hurt in my chest rise again. "What's wrong with me? Why am I losing my mind?" I ask as though he would have a clue.

"There's nothing wrong with you."

I sniffle and close my eyes. There is so much wrong with me. It's not even funny at this point. However, my latest series of mistakes are just icing on my shit cake.

My gaze meets his, and I wrap both hands around his wrists, holding him as he holds me. His thumb brushes the tear rolling down my cheek and then he smiles. "Other than the fact that we're stuck here and you're batshit crazy."

I laugh at the same time he does. I needed that. "Other than that."

"I know me offering you food set you off, but I mean it, I'm fine, just eat the bar and then take a nap or something."

I step back, nodding once. "Thank you."

"See, and here you think I'm the biggest dickhead on this planet. So far, I've fed you, comforted you, given you a series of pretty fantastic orgasms, and I haven't killed you. You know what?" Rowan asks, plucking the bar out of my hand. "I deserve a cookie, so this will be the substitute."

His playful demeanor shakes me out of my mini—okay, full-blown—meltdown. I grab it back. "I don't think so. I've also been nice, given you a blowjob as well as several orgasms, and haven't killed you. So, give it back, jackass."

"Ask nicely."

I snort. "Not on your life."

I reach toward his middle, tickling him, and when his arm drops to protect himself, I grab the half a bar and shove it in my mouth.

So ladylike.

Then, I limp away, trying to gain some distance, but Rowan is ten times faster and his stride is definitely longer. Not even two seconds later, an arm wraps around my middle.

I try to chew and swallow, but my mouth is stuffed.

"You stole my bar and ate it?" he asks as he spins me around.

"It's my bar," I try to say but it comes out more like, "If eye are."

"You're going to pay for this, you know that, right?"

I chew more and fight back my smile.

"Since you ate, I think it's only fair I get to do the same." Rowan's voice shifts, and gone is the playful guy. Now, he's a hunter and I'm his prey.

I rest my palms on his chest. "Then go eat."

"Your mouth has the remnants of my meal. Open up and let me taste."

I shouldn't. God, I shouldn't, but what the fuck? We've already made the mistakes now and agreed once we're out of here, we will never do it again. I lean forward, my lips almost touching his. "If you want to taste, go ahead."

The sound that comes from his chest curls my toes. Instead of kissing me, like I really want him to do, Rowan lifts me and brings me over to our makeshift bed.

"Rowan?"

"Pull your pants off."

I look up at him. "What?"

"Take your fucking pants off. I want to eat."

And then it hits me. Oh, well, I mean, if he's going to make a meal out of me, I'm not going to fight him.

An orgasm will totally change my mood.

However, I'm sure as hell not willing to make things easy for him. I stare back at him, knowing how much he loves when I challenge him. It's like the two of us feed off it. "If you want my pants off, then get on your knees and take them off."

I open my legs, showing him what he could be looking at if I was naked.

Rowan's eyes flare and I know I've hit that nerve. He drops down, eyes toward me. "You like pushing me, don't you?"

"I do."

"You like pissing me off, making me fuck you hard because you've driven me crazy."

"You like it too," I push back.

"I really wish I didn't," he admits.

Me too. I wish this was any other man but him.

"Tomorrow it'll end," I tell him, putting it out in the world that this will be the last time.

"Then we go back to just hating each other," he says as his hand moves to my waistband. "But right now, I'm going to make you scream my name as you come on my tongue."

"And I'm going to suck your dick until you yell as your cum drips out of my mouth."

"Good. Now lie back, and let me have what I want."

My pants are gone in an instant, and then Rowan removes his clothes. The two of us are naked, and the hunger I had before is different. It's no longer about food, it's about him and this and forgetting the absolute hell we've endured.

Rowan takes that away.

I'm not thinking about anything other than him and how he'll make me feel.

He lifts my knees up, exposing me completely. "Fuck, Charlotte. Look how wet you are for me." I close my eyes, first I can't see, but second, I'm slightly mortified. "You want my mouth on this sweet cunt, don't you?"

"Yes," I moan.

"It's clear you do. You know, I want to do nothing but lick you until you scream, but you ate my food, and I did say I was going to punish you."

Still my legs are wide apart, the cool air a stark contrast from the fire behind me.

"Consider me punished."

He chuckles low and dark. "Not even close to it, sweetheart."

Then my legs are lowered to the ground and Rowan shifts, lying back on the floor.

"What are you doing?"

"Get on your knees," he orders.

I won't even think about how much wetter I get at his gruff command. "Excuse me?"

"On your knees." I shift so I'm up on my knees. Rowan's eyes flash with approval, then his voice drops low. "Good girl. Now, crawl to me and sit on my face so I can have my meal."

Oh my fucking God. I might have just come.

The look in his eyes and the rasp of his voice, I swear I'm dead. Never has a man looked at me that way, and I'm not sure I'm ever going to recover.

I get on my hands and knees, watching him watch me with an unmistakable hunger in his eyes.

"That's it, baby. Come to me," he praises.

I keep going, wanting to stop and sink onto him and ruin his plan, but I don't. I want this time, our last time, to be something we both remember.

He grabs my ass, pulling me where he wants me after I apparently take too long. "Rowan!" I gasp as his tongue slides against my clit.

I have nothing to hold on to, so I have to keep myself upright, my legs begin to tremble as he brings me close. His tongue makes the most amazing circles and swipes, making my head spin. There's no softness in his touch, and I'm grateful for it. Rowan's fingers dig into my ass cheeks, and he keeps me from moving and just licks and licks.

"Oh, God, Rowan. I'm so close," I pant, sweat beginning to break out against my skin.

Then the bastard stops.

Not eases up, not changes positions to better make me come. No, he fucking stops.

"Rowan!" I protest.

"Hmm? What's wrong?"

I look down at him as he stares at me with a smirk on his wet lips. God, I need to come. I can't see him like this. "I need...please...I need."

"You need what, baby?" he asks, his thumb brushes my clit, just barely.

I shudder as a small ripple of pleasure washes through me. "Please."

"Please, what? Please more? Or please stop?"

Please God give me the strength.

"More," I say the word and I'm almost ashamed of the way it comes out as a cry.

"Say you're sorry for eating my food."

"I'm sorry!"

He laughs softly. "How sorry?"

I'm going to kill him. I want to slam my hips down and show him how sorry he's going to be, but his hands are cupping my ass, holding me still.

"Rowan, I can't take it. I'm sorry. So fucking sorry! Please, I need to come!"

His head lifts just a bit, his tongue swiping so slowly that I mewl. "God, yes."

"Who is pleasuring you, Charlotte?" The question is out and then he drops me so he can lick harder.

"You!"

"Say my fucking name as I make you come," he orders.

Then my legs begin to tremble as he licks, sucks, and swirls his tongue over and over while his thumb presses inside.

I want to defy him, to deny him the way he did me, but when I turn my head, I see him jerking off at the same rhythm he's fingering me, and I detonate while screaming his name, hating myself as I do.

fifteen
ROWAN

The wind isn't too bad today, so I head out to get more wood since we're low again. I can get a little farther out than I could the last few days, and I find a few hollowed-out evergreen trees and two that have fallen. When I went through the shack this morning, I found a ton of glass jars filled with random things, some were mushrooms, which we weren't touching. There were some birch bark shavings—grabbed those—and some other jars of shit I figured Charlotte might find some use of.

"Do you need help?" Charlotte asks as I'm carrying up another load of wood.

"Did you suddenly fix your ankle and can walk out here?"

"No, but . . . you've done everything so far."

I've done what I should, what was needed. "I'm good, just keep the fire going if you can."

She nods, grabs one log off the porch and hops in. I keep going, carrying the final logs up and go inside.

Charlotte is on the floor with a knife, cutting something off the log. "What are you doing?"

"Oh! Look!" Her voice is animated. "I found some sap."

"Sap?"

143

She nods. "Pine sap! I'm going to scrape all this down, so don't toss any of the pine tree wood in yet. I need to inspect it."

Is she for real? "What the hell are you going to do with it?"

"It has medicinal properties. You brought in all those jars from the murder shed and one has honeycombs in them, did you happen to find any old hives out there in the wilderness?"

I swear, I don't have adequate words to respond with. So, I keep it simple. "No."

"Okay, when you go back out, can you check old trees?"

"Charlotte, it's fucking freezing still, the ground is still an inch thick with ice, no I'm not going to scour the empty trees for a bees' nest."

She huffs. "Well, you could at least try."

"I'm sure I could, but no."

"Well, I have some here, I'm going to make a salve."

Oh, dear Lord. She's definitely lost it now. "Are you taking cues from *Little House on the Prairie* suddenly?"

Her eyes narrow. "I could be. I watch a lot of Alaska survival shows. Anyway, you can melt this down with the wax and make a sort of salve. I think it'll help with my chapped skin or maybe this honking zit that's growing on my cheek. It'll fix something, I'm sure of it."

I really don't know what to say to her, but she seems excited and in need of a win. So far, this trip has been nothing but losses—well, other than the sex. That part's been pretty fucking amazing.

"I'm sure it'll be great."

"You have that cut on your arm, maybe it'll work there!"

She's not putting pine sap on my arm, no way. "Isn't pine sap sticky?"

"Yes, which is why I'm melting the honeycomb, duh! Oh, and we'll use the oil that's in the cabinet."

"Oh, yes, duh. How did I not know that?"

"I bet this clears up that cut right away." She nearly preens at this idea.

"I bet you can try it on yourself first."

For the next three hours, Charlotte works diligently. She gathers a bunch of the sap from the wood I brought in, puts it in piles based on whatever theory she has about good resin and bad resin. As if she has a single clue.

Then she works on the honeycombs I grabbed from the murder shed that are probably as old as this cabin. She picks them apart, talking about it as she does as though I care, but she's busy, feeling useful, and seems genuinely happy, so I sort of listen.

"Okay, I don't have a strainer, so there might be chunks, but that's fine, it will just be more rustic," she explains as she's pouring things into a new jar.

"Yes, rustic medicine is all the rage."

"Hey, you'll be thanking me when your cut is healed, skin isn't chafed, and that redness is gone. I can't wait to hear you." She drops her voice low. "Oh, Charlotte, you're so resourceful. I wish I was as smart and amazing as you."

"I have other ways I'd like you to be resourceful." I wiggle my brows and grin.

Charlotte smiles, her eyes go all molten. "Well, if you let me rub my salve all over you, and I mean all over, I'll be very, very resourceful."

"Sweetheart, you can rub me down with anything you want."

She laughs and shakes her head. "Easy, boy, let me work."

I do and then after the salve cools, Charlotte makes good on her promise. I don't even fucking care about the shards of pine sap as she uses her hands to cover me in it, and then I enjoy every moment of rubbing my body against hers, ensuring we both get the benefits of her hard work.

※

"We're able to get about halfway, do you think you can get up the mountain a bit?" Sawyer asks on the walkie-talkie.

I look to Charlotte who has been despondent since this morning. Gone is the woman who fell apart while I fucked her hard and fast last night. Now she won't even look at me. She's tired, hurt, and short of breath as she tries to climb up without assistance.

"I'll get us there," I say, wanting this cabin to be in my past so I can focus on the future.

"Sounds good. Turn your tracking device on so I can send you my coordinates."

I do that, and the ping pops up. Not too far. Although, it'll take double the time to get there if I have to carry Charlotte. Which would require me to touch her, and she seems hell-bent on avoiding that.

I turn to her. "Do you think you can handle it?"

Her eyes flare with determination. "I'm not a simpering female. I can handle getting up the mountain."

"On your busted ankle?"

"I'll be fine," she says. "I just . . . I need to breathe for a second."

"So we're back to enemies?" I ask, tossing the jacket in my pack. "Just so I know how this goes?"

"The cabin is over, Rowan. We have to go back to what we were so no one suspects anything. Not to mention, we said this was what it was back there."

Her voice has gentled a bit, but it pisses me off. "Then the answer is yes."

While she's right, we said exactly that, I sort of liked the semi-truce we had. Even though Charlotte is complicated, and a Sullivan. If she has even a smidge of her sister in her, I'd rather walk away now, and we never think of it, but she's not Aurora. She's not even close to her.

"What did you want me to say?" Charlotte asks, her hand resting on her chest.

"Whatever you wanted, babe."

She nods once. "Okay. Good, then we're both in agreement, we don't talk about it, we never admit to it, we don't think about it, and we never do it again."

As if she didn't enjoy every fucking minute of it. Whatever. I give her my best smirk, the one that I know will piss her off. "Not unless we end up back in the cabin again. If we do, then you can fuck me until you can't walk again."

She scoffs. "Right. Unless that."

Let's be real, neither of us is ever coming back here.

I grab Charlotte's pack, adjusting a few things to balance the weight more. "If you can get at least part of the way, it'll help when I have to carry you. Not that I can't manage it completely, but we're both tired and haven't eaten much. I'll carry your pack to make it easier."

She looks to the bag and then to me. "I can do it. I don't want to make things harder for you."

"I know you can, but you need to work on not breaking the other ankle and getting as close as we can to Sawyer. You'll carry the tracking device, and I'll go behind you to catch you if you fall."

For a second, the mask slips, and I see the girl I spent five days with in this shitty cabin. "I appreciate that. Thank you."

"Let's go while the weather is in our favor. It's going to be slippery, so use the poles," I say, needing to create my own distance.

Charlotte's poles snapped when she fell, so I gave her mine and I'll use two sticks.

The trees are spaced so that we can use them almost like a ladder, getting to one, pulling ourselves up, using the pole or stick to leverage up.

"Fuck!" Charlotte yells as she starts to slip.

I put my hand on her ass, pushing her up. "Pull!" She does, and she gets to a tree, panting and leaning as I follow her footsteps. "You're doing amazing, Charlotte. So good. Keep it up. I'm right here."

Her head moves to the side, our gazes meeting. "It's like ten times harder than ever."

"It's still so slick. We probably should've waited another day."

"We can't, we don't have food."

That is definitely the driving force on this. The other option is to have Sawyer bring supplies and I hike up to get them. Without the pack, and Charlotte's bum ankle, I probably could've been halfway by now.

"What if you head back and I go meet Sawyer to get food?"

Her eyes widen and she looks panicked. "No. I'll do this. I have to do this."

I'm not about to argue with her. The idea doesn't exactly appeal to me either. "Then let's go."

She lets out a deep sigh and starts to climb. Several more times I have to push her up, and then the trees thin out and we've lost the one advantage we had. I sit Charlotte down under one of the trees, and we drink some water. She's completely beat. Her face is red, and her breathing is accelerated.

"Take off your other jacket," I tell her, worried she's sweating too much and will start to freeze.

Instead of asking questions or arguing, she does it. She fans herself and gets control of her breathing. "It's so much harder going up."

"You need to tell me to stop if it's too much. You can't sweat, we'll be in a different kind of danger, sweetheart."

I took two layers off midway, not wanting hypothermia to be the next obstacle.

"I didn't think I was hot until we sat for a second."

"About how far is the dot now?" I ask, placing her jacket in her pack.

"Maybe another half mile? I don't know, I'm so tired."

"I know you are, but we're close now. I won't let you fall, I'm right behind you."

She leans her head against the tree, eyes filled with so much emotion, but she won't let herself cry. "I know you won't."

I take the walkie-talkie out, ignoring the desire to pull her into my arms and kiss her senseless. "Come in Moist Beard."

Charlotte groans. "I can't wait for that thing to get run over by my car."

"Skittle Titties, this is Moist Beard." I love irritating the piss out of her. "Are you close?"

"We're about a half mile away still, Charlotte and I are trudging through thick ice and it's taking longer. Are you able to come any closer?"

There's silence for a moment. "I tried, Row, but I slid a good amount and almost got stuck. I really don't think I should risk it."

That's what I was afraid of. "All right. We're going to be a while. With her injury and the ice, it's a lot of work."

"I have a fire going up here and food. As soon as you get here, I'll get Charlotte to the house. Faye and Meagan had to leave this morning, but Joey is waiting."

"They *left*?" Charlotte screams. "What does he mean they left?"

Oh fucking hell. I hand her the walkie-talkie because I'm not playing the relay game, I've had to do it one too many times with Brynlee.

"Sawyer, you said Faye and Meagan left? Like to go to the store?"

There's a pause, and I'm pretty sure Sawyer is debating heading back to the house to avoid this. Finally he speaks. "Umm, Meagan had to get home, and Faye knew we'd drive you back to Sugarloaf. She left you a note explaining it."

Her jaw drops. "She left me?"

"Relax, Charlotte, you're not abandoned, we'll take you home and get you medical care. You know Meagan has to take care of her brother."

The anger drains from her face. "Right. I forgot. It's fine. We'll get back, and I can finally shower and go home."

I let Sawyer know we're starting to hike again and then I grab Charlotte's pack, hoisting it to my chest.

We climb for what feels like hours, stopping to cool down or add another layer. It's by far the most intense hike I've ever done and we're not even going all that far.

I see the smoke plume and Sawyer wasn't kidding about the ice in this area. It's thicker the higher altitude we go. Charlotte and I both slip, catching a tree or each other.

"Almost there," I say, as the smell of firewood gets stronger. "Come on, find a tree and pull."

Her arms must be screaming in agony, God knows mine are. Charlotte stops for a moment, looking back to me.

"I need to say something before we get up there."

Something in her eyes has me worried. "Okay."

"Whatever . . . that was between us, I don't really understand how two people who hate each other as much as we do could ever be that . . ."

"Good," I finish for her.

"I was going to say nice to each other, but sure, we'll go with good. I just appreciate you taking care of me."

"That could've all been summed up in two words: thank you."

She rolls her eyes. "You could've been nice and just said you're welcome."

"I could, but then I wouldn't get to see you pissed off." She turns, and I grab her wrist, not really sure why, I just don't want this entire fucked-up few days to end on me being a dick. "You don't have to thank me, as much as we dislike each other, which I think is misguided on your part, I would never let anything happen to you —you know, other than embarrassing shit. That's fine."

"Same. I wouldn't really let you suffer in pain. I mean, anything else is fair game."

I smile. "So we're in some kind of truce?"

"Some kind."

"Enough to let me have the Knight contract?"

"Not a chance in hell."

I lean my face close to hers and watch the desire pool in those green eyes. "Then may the best man win."

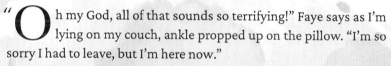

sixteen

CHARLOTTE

"Oh my God, all of that sounds so terrifying!" Faye says as I'm lying on my couch, ankle propped up on the pillow. "I'm so sorry I had to leave, but I'm here now."

She has no idea how bad it was, but then also great. Toward the last day, I really did start to panic about the food situation. I worried that we'd run out of food and wouldn't be able to get help. Then, my ankle was throbbing and I didn't know if it was broken.

"We survived."

"And your ankle?"

The doctor said it's just a severe sprain and gave me a lace up support stabilizer for a few weeks. Considering I walked miles on it, there really wasn't much they could do other than that.

"It's fine. I'm fine. Everything is fine. The doctor said the bruising wasn't so bad because of the salve I made too."

Faye lets out a huge huff and leans back in the large armchair my granny sat in every night to read her book. Thinking about her, even just briefly, makes my heart hurt. I miss her so much. She was my favorite person in the world. When my parents were alive, she'd sneak us bubble gum because my father wouldn't let us have any, he was so worried about it getting in our hair. Then, as we got older, she'd hide two-dollar bills all around the house that we could search for. She said they were special bills that we had to keep forever. I still have them in the safe upstairs.

I think about this farm, this house, this life I have because of her and I can't fail. I can't lose what they gave me. For sixty-three years they lived and worked here, built a legacy, and in the course of two years, I've let it fall apart.

"Well, that's good that you were able to find what you needed. Speaking of the cabin, how was spending five days trapped with Rowan?" she asks, her brows raised.

It was . . . orgasmic.

But not saying that.

"We endured," I say nonchalantly.

He dropped me off late last night after the guys insisted we go to the hospital for X-rays. So, I did. Then Joey, Sawyer, and Rowan got me settled here, where it was awkward saying goodbye to him.

"I see that, but still, I was going crazy, worried about the two of you being stuck out there. Joey had to keep me *very* busy so I could keep my mind off it."

I bet he did, and I was very busy as well, but I can't admit that. "So your week at the chalet was good, then?"

"Other than my best friend getting hurt and stranded? Sure."

I smile and laugh. "Other than that."

"I'm sorry your week was terrible. I know I convinced you to the leave the farm for just a few days and then it went a little stupid."

"A little?"

"Okay, extremely stupid."

There's nothing I can do about it and Faye is so tenderhearted that if I were to even hint at how bad of an idea it was to *think* about going away, she'll blame herself and it's not on her. It's on me.

I should've never left here. I should've stayed here and come up with some brilliant plan to save the farm, instead I was getting naked with my archenemy.

Faye leans forward. "I'll make it up to you with a spa day."

"As much as I appreciate that, I don't have time for a spa day, I need to work and see what else needs to be fixed."

Which is like . . . everything.

She sighs heavily. "You know, this farm isn't the only thing in life to worry about."

"It's what I'm worried about now," I admit.

"You need to date, have fun, have a *life*. All you do is work, work, work."

Anger wells up in me at her flippancy about it. This farm is more than just work, it's a *home*. It's the place my mother was raised. Her bedroom was the first on the left, it has yellow wallpaper with pink flowers. Her trophies from barrel racing are still up on the shelf. I slept in there for years, staring at the girl she was, the dreams she must've had about me and my sister in that four-poster bed.

She had it and then it was gone.

If I lose this place, this home that is my only tether to my mother, then what? Who am I without the roots that were planted here?

Faye has it so easy. Her family gives her money for whatever she wants. She lives a life without working hard because she doesn't have to, and I never begrudge her that, but to tell me I need to do more . . . I can't.

"For most of us, that's life, Faye. I have to work so I can pay bills. I don't have a rich daddy who will fund my fun and dating life. It's all on me."

Her eyes widen and she stands. "Charlotte, I didn't mean it like that."

And now I feel like shit for snapping at her. "I'm sorry, I know you didn't."

As spoiled and privileged as she is, she doesn't have a mean bone in her body. She's giving and loyal, and I know her heart.

"No, you're right. I don't have to worry about the things you do, and I shouldn't have said it that way. It's me who's sorry. You're hurt and had a shitty week because of me, I'm going to change and we're going to farm together."

Now it's my turn to look at her in shock. "I'm sorry, what?"

She's already heading to the stairs. "You wait there, I'm going to get changed and then you and I are going to go out to the range or land or pasture?" She purses her lips. "Whatever you call it, we'll go there, and you can teach me how to be a cowgirl. You're a cowgirl, right? I mean, you have cows and you're a girl. Pretty much defines what it is."

I sigh. "Faye, I love you, but I promise, you don't have to do that."

"It's what friends do. We help. Now, I'm going to get in uniform."

Oh Lord, I can only imagine what the hell this is going to be.

Ten minutes later I hear her clomping down the steps. Sure enough, she's a freaking mess wearing skin-tight jeans, a white tank, flannel shirt tied above her belly button, and my straw hat.

"What in the hell?" I ask when I see she's got my boots on too.

"Yee-haw!"

I roll my eyes. "Work boots would've been better, I don't need cow shit on my dancing boots."

"I'm working with very limited options up there. So many jeans, so many sweatshirts, not enough cute stuff."

"Yes, because the cows care," I say with a laugh as she bounces toward me.

"Maybe you can date one of them. You are *moo*-velous."

I laugh so hard that I have tears. "You're such a dork."

"That I am. Come on, let's go to work."

I grab my work coat and the extra I have, tossing it to her. "Well, cowgirl, you're going to need layers because it's freaking freezing out there."

"Wait, I have to cover up my outfit?"

"Yup, come on, time to get dirty."

Faye sighs dramatically. "Work sucks already."

"And we haven't even gotten started, spoken like a disgruntled employee already."

"Oh! Am I getting paid?"

I laugh. "Nope."

The two of us head out to the barn and laugh as we work the rest of the day without a single complaint.

※—⟶

"Hey, Charlotte!" Brynlee calls my name as I pass her in Sugarlips Diner.

"Oh, hey."

She motions her hand toward the chair beside her. "Sit. Let's catch up!"

Oh, shit, does she know I slept with her brother? Did he tell anyone? I'll kill him if he did. Seriously, I have land, they'll never find him.

As I plot the various ways to dispose of Rowan's body, I take a seat, forcing a smile as his sister watches me.

"How are you?" I ask, hoping maybe I can come at this from a friendly angle. Where she understands it was out of duress. I wasn't thinking clearly, therefore, it really was more of a moment of insanity versus a mistake.

That's a line of defense and it works, so I'm sticking with that.

"I'm good, just working on some contracts. I'm doing entertainment law as a consultant out in California. An agency needed a lawyer to review a few new options and Addison knew them, so, yeah, it's been amazing."

"Oh! Are you still working for Sydney Arrowood?"

"Sydney actually told me that she couldn't hire me because I needed to find what kind of law I wanted to practice. Which is crazy, because she's the reason I went through law school. However, she was right, I didn't love family law. Jacob Arrowood had me review one of his contracts and one thing led to another and another. Then Catherine Cole, his publicist, asked if I could review a few more clients' contracts since her lawyer is on maternity leave . . ." Brynn explains.

"That's seriously so cool. I'm happy for you," I say with a smile.

At least someone is getting to live out their dreams.

"It's definitely more fun than dealing with grieving family members upset with their settlements in the wills and custody crap. And how about you? How was the hiking trip that turned into a nightmare?"

Tread super carefully, Charlotte. She's smart and close with her brother.

"It's over. That's what I can say."

She laughs. "Trust me, I lived with Rowan for years and when he left, it was a very happy day. I can imagine how it would've been if we hated each other."

No, I really don't think she can. "He was terrible, but he also took amazing care of me."

Brynn's head tilts to the side. "I think that might have been a compliment."

"Might."

The door chime rings and in walks all three Whitlock brothers, laughing and pushing each other as they talk.

Great. There goes my nice lunch break.

Which isn't even really a break, it's more of a bribe for Donny to fix my truck and do an IOU. Right now I'm riding an ATV around town and telling everyone it's to conserve gas. However, if it rains tomorrow, I'm taking the tractor. I don't even care.

"Well, well, if it isn't our little sister and . . . Charlotte." Rowan approaches and Brynn points her finger at him.

"Be nice, asshat," Brynn warns.

"Nice, please, he wouldn't know nice if it kicked him in the balls," Asher says, kissing his sister's cheek. "Hey, Charlotte."

"Hey," I say back.

Grady wraps his arm around Brynn and kisses her other cheek. "We all know he doesn't have any balls. Good to see you, Charlotte."

"You too, Grady."

Then it's Rowan who practically lifts Brynn out of her chair to hug her. "You're both just jealous because I'm the only one who hasn't been castrated by a woman. Besides, it's not about the size of the balls, it's about the length of the bat. Right, Charlotte?"

I hate him.

"I wouldn't know, I'm sure you're batting with a T-ball size anyway," I say, knowing damn well he's in the majors.

Both of his brothers laugh, and Grady slaps his chest. "Damn, brother. You walked into that one."

Brynn sighs heavily. "I was having a nice lunch and talking to a friend, but it seems you three are going to ruin our day. Might as well sit."

Each of them does and I feel really fucking uncomfortable. I keep trying to make eye contact with anyone other than Rowan. I haven't seen him in days. Other than each night when I close my eyes and feel his hands skimming across my skin or hear his voice as he slammed into me, keeping my body exactly where he wanted to hit the perfect angle.

"Charlotte was just telling me a little about the hiking trip where she and Rowan managed not to kill each other," Brynn says in our awkward silence.

"I won't lie, I was shocked," Asher says with a smile. "I thought for sure we were coming to get his body. My money was on you." He elbows me and winks.

"Thank you."

Grady nods. "Mine too. Brynn was the only one betting on Rowan."

"Hey! I didn't bet at all! You two were the ones acting like idiots," Brynn corrects them.

Rowan shakes his head, looking at his two brothers. "Both of you are traitors."

"Maybe, but even with an injury, I think Charlotte could take you," Grady says.

I like his brothers. They're kind of fun and they're right. I could totally kick his ass if my ankle wasn't sprained. "You're both very smart."

"Could you tell our wives that?" Asher asks.

"Wives? When did either of you get married?" Brynn cuts in.

159

"Almost wives, whatever," Grady snaps back. "Asher and I could use the support."

I smile, thinking of how Phoebe must keep Asher on his toes and Addison with Grady. I didn't really know the brothers that well since Brynlee moved here when we were in middle school. Asher didn't move to town until his mother died and Rowan came around the same time. Grady never did until his wife passed away and he moved here to be near family.

"I'll be happy to put in a good word."

Brynn scoffs. "Please, they all know better. What brings you boys to Sugarlips?"

"It's our weekly brothers' lunch where we talk about you," Rowan answers and Brynn playfully slaps his chest. "Ow, that hurt."

"Serves you right," she replies.

"We were here to get some food." Rowan looks to me. "All I had today was a protein bar."

The way he says it, the look in his eyes, has me going back to the last day in the cabin where I took it from him and then he punished me. I shift in my seat and he smirks.

Asshole.

"Well, I hate to be the plus one in this family luncheon. I'm going to grab my food from Magnolia and see if Donny will take payments in cheeseburgers," I say as I stand.

Rowan stands too. "Is he working on your truck?"

"Yeah, it's fine, though. I'm hoping to pick it up in a few days."

"How did you get here?" he asks, looking out toward the parking lot.

"I didn't walk, you know, since I can't do that and all."

Then I remember him scooping me up and carrying me.

His gaze returns to mine. "If you didn't walk, how did you get here?"

"I rode the ATV. Now, I really need to go." I turn to the rest of the Whitlocks. "It was great seeing you all. I hope you have a wonderful lunch."

Brynn smiles. "Good luck with Donny. Maybe bring him a cupcake, he's a sucker for sweets."

"Thanks, I'll add that to my order." I wave to everyone and head over to pick up my food.

It takes all my self-control not to turn and look at Rowan as I leave. When I finally make it outside, I relax just a little.

Okay, I survived it.

I didn't mentally undress him too much. Just the appropriate amount when trying to forget the best sex ever with the worst guy ever.

Maybe not the worst, but he comes close.

I inhale and smile, preparing to schmooze Donny into giving me a very, very discounted rate on repairing my engine with payment plans and groveling. I start to step in that direction when a hand grips my wrist from behind.

I gasp, turning suddenly to see blue eyes that haunt me in my sleep. "Rowan? What the hell are you doing?" I ask, pulling my wrist out of his grasp.

"How's your ankle?"

"What?"

"Your ankle, how is it?" he asks again with exasperation in his voice.

"It's fine."

He glances behind him at his siblings who are clearly watching this. "I told them I needed to ask you about something I can't find from the trip."

"Ooookay." I'm so damn confused. "Why are you really out here talking to me?"

"I . . . fuck, I don't know. I just wanted to see you, ask if you're okay and . . ." He laughs once, which is kind of a huff more than anything. "I was concerned because your truck is broken and you're riding around on a damn ATV. I didn't save you to have you injure yourself again."

I roll my eyes and cross my arms, well, as much as I can with a bag of food dangling. "I've been riding around on it since I can remember. I'm pretty sure I'm fine since I'm not off-roading on it. Thanks for the concern. I'm good."

I'm also not good because the fact that he came out here made my stomach clench. He's concerned about me, and I don't know why that makes me feel anything other than annoyance, but here I am, being a girl with butterflies.

Not that he'll know that.

"Okay then," he says as though that's that.

"Okay then what?"

He smirks. "You're fine. Good luck with Donny."

And with that, Rowan turns and walks back into the diner, leaving me with more questions than answers.

Ugh, I hate men.

seventeen

ROWAN

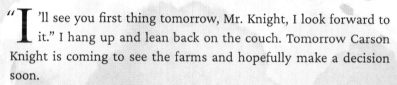

"I'll see you first thing tomorrow, Mr. Knight, I look forward to it." I hang up and lean back on the couch. Tomorrow Carson Knight is coming to see the farms and hopefully make a decision soon.

I'm not sure how I feel about taking this from Charlotte since she's hurt, but this deal will allow me to really add more cows. I had to sell a lot of calves that were born last year because we had way too many males. I need females. I need milk, therefore . . . I need this round of pregnant cows to actually birth some females.

With the new bull I got, it'll also ensure we don't breed incorrectly, not that we have before, but it's important to keep records of it all.

I send Micah a text, informing him of the visit and what time I expect him here tomorrow. According to Mr. Knight, he'll be here mid-morning. Which is a pretty broad time of day.

There's a knock at my door, which is probably Micah. Getting up, I groan, my back is still killing me from sleeping on the damn floor with Charlotte.

"Coming!" I yell when he knocks again. I open the door and find not Micah there, but Charlotte.

"Hi," she says, her cheeks red stained.

CORINNE MICHAELS

"Hello." I lean against the doorjamb, both confused and intrigued why she's here. "What brings you by?"

Charlotte pulls her lips into her mouth, and then makes a smacking noise. "I'm not sure."

"You're not sure?"

"No. I mean, I am sure, but I'm not sure at the same time."

I stay quiet for a moment, staring up at the dark night sky. Then step back. "Do you want to come in to see if you can work out exactly what brought you here?"

Her green eyes find mine, she nods and then shakes her head. "No, I don't need to come in. I found this." Charlotte lifts her hand and extends a hat I've never seen before toward me. "I knew it was yours and didn't know if you needed it."

She's full of shit. She's here for something else, something I think the two of us want and have been trying to pretend never happened.

"I do need it," I say, playing along, my voice rough as I think about the other things I need that have nothing to do with putting clothes on.

"Good. Then, I'm glad I brought it by."

I step toward her. "Charlotte?"

Her lips part and she sucks in a breath. "Yeah?"

"Come in."

I wait for her to tell me to fuck off, to run, to do anything, but instead, she steps inside. I close the door, turn to her, and we both collide against each other.

Her hands are in my hair, pulling my lips to hers, and I'm lifting her in my arms. We kiss so hard I swear we'll both be bruised, but I don't fucking care. I don't know why or what is going on, but for the first time in days I feel like I'm free and alive.

I push her back against the door, her legs wrapped around me as I bite her lip. "Is this what you really came for?" I ask before crushing our mouths back together.

When I pull away, I kiss down her neck and she moans, "I'm not answering that."

My smile is automatic and I move back up to her ear. "I think we know the answer."

Charlotte turns to me, meeting my gaze. "This never happened."

"Never."

"Good. Now please give me an orgasm."

I grin. "My pleasure."

"And mine."

Yes, it definitely will be hers.

I carry her into my bedroom, dropping her on the bed, and she squeaks.

Charlotte leans up on her elbows, watching as I pull my shirt off, throwing it over to the chair. Then I move to my buckle and she licks her lips. "You like the show?"

"I mean, it's a very . . . average show."

Fuck, I'm going to enjoy making her saucy mouth do something else very soon. "Average? Is that what has you showing up at my door with some bullshit about a hat?"

Charlotte shrugs as much as she can. "I'm clearly deranged and confused."

"Clearly." I unbutton my jeans and stand there, not moving. "Take off your clothes," I command her.

"Or what?"

"Or I get dressed and kick you out, making you wonder if I'm jerking off, remembering your taste, the way you ride my cock like I was made for you, and how your cunt feels when it's contracting because I made you come like no other man ever has."

She shudders and then pushes up, lifting her shirt over her head, revealing a purple lace bra that does nothing to hide her hard nipples. "And would you be doing that?"

"I do every fucking night since we got back," I admit. "I wake up, my dick in my hand, hating that I want you again."

Charlotte's breathing accelerates. "I want you too."

"I know, baby, that's why you're here with your bullshit hat excuse. You want me to lick you until you scream. You need me to bury myself deep inside you until you feel nothing but me."

She unhooks her bra, throwing it off the bed. "Stop talking."

"Take your pants off and let me see what I want."

There's a hunger in her eyes and it fucking turns me on even more. She lifts her hips, sliding her jeans and underwear off, letting me look at her naked on my bed.

"I've imagined this," I admit. "I thought about you lying here, legs spread, wet and waiting for me."

"I've tried not to think about it."

I move to the bed, drop down on my knees, grab her calves, and pull her to me. "Enough thinking," I say before I bring my tongue to her clit.

"Oh God," she pants and I do it again. "Yes, please."

"That's it, baby, beg for what you want."

But it's not just her who wants, it's me too. I wasn't lying when I told her that I wake up stroking my dick, imagining it's Charlotte's mouth wrapped around it. I'm like a fucking teenager waking up with a wet dream because I spent the middle of the night dreaming of being inside her again.

I don't know what this woman did to me, but I need this to get it out of my system. I need to fuck her out, like if it was a fever and I sweated it out.

Maybe that'll be the cure.

And if it's not, then we'll just have to keep trying to find a way, because I do not like her.

I don't want her. I don't need her. I refuse to be in any kind of a relationship.

Even doing this is fucking stupid. I've already seen the ending of this play with her damn sister, but here I am with my head between her legs.

Charlotte's fingers slide through my hair as she begins to pant louder. "Yes, right there. Goddamn it, why is it so good with you?"

I can feel her body tighten as I bring her closer to her orgasm. A part of me wants to make her feel the frustration I have, but the other part of me needs to make her come so she is just as fucked in the head as I seem to be right now.

"Rowan, please, I can't!" she moans and pulls my hair. "I can't stop it!"

Good. I don't stop either. I flick and move my tongue in different directions as her legs squeeze my head. She yells out my name over and over as her body goes limp.

I need to fuck her. I stand, pulling my pants off and kicking them as I move to the edge of the bed. She's lying there trying to catch her breath and I climb on top of her, moving my hips right to her soaked entrance.

"One more time," I say as an oath. "One more time."

And then I slide into her and fuck her for the last time.

Charlotte is passed out in the bed after we had sex for the second time. I was really full of shit when I said it was the last time because really, what I think I meant was the last time before the sun came up.

Which is in like three hours.

So, I mean, if I were to take her now, surely it wouldn't be breaking any promises.

She moves her ass toward me, as though she knows my thoughts, so I take full advantage and find her clit with my finger.

Already she's soaked and I adjust her leg so I can just slip right in from behind.

"Oh," she moans sleepily. "Rowan?"

"Shhh," I say against her ear. "I want to fuck you slowly this time."

She moves her hand up to my neck and drops her head to my shoulder. "I'm not going to be able to walk tomorrow."

"That's the idea, but I think you mean today."

Her laughter is soft and she moves her hips with me. "I'm close already."

I keep playing with her clit as I just rock at this steady pace. "It's because I know what you like," I tell her and kiss the side of her neck. "Your moans get louder when I do this." I run my tongue along the shell of her ear, and sure enough, she moans. "You tend to gasp when I do this." I push against her clit and I get the response I want. "And if I can hit this spot, you come."

I feel her body tense as I rub that spot inside her over and over as well as play with her clit, and she detonates, and I follow her right over the edge.

✎—ø

"Rowan?" There's a knock on the door and I swear I just fell asleep.

I groan, pulling Charlotte closer against me.

"Rowan? Are you here?" The voice calls louder and my eyes open.

Fuck.

It's morning.

Another pounding on the door and Charlotte moans. "Go away, I'm sleepy."

Yeah, this can't happen. She can't be caught in my damn house. "Charlotte," I whisper. "Wake up and be quiet. Micah is outside. We must've passed out."

Her eyelids fly open and her hand covers her eyes. "No!" she whisper-yells.

"Get dressed, I'm going to stall. Slip out the back door and I'll let you back in when he leaves. He likes to come in and talk."

I slip out of the bed, throw my shorts on, and Charlotte is already getting dressed.

"You can't let him see me."

He knocks on my window and she drops to the floor. "The curtains are closed, he can't see."

She glares at me. "Go! I'll hide out back."

I fight back a laugh and head out to the main room, closing the bedroom door behind me.

"Hey, Micah," I say, stepping out onto the front deck. Fuck it's cold. I should've grabbed a sweatshirt.

"Hey, I got your text, went to the barn at five—like you said—but you're sleeping in?"

"I didn't get much sleep, I fell asleep about an hour ago, sorry about that. You head to the barn, and I'll be there after I get dressed."

I'm really hoping Charlotte got out the back because I'm freezing my balls off here. "Dude, why are you out here in shorts?"

Because Charlotte Sullivan was naked in bed when you woke us up.

"You woke me up, I just wanted to see what was wrong."

"Well, let's go in the damn house, you get dressed and we can discuss what you wanted to go over."

This is not exactly how I planned for this to go, but I'm really fucking hoping Charlotte snuck out the back and has a way to get back home that doesn't involve her ATV.

I clear my throat and head in the house. The bedroom door is open and she's not in the living room, which means the coast should be clear and now I have a reason to go to her tonight to discuss what the fuck last night was.

eighteen

CHARLOTTE

C arson Knight has to be the most terrifying man I've ever met. Ever. He's maybe five years older than me, but he's tall, dark, intimidating, and he's said maybe a total of ten words in the hour that he's been touring the facility with me.

"Do you have any questions?" I ask, as we're nearing the end of what was a very awkward tour.

"You've answered most. My sister was very impressed with the farm, and I agree, there are some great things you're doing here," he says and I finally feel like I can breathe.

"Thank you."

"How many full-time workers are you employing right now?"

Yeah, I'm not sure how to answer this, but I'm going to heed my grandpa's advice and always speak the truth.

"I'd love to tell you I have ten full-time employees right now, but I can't do that. This farm operated at its top with ten, and that's what I wish I had. However, the last two years have been incredibly hard on this farm. I bought my sister out, and then when we made the farm one hundred percent organic, it depleted more of my funds. I've had to make hard decisions, but I'm completely positive even with my small staff, we're able to fulfill this contract without issue."

Most of that last part is true. I'm going to have to work myself to death, and then hopefully have enough money to revive the farm and hire staff.

"I see," Carson says, nodding slowly. "Not many people are that honest, most would lie in your situation."

"That's not how I was raised."

He smiles, just the corners of his lips tip up. "Neither was I, which is why I'll tell you that one of the things I'll need assurance on is that you can maintain the production level promised."

"My word is all I have to assure you at this point."

"Yes, it's really all we have," he says, now looking around the barn. "You know that there are other farms vying for the same contract?"

Yeah, my fuck buddy. "I know, one is my neighbor."

"His farm is significantly bigger than yours."

"Yes, but that doesn't mean that it's better. I produce high quality, organic milk. Which no other farm in this area does. I'm certified, which means that while you may pay a little more, you get to charge a lot more. This isn't some new wave of consumers who want organic for their children, this trend isn't going anywhere."

At least, that's what Faye convinced me of and I'm dying on this hill. Literally.

He inhales and walks around a bit. "I agree, the organic market is only growing, which is the major appeal in working with you."

I smile confidently, even though I feel anything but that. "I won't let you down."

"You know, I believe you wouldn't."

And I pray that means I have the best shot at this.

⚷

"I'm sorry, Charlotte," Aurora says again on our video chat. I've avoided her calls the past few weeks, still angry about the way she acted the first night I slept at Rowan's.

Since things have . . . well, changed, my anger has subsided and been more guilt and self-hatred for breaking the code of sisterhood.

I should not have slept with Rowan—several times. The worst was me going there last night. It wasn't some mistake in the woods. It was me showing up there, with a hat that wasn't even his, because I was feeling sad and alone.

Donny refused to fix the truck on a payment plan and ate all the food I brought. I don't know what I'm going to do, and I'm falling apart at the seams.

"I'm more sorry," I say, fighting back tears. "I was wrong to yell at you. You were concerned and I . . ."

"No, I was wrong. You're right. You're doing this on your own and I'm here, in New York because I hated small town living. I wanted to come back to where Mom and Dad raised us. Where we had food, fun, and options. You loved the life Granny and Pop had. I should've never ever thought you were doing anything with Rowan. I know you'd never be so stupid."

Oh, how wrong you are, sister.

"Are you happy there?" I ask. There's no way I can listen to her talk about how I didn't or wouldn't betray her because, that's exactly what I did.

Not that it hasn't been two years.

Not that she hasn't spoken to him in that time or that they were ever really dating. At least not according to him.

But . . . in the end, none of that matters. She's my sister and she was hurt by him.

God, I'm the worst human alive.

"I'm so happy here. I really like Ryan, too. He's funny, sweet, and spoils me rotten. It's amazing the difference dating a man who has his life together and isn't slumming it on some farm."

I let out a huff. "Slumming it on some farm?"

"I didn't mean it like that," she says quickly.

But she did. She always does.

"You seemed to like slumming it when you were here," I remind her. With that same guy she hates and refuses to stop talking about.

"Again, I didn't mean it like that, Charlotte. Please don't take it the wrong way. It's just different. I don't go on dates in the woods and have sex by the creek. This is dress up and dinners at the best restaurants, shows, and so much more. Two nights ago, he sent a box with a dress and instructions on what to do. I showed up, completely unsure of what the hell was going on, and we went to this weird place that looked like a library. Then, oh my God, it was so cool. We said a password of some sort and they took us back where this door opened and it was a speakeasy!"

A part of me wants to yell at her, to tell her how shallow and ridiculous she sounds because, to me, a picnic and sex at the creek sounds pretty damn perfect. The idea of having to dress up and all that sounds complicated and over the top. It just further goes to show the difference between Aurora and myself.

"Well," I say, refusing to fight with her. "I'm glad you enjoyed it."

"You could at least sound semi-happy for me."

"I am happy for you." I just think you're a selfish twat.

She flops back on her mattress. "If you were, you'd come here for my birthday next month."

"I can't, Aurora. I can't leave the farm."

"Don't you have workers?"

"No, I had to let a lot of them go," I say, frustration building once again with her. Not once has she asked about the farm or me. She doesn't care about anything other than telling me about her fabulous life.

"Oh, I get it. We had to do that at work too. I wasn't really worried I'd be one of them since I've really worked to ensure I'm indispensable. Too bad your . . . people . . . didn't do the same. It's hard being on top, isn't it?"

"Sure."

"I have a new client that I was able to get away from our competitor, you'd be impressed with me . . ." my sister drones on and on about herself and her amazingness.

Was she always this self-centered?

I try to remember, but my whole life I idolized her. I dreamed of being her because she was beautiful, funny, smart, and knew what she wanted.

Aurora didn't wait for things to happen, she made them happen.

I wanted that life. I wanted to command the world to bend to my will.

But now I see her as a spoiled brat who only wants to talk about herself.

She could've asked why I let the people go, but she didn't. Surprise, surprise.

"Aurora," I cut her off. "I have to go. Thank you for calling and I'm glad we could clear the air. Love you."

"Oh. Love you too, byeeee!"

I disconnect the phone, tossing it over on the side table, and head out to the back patio.

On my way out, I grab a six-pack of beer and a blanket. The air is still unseasonably cool, but right now, I just want to sit under the stars and enjoy the land while I still have it.

Mr. Knight said he'll have a decision in the next three weeks.

I need to hold on until then. Once I get the contract, I'll get a portion upfront, which will allow me to hire people and start getting the production back to what it needs to be. With just me and Perry working on the farm, there's not much we can do.

He's also now an unpaid worker, so while he's earning free rent, he's not working as hard as before and spending much more time drinking at Peakness.

Which is where Faye is tonight and I refused to meet her, much to her irritation.

Tonight, I need fresh air, and complete and utter peace.

However, it's really freaking cold so I toss a few logs in the pit and start a fire, listening to the crackling and enjoying the smell of smoke in the air. It reminds me of the fires in the cabin.

I mentally slap myself. I do not need *that* to be the memory that comes with this smell. I have a million other memories with bonfires and camping that I can recall that do not include a damn Whitlock.

"Ugh!" I groan to the sky. "Why do I think about him all the time?" I ask the universe because surely it must know.

"Because I'm good in bed," a deep male voice says, and I scream, jumping out of the chair.

My heart is pounding as I stare at the man I can't seem to forget. "You asshole! You don't just sneak up on a girl when she's talking to the moon!"

He chuckles and makes his way out of the shadows. "You asked a question. I figured you wanted an answer."

Of course this is my damn luck. "Why are you here?"

"To return the hat that isn't mine." Rowan lifts the object and grins.

I hate him.

"It's not mine."

Technically, that's not a lie. It's mine in the fact that I've had it in my possession for about two years, but it's not mine because it's actually Sawyer's. Semantics don't really need to be debated in this case.

"Then whose is it?" he asks, walking toward me.

"Yours."

Possession is nine tenths of the law and all that.

He laughs, low and throaty as he squats in front of me, placing the hat on my leg and his hands on each arm of the chair. "Is this going to be our excuse to keep doing what we both know we shouldn't?"

"No, we aren't going to do what we shouldn't have to begin with."

"We're not?" he asks as though he already knows the answer.

"No. We're not. Whatever we did can't happen again."

The corners of his lips tip up. "I agree. I just came to bring your hat."

I sigh. "I'm serious."

"I am too."

"I had to lie to Aurora today," I admit, feeling like shit.

"She asked if you've been sleeping with me?" Rowan's voice is filled with surprise.

I shake my head. "No, I just . . . avoided anything about it, which isn't hard because Aurora likes to talk about herself more than she cares about what I'm doing."

Just saying it makes me feel sad and disloyal, but Rowan, if anyone, might understand.

He stands, pulling the other chair over beside me. "Do you have another one of those?" I hand him a bottle of beer, after he takes a long drag and I do my best not to watch his throat as he drinks—and fail—he looks to me. "I don't know Aurora better than you. I don't really know her much at all. We never dated." He raises his hands. "I know, I know, you don't believe it, but it's true. We were fucking around, which I was honest about. We never had deep, meaningful conversations, but she did talk about how she loved you a lot."

"I don't doubt she loves me. I just don't think she cares about what I'm going through right now."

Rowan watches me, drains his beer and grabs two more. He opens the top and hands me one. "Your farm is in trouble."

It's not a question, it's just a fact and he knows it. "I'm handling it."

"I know you are."

The way he says it is like he has all the faith in the world that I'll do what I have to. It's strange, us talking like this. There's no anger, for one. Also, he's not giving me some grand pep talk, he's just believing in me, and I didn't realize until now that I needed that more than anything.

"Why are you really here?" I ask.

Rowan looks to me. "Because I was lying in my bed and I could still smell your perfume. Next thing I know I was throwing my sweatshirt on and walking here."

The butterflies in my stomach take flight. "Do you know why I came over last night?"

"Tell me."

Our eyes are locked and I can see the desire pooling. Why do I feel this way? Why do I want to leap out of my chair into his arms?

"I felt vulnerable and I didn't want to. I knew you'd take it away," I admit the truth and wait.

"I can make it go away now, Charlotte. Just say the word."

I can't.

I won't.

It's a bad idea.

I open my mouth to say those things. To tell him that we are enemies and I'm not vulnerable now. I'm going to get the contract, save my farm, and then I won't be weak again. I'll be stronger than ever and ready to rebuild into a force that can't be stopped.

"Word," I say instead, and I let him carry me inside to start a different kind of fire.

"How was your meeting with Carson?" Rowan asks as I'm lying with my hand on his chest, head resting atop it.

"He's a weird guy."

I laugh at that in my head. "He's very serious."

"He would have to be since he's a billionaire and all."

I'm not sure that all billionaires are like that, but given that he's the first one I've met, I'll take his word for it. "How did you even find out about this contract? It's supposed to be strictly organic farms."

This part always made me curious. I found out through the certified organic letters. They often put notices and opportunities there, and Rowan and I both know he is not certified, no matter what he feeds his cows.

"I'm working on becoming organic."

Great. "It's not easy."

In fact, it's a pain in the ass and took me almost two full years to get the paperwork through.

"I know, and it probably won't happen for another year or two, but Carson knows I can produce and while it won't be technically organic, we will be able to make claims on how we handle our cows."

I inhale deeply. "Well, that right there puts you out of the running."

Rowan chuckles. "You'd like that to be true."

"Considering you can't just be like, 'oh, look, I'm an organic farm'," I say in my manliest voice. "I know it's true. The contract clearly states it must be a certified farm. They want to be able to slap organic milk on the carton."

I feel so much better now. I thought maybe Rowan was close to being certified and I just hadn't heard about it. Knowing he's just at the beginning, there's no way Knight Food Distribution can choose him, it would be completely stupid.

"Well, he hasn't completely cut me out of the running since he came to my farm today too. He liked the facility and he works with Grady."

"And that's how you know about the contract." I roll onto my back, staring up at the ceiling.

Rowan follows me, hovering over me, and playfully bites my shoulder. "It's how I heard about it, yes. Grady was doing a job for Carson and he mentioned it."

Nothing I can do about it. "You think you'll get the contract?" I ask, running the tip of my finger up his side.

"Not sure, but it's good for either of our business."

No, it's not good for mine, it's essential. If I don't get this, I'm going to lose everything. "That it is," I say, not wanting him to know just how bad things are here.

"And you know what else will be good for either of us?" he asks, his eyes going soft as his lips move to mine.

"What's that?"

"The angry sex that'll follow when the other wins."

Not wanting to even think about it, I wrap my arms around him and kiss him to shut him up and end the conversation.

nineteen

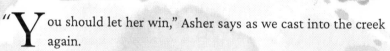

ROWAN

"You should let her win," Asher says as we cast into the creek again.

"Yeah, that so sounds like me," I toss back at him. Olivia wagered that she'd catch more than us combined.

My brother, the candy ass that he is, has conveniently lost every fish he's hooked. I swear, these girls have made him into a pansy.

"She's feeling left out, I think, since Sienna was born."

"Do a better job then," I say as Olivia claps her hands and lifts her fish in the air.

Of course she's going to win now. I put my pole between my legs to sign to her. *"Good job. I am still going to win."*

"You can try, but you never will."

I wink at her. She's seriously the best kid. So fun. Such a smart-ass.

Asher elbows me. "Seriously, she's a kid, let her fucking win."

"She's kicking our ass because you keep cutting your line or you dropped the fish. She doesn't need me to do anything, you're already taking care of it."

He huffs and goes back to fishing. "Brynn said you were out late last night."

"Brynn needs to mind her own business."

I love where my house is located, but hate that I have to pass her damn house to get there. She's so fucking nosey sometimes. It's why I walked to Charlotte's the other night. Since she brought me back the hat three days ago, it was my turn to return it.

Taking my truck was a risk, but I wasn't hiking over there in the pouring rain.

"Did you go out drinking?"

"Am I under investigation?" I toss back.

"Should you be?"

I swear, siblings are annoying. "It sure as hell feels like it."

Asher's eyes narrow. "Evasive."

"Intrusive," I fire back.

"So, where were you last night?"

I swear to God. "Listen, Officer—"

"It's Sheriff, if you don't mind."

Asshole. "Sorry, Sheriff Whitlock, kindly go fuck right the hell off with your questioning."

My brother huffs a laugh. "So you were with a girl, and you don't want me to know. Interesting."

I could've lied and said I was at a bar a few towns away, but Asher would've asked follow-up questions and then the lie would've been worse. So, evasive tactics are my best shot at avoiding this.

"I wasn't with a girl, but thanks."

"A guy?"

I give him a look that should make him shit his pants, but he doesn't. Instead he laughs. "I swear to God, if I didn't know better, I'd think you were with someone like Charlotte or something with the way you're evading the questions."

How in the hell could he be so right?

I force myself to laugh hard, but not too hard or he'll figure out my big secret. "Yeah, like that would ever happen. I'm sorry but our time in the woods was enough time in hell."

He shakes his head with a laugh. "Then who was she? Come on, I need to have something to hold over Brynn's head."

"It's seriously nothing. You know me, I don't fucking do relationships. We used to have that in common until you found Phoebe."

Immediately my brother's eyes go all mushy and shit. Unreal.

"I learned that there are some things worth giving up your ideas about what love could be," Asher says before looking at Olivia. "And we don't have to follow in our parents' footsteps. I'm the father that we never had for my girls. Even though Liv doesn't live with me, I give her everything our dad never did."

He's really a fantastic father, no one can ever say different. When he met Sara, Olivia's mother, they were literally what all my relationships have been—sex. Nothing more. No feelings got involved, no late-night cuddling. Just hooking up with clear expectations. Then, Asher got the surprise news that Olivia was created.

He never once faltered. He stepped up, has been there for every possible situation that his daughter could ever face. When she was born, and they realized she was deaf, he called everywhere to find ASL classes, and we all went with him. When Olivia needed surgery, he was there, side by side with Sara, being there for both of them.

They co-parent in a way that's truly amazing and Phoebe fit into their unit like she was there from day one.

"I know you do, and it's really great that you, Sara, and Phoebe have figured it out. I just have zero desire to ever walk down that path," I say with a smile. "I'm perfectly content with my only marriage being with this farm."

He snorts and shakes his head. "Until you knock some girl up."

"Shut your fucking mouth. Why would you curse me like that? Dickhead."

I'd be lying if I wasn't a little anxious by that comment. Yes, Charlotte has that IUD, but . . .

No.

No, no, no. I'm not going there. However, I am going to buy a box of condoms to double up that protection.

"Why would it matter? You're not boinking anyone, are you?"

Shit. "No, not right now. Why, do you have any prospects for me? Maybe Phoebe's bestie from Michigan?" Emmeline was hot as hell and I wouldn't mind having a long-distance fling. There'd be no risk of feelings there.

"Not a chance in hell. That woman would eat you alive."

"Probably," I say, hoping we're off the topics of accidental pregnancies and marriage. Seriously, this was supposed to be a fun day of fishing with my brother and niece.

Olivia, bless the Lord above, comes running over. We both turn as she's holding up a huge ass fish.

My eyes go wide and we both walk over, tossing our poles to the side.

"Wow!" I sign.

She beams.

Asher starts signing, but I'm not sure what he says as I'm still staring at the freaking fish.

Olivia puts it down. *"You were talking so I got it in all by myself."*

Asher laughs and signs and speaks this time. *"You sure did. That's the biggest fish any of us have caught. I'm so proud of you."*

She claps her hands and rushes over to Asher, wrapping her arms around him before signing. *"Thank you, Daddy."*

Olivia is non-verbal and we usually do a much better job at ensuring we check in on her.

"You win," I tell her.

She grins and nods. *"I knew I would."*

I rush over to her, lifting her up in the air as she smiles, and kiss her cheek. Then, when I put her down, I lift my hands. *"You are the only one who has ever beat me."*

Olivia tilts her head to the side. *"That is not true. Charlotte beat you at the auction."*

Asher bursts out laughing and I groan while keeping my smile.

"Surprise!" What feels like the entire town yells as I walk into Peakness.

Fuckers. They got me.

I got a call fifteen minutes ago from Brynn that she needed me to come to the bar, there was something wrong.

I ran back to my truck from the back pasture, faster than I'd ever run before, and flew here. My sister never needed saving, she needs to get her ass kicked.

I stand here, eyes wide as the bar is decorated with streamers, balloons, and other decorations everywhere. "Wow, umm," I say as Brynn approaches with her head tilted.

"Don't be mad."

"I'm not."

"You are, but please know this was Olivia's idea." Brynn pulls me in for a hug and kisses my cheek. "She loves you and you will not make her cry."

Of course I won't. The guilty girl comes running up to me, and I squat down to pull her in for a hug. *"You did this?"*

She nods. *"Happy birthday, Uncle Rowan."*

"Thank you. I love you very much."

"I know."

I laugh and kiss her forehead. She runs back to her dad and I clap my hands. "Someone get me a beer."

The crowd yells and sure enough, I have a beer in my hand a moment later. Both of my brothers and their fiancées come over, Micah, and the old ladies of the town as well. I look around and see Charlotte over against the wall. She's wearing a light blue sundress with white cowboy boots, one leg up on the wall and a beer in her hand as she talks to Faye. Our eyes meet and she smiles and winks before taking a long drink.

Tonight was not supposed to have us here.

It was supposed to have her naked, in my bed, tied to the headboard.

That was my fucking plan for tonight.

Not a damn surprise party.

However, it seems she will not be there waiting for me to

restrain her so I can make her come sixteen times before I fuck her senseless.

Nope, we're here, having to ignore each other.

I say hi to a few more people, some former ranch hands who are finding happiness at new ranches, one or two guys from the baseball team that ended up being a drinking league because we couldn't find other teams to play.

"Happy birthday, asshole," I hear her sexy voice interrupt my conversation.

I turn to see her there with a shit-eating grin. "I didn't know they let demons out of hell to celebrate birthdays."

She shakes her head with a laugh. "Only when it's to commemorate another demon. We tend to stick to our own kind."

"Good to know."

"Feel free to celebrate my birthday, it's on the sixth."

I nod slowly. "The sixth? Interesting. That's one of Satan's favorite numbers."

"You're such a dick."

I lean in so only she can hear. "You like my dick."

Charlotte leans back and slaps a wrapped package on my chest. "May you wear this and think of me."

Oh, I can only imagine what this is. Probably some kind of shirt that will embarrass me forever.

"I'll open it later."

She raises one brow. "Scared?"

Faye comes up next to her, laughing and wrapping her arm around Charlotte's shoulder. "Happy birthday, Rowan."

"Thanks, Faye."

Charlotte scoffs. "Oh, sure, you're nice to her when she says it."

"Well, if I recall she said it nicely, you called me an asshole."

She shrugs. "At least I'm honest."

"Sure, we'll go with that. Isn't it some kind of unwritten rule you're supposed to be nice on someone's birthday?" I toss back.

"This is me being nice. I brought you a present."

I look down at the gift in my hand, terrified of what could be in this. I exhale, decide it's not going to change if I don't open it, and tear the paper open.

The laughter that comes from deep inside me causes several people to stop and look at me. I can't believe it. In my hands is the skull cap that we've been tossing back and forth for the last week.

My eyes find hers and she's smiling and laughing softly.

Oh, Charlotte, I'm going to fuck you senseless in this bar.

Faye, completely unaware of what the hat means, stares at it. "A hat? I feel like I'm missing something."

Charlotte loops her arm through her best friend's. "Rowan lost his at the cabin, I felt he needed to have it back in his possession."

I smile at her. "I can't wait to wear it in a bit."

"You're planning to wear it soon, are you?"

As soon as I can get her alone. "In about ten minutes, when I need to step outside."

I see the awareness flash in her eyes. "Wow, are you planning to go outside alone?"

I shake my head. "Maybe, but I'm sure someone will be willing to go with me."

Faye purses her lips. "I really wish I knew what happened in that cabin. You both are weird and—oh! Joey!" she yells as he enters the bar, and he heads to her, lifting her in his arms and kissing her.

I move around the two idiots, where I'm beside Charlotte. "Meet me in the back in ten."

Then I walk away, greeting the rest of my guests, watching the clock until I can get to her.

It's been nine minutes and I'm heading away from everyone, explaining I need to use the bathroom, but seriously, it's like Declan Arrowood knows what I'm trying to do.

"How did the meeting go with Carson Knight?" he asks, leaning against the bar.

"Good. I think there's a good possibility I'll get it."

I really think it's mine. While he wanted an organic farm, he wants a high producing and growing farm more. He'd like to expand business into several different areas, not just milk alone.

We're able to give him a high-quality organic even though we're not certified, at a steady rate. Micah and I have been working tirelessly to become more efficient and we're doing great things.

"Charlotte has the certification, though. Don't count her out," he urges.

"I'm not. But she's maybe doing a quarter of what we're doing production wise."

"That doesn't discount her. Charlotte is smart and determined. She also knows her ass is on the line."

Her ass was about to get tapped, but he won't shut up.

I glance over to where she's standing, she smiles, places her beer down, and heads toward the bathroom area.

"I'll talk to you later, Dec," I say, slapping his shoulder. "We'll talk business another time. Tonight is for pleasure."

He laughs and nods. "Go have fun."

If he only knew.

When I get toward the back area, I rest against the door outside the bathroom. There's no way I can take her in there, someone will walk in, and considering the entire party is friends and family, we won't be able to hide for long.

She walks out of the bathroom, and I push open the door to the storage closet, grab her wrist, and pull her in.

"Rowan!" she gasps.

I don't wait or say anything, my hands cup her jaw and I pull her mouth to mine. Our tongues slide against the other's while her hands clutch my back. I kiss her hard, pressing her against the wood column of the shelving unit.

"You gave me the hat," I murmur against her skin.

"I did."

"Is this what you wanted?"

Her hands move to my face, pulling me so we're eye to eye. "I wanted you."

"I'm going to fuck you here, while everyone is out there, where anyone can walk in and see you coming apart on my cock."

"Rowan," she moans my name softly.

"Are you wet for me? Just thinking about what I was going to do when I had you alone?" I reach under her dress, sliding my finger against her bare pussy. "No underwear?"

She grins. "I took them off in the bathroom. Less obstacles."

"Good girl. Undo my pants."

Charlotte unbuttons my jeans, pushing them down and freeing my dick. "This is the last time," she says, like we do every last time.

"Never again."

"Make it count."

I lift her by her thighs and she wraps her legs around me as I slide in. Her jaw falls slack and I bounce her on my cock. This is rough and hard. There's no finesse or foreplay. I just fuck her, in the dirty closet, with a party going on around us.

It's like the cabin all over again. The two of us isolated where there is a world around us but we are the only two who exist.

Charlotte makes me crazy and I can't seem to get enough of her.

"When I saw that hat, all I wanted was to take you right there."

"I know," she says against my ear, in between panting. "I hate you for it."

"I hate you for this." I bounce her harder and then slide out before turning her around. "Grab the column." Her fingers wrap around the wood. I spread her legs wider and enter her from behind. I grab her long brown hair in my hand, pulling her head back.

I keep my grasp, fucking her hard, and I know I'm not going to last. We don't have time and seeing her like this, at my mercy, has me ready to explode.

"I'm close," I warn her, and I can feel her tighten around me.

"Hurry," she whimpers.

I slam into her four more times and she bites down on her arm as the two of us fall over the edge together.

I have sweat trickling down my temple and Charlotte grabs for the paper towels in front of her to clean up.

"This was convenient."

I hold back a laugh and brush her hair back. "The last time," I say again, needing it to be true.

She pulls her underwear on and fixes her dress. "No more, Rowan. We can't. We both know this is stupid."

"It is."

Charlotte runs her fingers through her hair. "Besides, we hate each other."

"We do."

"Now, how do we get out of here unnoticed?"

"I'll go out first, you wait a few, listen for me to knock on the door twice, and then you can come out."

She laughs softly. "This was fun. I know that sounds terrible, but . . . you're not the guy I thought, and I guess for that, I'm glad we made this mistake several times."

"You're not the girl I thought I knew."

"There will always be that. However, I'm still going to get that contract and then I'll be kicking your ass in every way."

"I can't wait to see you try."

"Well, happy birthday." She lifts up on her toes and gives me a sweet kiss.

If this is the last time I'm going to kiss her, it won't be that. I shift closer, cupping her face, and bring my lips to hers. It's a slow kiss, one that if I were another man and she were another woman, would be one that people wrote songs about.

I pull back, and her eyes slowly flutter open and find mine. "I'm going to need that hat back."

"I'll bring it tonight."

twenty
CHARLOTTE

"Happy birthday, Rowan," I say, walking out to the back patio with a cupcake.

"You made this?"

I nod. "Don't get too excited. I made them for Micah's niece and just kept one."

"Be still my heart. And they say you're heartless."

He opens the blanket and I climb on his lap. "I don't think I'm heartless, I just don't feel the need to lie to people."

"A trait I've noted since I first met you."

I smile and then look up at the sky. "This is one thing about Sugarloaf that I will never get tired of."

"The stars?"

"Yeah, it's so magical, sort of makes you remember we're just a tiny part of this world."

"That we are," Rowan agrees. "Sugarloaf has that effect on us. I know Michigan felt like its own world too."

I nestle against him, exhausted after the intense bout of sex we had once he got to my house. "Tell me about when you moved here. I know it was for Brynn after your mom died, but it couldn't have been easy."

Rowan's arms tighten around me and he shifts me to his other side. "It wasn't easy, but it also wasn't a hard decision. Brynn was young and she needed her family. I was definitely not in any position to be her guardian, that was all Asher, but I could be her friend."

"So you just packed up, left Michigan and school?"

"Pretty much."

I smile, resting my head on his shoulder and seeing a shooting star fly across the dark sky. "No wonder she thinks her brothers are all amazing."

"It's also because we actually *are* amazing."

I roll my eyes, even though he can't see it. "Your mom was always so nice to me. I remember she made the best brownies in the bake sale. She'd always sell out before anyone else and it upset Mrs. Cooke so much."

Each year she had to make a bigger batch and it always irritated the other moms because she sold out no matter what.

"She put coffee in them," Rowan says, almost absently.

"Coffee?"

"That was her secret ingredient. Brynlee makes them for our birthdays after she found the recipe buried in a false drawer."

I turn to look at him. "What?"

He smiles and nods. "She substituted used coffee grounds for something and it worked. She loved to bake. I remember that as a kid."

"What was your childhood like?" I ask, snuggling back in.

Rowan had the picturesque family. He and his brothers were all close in age and they had a little sister to dote on. I would've given anything to have had the life he did. I was an orphan at six, ripped away from my life in a city I loved, and stuck out in cow country with Aurora who was angry at the world.

But I had my gran and pop. They were what made all of it okay. Her kind words and his warm hugs always made me feel better.

Rowan sighs heavily. "It was nothing like you're probably imagining."

"How so?"

"For one, my father was a piece of shit. He took off after I was born, and after that, my mother was . . . well, a mess is a kind way of saying it."

"You're right," I tell him. "I was definitely not picturing that. How was your mom a mess?"

I try to remember something about her as a person, but I really just remember the way she was always there for Brynn.

"For one, she got married three times in three years."

I sit up, turning to look at him at that news. "Three in three years? How is that possible?"

He laughs once. "She got married a week after her divorce was final to my father, divorced him a month later because she met someone else, married him, found out he was a donkey's ass, left him two months later. I guess that one was at least double the other. Then, she met husband number three and stayed with him for about six months until she caught him cheating and that was the end of that one."

"Wow."

"It gets better, then she met Howie, who is Brynlee's father. Howie was a piece of shit that I almost killed one night."

My hand rests on his chest as I listen to his story. "What happened?"

"He was drunk, like always, and I walked in right as he slapped my mother. I swear, I've never felt rage like that in my life. I was home from college for winter break. Asher was in the basement and heard me roar. He got me off him as I was ramming my fist in his face."

"As you should have!" I say, feeling my own rage. No one should ever hit their spouse. Ever. If I had ever seen someone hurt my mom or grandma, I would be no different than him.

"I felt the same, but it did a number on me. My mother packed her shit two days later and came to Sugarloaf with Brynn since she owned the farm after my grandparents passed. Mom and Howie got divorced and Brynn was never the same toward her father."

197

"Again, rightfully so."

He sighs heavily, pulling me back against him. "I feel bad for her, though. She witnessed her brother beat the shit out of her father. She understood why, she was almost ten and definitely knew what was going on."

I try to imagine what Brynlee must've felt, seeing her brother and father. Knowing her mother was hit by her dad. I don't know that I would've been okay after that. My father loved my mother beyond reason. There was nothing in the world he cared about more than his girlies, as he called us. I swear, my mother walked on water if you ever asked him.

"She had three amazing brothers and her mother to help her."

"Now I'm amazing, am I?"

"You have your moments," I say with a smile. "I still think you're an asshole."

Rowan chuckles. "What about you? I know you lived with your grandparents because you lost your parents."

"I did. I was six and Aurora was eight. We hated it here."

"What? Sugarloaf was not the beautiful metropolis you dreamed of?"

I snort. "Not even a little. We lived in a penthouse in New York City. We had our nanny, Minnie, who was fun and always made us smile. There was our butler, Victor, who never smiled but winked whenever we did something funny. Visiting here was like stepping into a story that we read as kids with horses and cows."

"I never knew that," Rowan admits. "I knew you lived in New York but not that you were loaded."

Sometimes I think that's the most ironic part of it. I was rich. Well, my parents were. Stupid rich, and when my parents died, we got a good portion of it. However, I used all of my inheritance to buy Aurora out of this farm, and the rest to improve it to get the organic certification.

Only to now be on the brink of losing it all.

I sigh heavily, pushing that sad thought away. "My parents

were, and the money is pretty much gone now, so a lot of good it did me."

"How did you lose your parents?"

"They say there are moments in a person's life when something happens that no matter what or where you go in life, you'll always remember every detail."

Rowan nods. "Yes, moments in history. Like when President Kennedy was assassinated."

I turn to him. "Yes! And Pearl Harbor, my pop could tell you exact details of where he was when he heard about it, the Challenger exploding, September 11th, and for me, when I found out my parents were killed by a drunk driver."

Rowan takes my hand in his, lacing our fingers together. "I'm sorry. It never should've happened."

"No, it shouldn't have, but it did. For so long I made up a hundred stories on how it went down instead of a drunk driver. Like, I would pretend they were killed by doing something heroic, like rescuing kittens on the road or stopping a robbery." I laugh at myself, remembering the ways I would weave these stories.

"I don't think that's funny or strange."

I shrug a little, rubbing my thumb against his. "When I turned sixteen, my grandparents felt like Aurora and I were finally old enough to know the details of our parents' accident. They let us read the report of how the drunk driver, who said she always drove better drunk, came across the two lanes of traffic, into my parents' lane and slammed into them. We read how my father was alive when they responded, and when he found out my mother was killed at the scene, he died in the ambulance. I always wonder if he didn't just give up because his heart was broken."

Rowan squeezes his fingers tighter around mine and we fall into a comfortable silence. I close my eyes and relax against him.

How is it that I'm so comfortable with him? I can't help but wonder if it's because there's nothing here. We're not even friends, so I can talk about all this without worrying he'll use the broken parts of me as a weapon later on, which is what the last guy I dated did.

In an argument, he'd bring up my insecurities. With Rowan, there's no reason to be insecure since we're nothing but fuck buddies.

Maybe we could be friends, but most likely not. He'll say something that'll piss me off soon enough.

Not to mention we're both vying for the contract that he shouldn't even be eligible for.

"It's almost midnight," Rowan says softly as I start to drift to sleep.

"Hmm?"

"My birthday is almost over."

I nuzzle more into his embrace. "I used to love my birthday."

"Used to?" he asks.

"My mom was the best at birthdays. Our day was whatever the birthday girl wanted. If we wanted cookies and ice cream for breakfast, we got it. It was the day of 'yes' and we looked forward to it every single year. I would always pick the same thing for breakfast, waffles with ice cream, and for dinner it was steak."

"Steak, at six?" Rowan laughs. "And now you run a dairy farm where it's basically steak everywhere."

"My dad loved steak. I did it because I knew he wanted it."

Rowan rubs his scruffy cheek against my neck. "Always doing for others."

Story of my life. I take care of everyone so they stay, only to end up alone. It's really working out well for me.

"Better than being selfish."

"Hey, don't knock it till you try it. I like the selfish life."

I roll my eyes, even though he can't see it. "Says the man who moved back here when his mother died to help raise his sister."

"Touché."

I yawn, feeling tired and comforted at the same time.

"I should probably leave before the clock strikes twelve."

I smile and twist in his lap, trapping him. "Do you turn into a pumpkin at midnight?"

"I think you're more Cinderella than I am. I was worried you'd grow horns or something hideous."

Such an ass. I get up, pulling the blanket with me, and he jumps as the cold air hits him. I giggle and he rushes after me and he doesn't leave for another two hours.

twenty-one

CHARLOTTE

"What about this dress?" Faye asks as she lifts something I would never wear off the rack.

It's practically see-through and way too short.

"Are you drunk?"

"I might be."

I smile and shake my head. "Keep looking."

We go through the rack and I remember I have something for Faye in my bag. "Oh! I got you something. As a thank you for shopping with me."

She laughs. "You never have to thank me for shopping, it's my favorite thing in the world."

This is true. However, since my adventure in the woods and the fact I keep using the salve I made on bruises, cuts, and pimples, I keep making it. Of course, now I have added a few extras to make it smell divine, used a couple of different oils instead of the crappy olive oil we had, and found someone local in New Hampshire who sent me some really good pine sap. It's actually really therapeutic and a lot of fun.

I hand her the little jar, wrapped with some brown burlap ribbon and a sprig of pine, just for a cute touch.

"Oh my God! Did you make this?"

I nod.

"It's adorable, what is it?"

I tell her all about my pine sap making in the woods and how it really helped with the bruises and the cuts we had. "Oh, and it worked on my zit! I tried it two days ago and look." I tilt my face to show it's completely gone. "It like, makes it come to the surface so fast that it goes away ten times faster. It's a miracle and I put some extra oils and things to help with different ailments."

"Wow, this is amazing."

"It's been a great stress reliever."

She smiles and opens the lid. "What is that smell?"

"Well, pine is really strong, so I've been playing with scents that will not really mask it, but work with it in a way to make it less . . . harsh."

"I love it. I'm totally going to use this!"

That makes me happy. I wanted to do something nice for Faye since Lord knows she does a lot for me. To know that she appreciates it really warms my heart. "I hope it works."

"Only one way to find out."

We keep looking at dresses, shaking my head at bad ones, laughing at the truly hideous ones, and really freaking hoping we find one that isn't horrible.

She lifts another off the rack that is completely inappropriate. Worse than the last one. "Okay, I'm convinced you want me to look unprofessional. You realize this is a work dinner where I'll meet the rest of the Knight family. The last thing I need to do is show up dressed like that."

"Maybe the way into the business is to show up like that," she says with a wiggle of her brows. "A little naughty time with the boss."

"No."

"I'm kidding. Okay, tell me more about this dinner so I can use my shopping superpowers."

I fill her in on the details I have. It's a fancy dinner party where there will be a lot of existing clients and potential ones. It's at an opera house in Manhattan and I'm going to have to drive in and back that night because there's no way I can afford a hotel for the night.

"Wait, you're going to drive back? After a night of what I assume will be dancing and drinking?" Faye asks, her eyes wide.

"I can't afford a hotel."

"I'll get you one."

"No, you won't," I say firmly. "I don't need you to when I can drive back."

Faye sighs heavily. "And, how, pray tell, are you driving into the city?"

I haven't worked that part out yet. My truck is about halfway done now, I need to give Donny another five hundred to finish the rest. I was able to convince him to drop the price a lot on the fact that I babysat for him.

"I'm not sure."

She smirks. "No shit, because your hooptie of a truck is dead."

"I'll figure it out."

"Just ask Rowan," she says while going back to looking at the rack.

"I'm not asking Rowan to drive me into the city."

Her gaze meets mine. "Why not? You two seem to be in a much nicer place since the ice storm debacle. He's going, right?"

I know he is, but I shouldn't know that. "I assume he was invited."

"Okay, then just tell him that it makes more sense to drive in together, which it does."

"Oh, sure, and then I can just casually drop that I should stay with him in his room since again, I have no money for a hotel?" I ask, crossing my arms over my chest.

Faye laughs at that. "Or you can stay with Aurora."

My sister. I forgot about that option, but I really don't want to see her. After the last few calls, I'm just not in the right place to be around her, but it would make the most sense.

"All the more reason not to drive in with Rowan, then. If she found out I drove with him, forget it."

"What the hell does she think happened in the woods when you spent days trapped with the man?"

I look away, biting my lip, and say under my breath, "I didn't tell her I was with him."

"You didn't *tell* her?" The shock in Faye's voice makes me feel defensive.

"Look, Aurora and I aren't exactly on the greatest of terms right now. She's pissed at me for a multitude of reasons and, honestly, I'm not exactly all that happy with her."

Faye rests her arm on the top of the clothes rack. "Why are you mad?"

"Because she won't stop pestering me about coming to visit her, she judges me for everything I do, and she went off after we spent the night when I got hammered at Rowan's."

She rolls her eyes. "Your sister is such a drama queen." She lifts her hands in surrender. "I know, I know, he broke her cold, black heart, but give me a break. Rowan is not a bad guy. He's been incredibly nice to you, took care of you, and I totally saw you smile at him at his party before we left."

I focus on the dresses in front of me to keep from letting her see my red cheeks. I did a lot more than smile at him that night.

However, my best friend stops talking and I look up to see her staring. "What?"

"Why are you blushing?"

"I'm not, I'm just hot."

"The hell you are. It's not even warm in this place," Faye calls me out on my lie. "What's going on with you? You've been weird since that hiking trip. If I didn't know you better, I'd think that something happened between you and Rowan, but . . ."

One thing I've never been good at is lying to Faye. She knows all my secrets, except this one. For weeks I've kept this to myself, and I feel like I'm going to explode.

"I've been sleeping with Rowan since the ice storm," I admit, and I wish I could take the words back.

Her brows shoot up and jaw drops. "You're *what*?"

I nod. "It's . . . yeah, I don't know. I'm clearly insane and a horrible person."

She comes around the rack and takes my hands in hers. "Explain everything."

The lack of judgment on her face is the only reason I spill my guts. I tell her about the entire ice storm, how we slept together, stating it all ended when we left the woods, because it was clearly just because we were bored and frustrated. Then, I tell her about how I went to his house to return that hat, and she just stares at me. All of it comes out in such a rush that I'm not even sure what I've said anymore.

"You're sleeping with him as in present tense?"

"Last night was the last time . . ."

I mean, I guess that's present tense.

For the first time since I've known her, she's at a loss for words. She keeps opening and closing her mouth while shaking her head.

Not that I can blame her. It would be more plausible if I had said I was moving to Hawaii to be a pirate than sleeping with the man I've vowed to hate in solidarity with my sister. But, here I am, absolutely not hating him.

"I'm . . . well, okay, wow. You and Rowan . . ."

"I'm insane, right?" I ask, needing her to tell me I am, because then, at least, I can get help for this affliction. It's not just bad decision making, which is a me problem.

"Is he nice to you?" Faye asks, still not really blinking.

"In bed?"

"Yes."

"Very nice," I say, thinking about how very nice the orgasms are.

She smiles at that. "Not even a little surprised. God, your sister is going to freak the fuck out. Now that I'm over the initial shock, I'm not sure what to say. The girl code says you definitely don't sleep with your sister's ex who she claimed cheated on her."

And that feeling of relief is gone. "I know."

"And that's why, I'm assuming, it took you weeks to tell me?"

I nod. "That and other reasons."

"Such as?"

"It's never going anywhere but here. Rowan is my rival in every way. He bought the damn land I wanted, and the bull, and he makes me insane, and he fights with me about everything, and he is stupid." I say that last part and feel stupid myself.

She laughs. "So you like him?"

"*No!*"

The word flies from me so fast that Faye laughs. "So then why did you sleep with him last night?"

"Because the sex is great."

We both know that's not the only reason. I've only ever been in one real relationship and it was in college. He was my first and my only, until Rowan. I wanted a love like my parents had. They met in college, fell madly in love, and had only been with each other. It was one of those love stories that was so perfect it was almost unbelievable.

That was what I wanted.

A love story for the ages.

My college boyfriend didn't. He wanted to get laid consistently, and then when we were nearing the end of my junior year, he ended it. No reason. No big fight, just that he thought we were moving in different directions and his was to the west where a blonde with big boobs was.

"If you were anyone else, I'd believe that line, but you're not that way and we both know it. You like him?"

"I don't want to."

I can see the sympathy in her eyes. "I'm going to give it to you straight, which is why I think you told me this. You have to stop if you don't want to face Aurora. If you care about him, or think there's something more than the fun you've been having, then you need to tell your sister and face that storm."

She's right. I know that's exactly why I told her. I need someone to tell me to stop because clearly I'm not able to do it myself.

"There's no future with Rowan Whitlock."

And there can't be.

In a few days or a week from now, we're going to find out who got the contract and then what? How do we navigate that mine-field? We both know we can't, which is why neither of us have spoken about it.

"Then, this will be one of those things that you and I will laugh about when we're living on our compound in our old age. I'll be like, remember that time you were banging your sister's ex? And you'll be all, do I ever, the sex was so good, I still tingle when I think about it."

I burst out laughing and sigh heavily. "I knew it was wrong."

"Look, I'm the last person in the world who will ever tell you it's wrong. I live on the wrong side of choices, but you're not me. You're loyal, amazing, smart, funny, and will cut someone if they hurt some-body you love. I get why it happened in the woods, but since you're back home . . ." She lifts one shoulder and her lips are in a flat line.

"You're right."

"Plus, you need this contract and you're going against him. How about we focus on getting a killer dress and making the money?"

I like that plan. "Deal."

"And you can borrow my car to get into New York and I'll get you a hotel."

I roll my eyes. "Not a chance, but I love you for offering."

She grumbles something and then walks over to the clearance rack and lifts a dress that is absolutely perfect. "Superpowers for the win!"

⚷

I grab my overnight bag, which is stuffed with every possible beauty product I could ever need, and my killer dress that was seventy percent off, which means I took the tags off and don't need to be insanely careful so I can return it, and then I head downstairs to wait for Faye to get here.

After much hemming and hawing, I accepted her offer to borrow her car. She's going to spend the night at my place, and I'll drive back tonight.

Only she's late.

Like freaking always.

I tap my foot as I look out the window, waiting to see her bright red car, but nothing yet.

I shoot off a text:

ME

Where are you? I needed to leave ten minutes ago.

FAYE

I'm sooooooo sorry. I love you, and I promise it'll be okay.

Oh, that sounds great.

ME

What the hell is going on?

FAYE

I got stuck and I can't get there for another hour, but I called for help

.

Help can only mean one damn thing.

I look back out the window and sure enough, a large truck is coming, leaving a cloud of dust behind it.

Great.

I have two options. I can refuse this ride and skip the party, probably screwing myself out of the deal I desperately need, or I can go in the truck and control myself.

ME

I hate you.

FAYE

I don't blame you. I did book you a room at the same hotel that Rowan is at. So, you don't have to worry about trying to control yourself in a room with him. You're welcome.

ME

You are going to owe me so damn much.

FAYE

Expect a grand payment. Love you.

I toss my phone in my purse and head out to where Rowan is waiting in the truck. It's been three days since we've spoken. I didn't really see any reason to talk and it isn't like he called me either.

This will be fine. We can just co-exist and get through the next twenty-four hours.

I get in the car, and sitting on the console is the hat, and the man sitting there has a wide grin on his face.

I'm so screwed.

twenty-two
ROWAN

I shouldn't be this damn happy to see her, but I am. For the last few days, I've focused on the farm and getting things ready to be out of town. We received information from our certifier two days ago that he needed some additional records because we may have been in violation of a pesticide a year ago.

I spent two days searching to make sure that isn't the case.

However, it took just one look at Charlotte and I feel better.

"Hi," she says as she puts her bag in the back. "Thanks for the ride."

Something is off. I can hear it in her voice. "What? No hello kiss?"

She straightens and then focuses extremely hard on putting her seatbelt on. "No."

All right then. "Got it, back to enemies."

Charlotte clasps her hands in her lap. "Not enemies, but not whatever the hell we were since the hiking trip either."

"Sounds good to me," I say as though I give two shits. Which I don't. Charlotte and I are nothing more than two people who have fantastic sex.

There aren't any feelings. Not real ones.

We have sex and we go about our lives.

It was good while it lasted, but it's over and that's fine. Now I can go back to focusing on what matters, my farm, my life, and the future expansions I want to make.

"Good. Then we're both in agreement? You can keep the hat?"

Fuck the hat. I lift it and throw it behind me. "Hat no more."

"Okay."

"Okay."

This is going to be a fucking fantastic two-hour car ride. Someone kill me now.

We get onto the highway and she finally drops her shoulders and looks to me. "This is weird."

"It doesn't have to be."

"No?"

I shake my head. "Not if you don't want it to be."

I've had enough fuck buddies and non-relationships that went perfectly fine after we decided to call it off. We're not all friends, but it's not like her asshole sister either.

"So, how does it work?"

"How does what work?" I throw back, wanting to goad her a bit.

"Well, do we just pretend we don't know what the other looks like naked? Do we talk? Do we go back to how it was before?" Charlotte shifts to look at me.

"I'll never be able to pretend I don't know what you look like naked, so that's out. As for the talking, I'd like us to be civil and you to finally believe I'm not the monster Aurora made me out to be."

She flinches, just barely, but enough I catch it. "I don't think you're a monster."

That's something, I guess. "No?"

She shakes her head. "No, you're maybe a dick, but not a monster."

I smile and wink at her. "You like my dick."

"I *liked* your dick. Past tense."

"My apologies."

The rest of the drive goes well. We get into Manhattan and I swear I'm starting to itch. I miss the quiet, the fresh air, and the stars in the sky.

Charlotte, on the other hand, looks like a pig in shit.

Her smile is wide as she looks at everything going on around us. "I love it here," she says, almost absently.

"Love?"

She turns to me. "What's not to love? The sights, the lights, the smells, the sounds, it's all magical."

Okay, I'm convinced she's lost her mind. "Oh, yes, who doesn't love the smell of garbage?"

Charlotte scoffs. "Garbage? It's not garbage, you idiot. It smells like food and people and a world where we move fast and get things done."

"Don't forget the smell of weed," I remind her. Seriously, I'm going to get a second-hand high.

"Shut up."

"You love it here?" I ask.

"I grew up here. It's home. I know you think it's gross, but to me, it's where my parents wanted to raise us. Where is our hotel?"

I look at the address on my phone. "I had us somewhere else, and Faye vehemently refused. She put us at some place around 5th and 55th."

She rolls her eyes. "Of course she did."

"She said she owed us, I wasn't going to argue."

Charlotte smiles. "She does owe us. It would be rude to deny her the grovel."

The way her smile widens at the end makes me want to pull the truck over and say fuck her stupid idea of calling this off, but that would be asinine because I don't need or want Charlotte Sullivan.

I can find someone else.

In fact, tonight, I'll do just that. There's bound to be a lonely woman who needs a little excitement at this party tonight. I'll be happy to show her why country boys are better.

"Oh!" Charlotte bounces in her seat as we drive down the street.

"There! We just passed the absolute best pizza in all of Manhattan. We have to go there."

"I'm pretty sure they're going to feed us," I say, as I pull up in front of the hotel.

"Yeah, but there's nothing like pizza at this place."

"If you say so." I park the truck and two men come rushing toward the door.

"Mr. and Mrs. Whitlock, welcome to the Magnifique. I'm Hugh, and I will be your butler during your stay. We'll go ahead and valet the truck for you and get your bags up to your room."

Charlotte and I both, at the same time, talk over each other. "*What?*"

"Fucking, Faye!"

Hugh blinks and then looks down at his paper. "I'm so sorry, your travel agent called about an hour ago to upgrade your room to the honeymoon suite."

Charlotte barks a laugh. "She did, did she?"

Poor Hugh looks like he's ready to crawl into a hole. "Yes, we have everything set up for you both. Your agent was very specific it had to be our best room. I could always downgrade you to a regular room, but . . ."

Oh, I want to laugh because it's comical, but the way that Charlotte's face is contorted, I keep it in. She looks like she's ready to blow. "Thank you, but we'll keep the honeymoon suite. I assume our agent who made the change put her credit card on file?"

He nods. "Yes, sir."

"Thank you, my wife and I will be ordering room service when we get to our room."

Charlotte makes a noise and then her face softens. "Yes, yes we will."

"Come on, sweetheart, let's go." Hugh rushes around us, opening the door. I place my hand on her back and we enter the hotel.

Okay, this place is impressive. The entire lobby looks like an old library. There are books lining the entire space, the floor is black and white checkered marble with sofas that look like they're from the 1930s. It's old, vintage, and really freaking nice.

Hugh hands the two of us a glass of champagne and barks orders at two guys standing to the side. They rush and take the bags that are sitting on the floor beside us and he takes us up to the penthouse.

"I think you'll both be very comfortable in the suite, and you need only text the number and either myself or Chase, the other butler, will answer," Hugh explains as we near the top floor.

"Thank you."

He smiles warmly and then escorts us to the room. "Here is your key, there is only one suite on this level. The other room to the left is the butler's quarters. We do also service the floor below, but are primarily reserved for your needs. Your bags should be in the room already. Please don't hesitate to ask for anything you need."

I don't think we're going to need anything, but Charlotte loops her hand around my arm, leaning against me. "I'm sure Rowan and I will be fine, thank you, Hugh."

"Of course, Miss."

Hugh goes back in the elevator, leaving us standing in the hallway. Charlotte looks at me. "I'm going to kill her."

"It would be warranted."

"Well, let's go see the room."

I unlock the door and we enter.

The two of us freeze at the entryway.

This place makes the lobby look like a dump. I've never, in my life, seen anything like this. "What the fuck?" I say more to myself than anything.

"This is incredible," Charlotte whispers.

This is not a room, it's a freaking palace. We step farther in, where there's a sunken living room with the biggest freaking television I've ever seen. Everything is shiny and white, the floors, the walls, the furniture, it's all glowing.

Charlotte walks deeper, her fingertips grazing the sofa table, and she turns to me with a huge smile and big eyes. "This is ours?"

"For one night, it seems."

"There's a whole second floor," she says, pointing to the spiral staircase.

I seriously can't even take this all in. It's insane. She's upstairs already, calling down and explaining there's a loft with a pool table and other games. "Why couldn't we get stranded here during the ice storm?"

"Right!" Charlotte yells back.

"Hey, Dora the Explorer, the party is in an hour, do you have to get ready?" I remember all too well her sister needing three hours just to go to Peakness.

I don't know how I ever thought sleeping with her was a good idea.

She comes back down and smiles. "I do. I'll go get ready and you can . . . do whatever guys do while girls get ready."

I nod once, grab the remote, and flop on the couch. "Baseball it is." I will get lost in the game that's on, relax, and get ready ten minutes before we're walking out the door.

Charlotte grabs her bag and heads down the hallway and gasps. "This bed is *huge!*"

And now I'm not thinking about the game that's on, I'm playing a much better game in my head with Charlotte and that bed.

Fuck.

***

"I don't know how you do this shit," I say to my brother Grady as he hands me a beer.

"Do what?"

"These parties all the time."

He shrugs. "It's part of business. Carson is a huge client and wants in on my company. He flies a lot, needs a pilot who will be at his beck and call, so these parties allow me opportunities that I need to keep growing."

Grady is by far the smartest out of us. Well, maybe Brynlee is smarter than all of us, but none of us will admit that. Still, Grady was a pilot in the navy and then got out, came home to raise his son, and started two different businesses that are both flourishing—and he's engaged to Addison, which was the smartest thing he ever did.

"So business is good?"

"The private plane section is going well, a little slower than I hoped, but the courier section is booming. It's stupid how much the companies are willing to pay for us to transport documents." Grady shakes his head and sighs. "I'm not complaining."

"I bet not."

Charlotte and Addison walk toward us and I have to force myself to appear calm, but Charlotte in that dress has me feeling anything but calm.

She's beautiful. Absolutely stunning. Her long brown hair flows in curls down her back and she's wearing a one-shoulder emerald dress that clings to every perfect curve. I had to feign disinterest when she came out of the room, go in the bathroom and jerk off, just to get through tonight.

Not my proudest moment.

"Hello, beautiful ladies," Grady says smoothly, wrapping his arm around his fiancée.

"Handsome Whitlock boys," Addy replies.

I fake a gagging noise. Seriously, my brothers have always been idiots, but in love, they're absolutely brainless.

Charlotte playfully slaps my chest. "You're so ridiculous. Are you saying we're not beautiful?"

"Never once even thought that," I tell her. "You're both stunning."

Her eyes find mine and there's a flash of something before it disappears. "Well, thank you. You clean up nicely, too."

"Was that a compliment?" I ask with mock horror.

Charlotte sighs heavily. "I take it back."

"No, no, princess, you can't do that. We have witnesses."

Grady raises one hand. "I heard nothing."

Addy smiles. "Me either, the music is really loud."

"Traitors," I tell them both.

Grady looks to Addison. "Dance with me?"

"I thought you'd never ask."

Cue the gagging feeling again. Before my brother can get too far away, he turns to me. "Dance with Charlotte, maybe she'll compliment you again."

Way to put me on the spot, asshole.

Charlotte looks anywhere but at me. I wait, because there's nothing more I'd like than to take her in my arms right now. She's like an addiction and I could use even a small taste right now, so I don't want to overdose on her.

Finally, her eyes find mine and I extend my hand.

"You don't have to just because he said it."

"I've never done something I don't want to because my family suggests it."

She hesitantly lifts her hand, placing it in mine. Neither of us speak as we walk to the dance floor, away from Grady because I don't want any more of his unhelpful suggestions. We stop, and her hands rest on my chest as mine are against her lower back.

We sway to the music, just looking at each other, and I clear my voice. "You really do look beautiful."

"That's twice now," she tries for humor, but I hear the tinge of hope in her voice.

"I meant it both times."

"I meant it too, you clean up very nicely. I don't think I've ever seen you in anything other than jeans and a T-shirt."

"It's the uniform of ranchers, isn't it?" I ask, teasingly. "I don't know that I've seen you in a dress before either."

She smiles. "I, too, wear the uniform of ranchers."

"I like this on you."

Her blush is so fucking alluring.

"Thank you."

I stretch my neck, hating the way this tie feels like it's choking me. "I'm starting to believe this was a way to torture farmers who are looking for contracts."

She smiles. "My feet are killing me, too. How much longer do we have to stay?"

"Well, I have my meeting tomorrow and the last thing I want to answer is why he didn't see us at the party."

So far, I haven't seen Carson, or I would've already found a reason to get out of this place.

Charlotte's fingers move up my chest, her arms now resting on my shoulders. "Well, if I have to suffer, it's nice to know you are as well."

I'm not suffering all that much at the moment. Lord knows when we get back to that fucking hotel room I will be.

"So, are you going to see Aurora after this?" I ask, stupidly.

"No, she doesn't know I'm here."

My eyes widen at that. "Really?"

"First, I didn't want to hear anything because I wouldn't be able to lie about you being here as well. Second, I just . . . I need to focus on the contract, not deal with any outside influences."

Charlotte and Aurora were insanely close when I was diddling with her fiddle. I'm a little surprised at how little she talks about her now.

"So after this ends in an hour, you're planning to what?"

Charlotte laughs softly. "I was planning to get out of this dress, get in my pajamas, and watch a movie in my hotel room. That was before we ended up in a honeymoon penthouse. Now, I'm not so sure that being cooped up with you is a good idea."

"Afraid you'll want to get the hat from the car?" I tease.

Her green eyes meet mine. "Yes."

The admission rocks me back a moment and I give her one of my own. "I've thought of doing it a hundred times."

"That's what I was afraid of."

"Then what options do we have? I'm sure as fuck not staying in Grady's hotel."

Her mischievous smile grows. "I think that sounds like a perfect idea."

"Not a chance, sweetheart."

"Hmm . . ." she ponders, looking around. "*Oh*! I know."

"I'm a little terrified."

"I'm going to make you fall in love."

Yeah, terrified was the absolute right response. "Umm . . ."

She shakes her head. "With my city."

twenty-three

CHARLOTTE

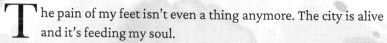

The pain of my feet isn't even a thing anymore. The city is alive and it's feeding my soul.

"You've got to be kidding me," Rowan says as we're standing in the center of Times Square. "This is what you thought would make me fall in love?"

"Can't you feel it?"

"Oh, I feel something," he quips.

I ignore him because nothing in the world can make me upset when I'm here. Each year, my gran and pop would take us back to Manhattan so Aurora and I could see all the things our parents loved. Not that I could ever forget, it's a part of my DNA. "You need to really feel it, in your soul. Come here," I say, pulling him close. "Close your eyes."

Rowan raises one brow. "And get mugged? No thanks."

"Oh for fuck's sake. You're not going to get mugged. Stop being dramatic. Close your eyes," I practically demand. He does it this time. "Now, listen to the sounds."

"The sounds of sirens, music to my ears."

I swear, he needs to be slapped some days. "Inhale through your nose. Do you smell that?" It's a mix of roasting nuts, hot dogs, car exhaust, and life. "It's the smell of living."

Rowan opens his eyes, staring at me like I might be in need of medical intervention. "You're kidding me, right?"

"You really don't feel that?"

"I feel like a sardine getting shaken around. There are so many freaking people. It's noisy as fuck, I can't hear myself think, and your whole smell-the-city thing is really a bad idea."

I sigh heavily. He's going to be a tough nut to crack, that's for sure. "Fine. Maybe Times Square isn't your thing. That's okay, this is the city that has it all. Let's go."

I pull his arm, dragging him uptown, where I know he'll love. Rowan pulls me to his side, his hand clutching my waist. "For your protection."

Sure it is. I roll my eyes. "There are a million people walking around, no one is going to get mugged."

Rowan scoffs. "Please, I do have access to the news. There are also a million crimes committed here, so let's not pretend we're in Mayberry where Opie is just riding his bike around town."

"Don't worry, Rowan, I'll protect you."

He laughs once. "Yeah, but who will protect me against you? You're the most likely suspect if I go missing."

"This is true, but . . . I like my odds."

I pull him along, up 5th Ave until we reach Central Park. It's everything I love about this city. A quiet oasis in the city that never sleeps. My smile grows as I allow the peace to settle over me.

"See over there?" I point toward the west where there are a bunch of buildings.

"Sure."

"Do not ruin this for me," I warn. "I lived in the cream-colored building in between the glass and the dark brown. My parents had a three bedroom on the top floor. I can remember waking up and seeing the park every morning."

"So, the view you have now?"

I give him a dirty look. "This view is nothing like what we have at home."

"It's grass."

"It's not just grass!" I say in horror. "It's a huge park. It has trails and ponds and horses pulling carriages. There are people everywhere who are just taking a break from their busy lives, reading, or having a picnic."

Rowan crosses his arms over his chest. "Okay, it's a big park, and I guess we don't have a whole sub-city that is nothing but a park, so I'll give you that. However, we have trails, you took one to get to my house. We have ponds and we have creeks if you want to take it a step farther. Horses? Well, we know we have those and contrary to whatever garbage you think, some people in Sugarloaf can read and eat."

He is not going to sway me on this, damn him.

"It's not the same and you know it."

Of course, just then a car horn blares, one that the guy is just laying on nonstop.

"You're right. Not the same at all."

I'm not even sure how to top this. I thought this country boy would appreciate that we have some of that here too.

Seems I was wrong.

"Okay, food. That's what we need." I change tactics. Guys love to eat, and Rowan needs to experience the cuisine here. It's different and amazing. No matter what, there is nothing like the options we have here.

"We ate at the party."

"Did we?" I throw back. While there was finger food, it was nothing, and I can always go for a pretzel and hot dog.

"All right, wow me with your food."

I smile, taking his hand in mine and tugging him toward the street vendor. It's just now six at night and I feel like this is the best time for some food from a truck. "You have to have a dirty water dog."

"A what?"

"A hot dog from the cart."

I stand in front of the guy with a thick New York accent. "Whadya want?"

227

"Two hot dogs. One with ketchup and sauerkraut and the other with . . ."

Rowan looks at me, shakes his head like he's shivering, and then turns to the vendor. "One with mustard."

"Eww," I say immediately.

"Oh, and ketchup and sauerkraut is a better option?"

I shrug. "It's better than mustard."

He hands us the hot dogs and Rowan offers to pay, and this broke girl isn't going to complain. Then we walk over to the bench in the park. "Okay, take a bite."

"It's a hot dog that was in a cart."

"Soaking in the water all day, getting all the flavor."

His brows lift and then he sighs. "Okay then."

He takes a bite and I sit here, anxious to hear. Although, I don't know why I'm anxious since I'm sure he'll find something wrong with it. "Not bad," Rowan says.

"See! The city has hot dogs on every corner. You can literally never be hungry here."

Rowan laughs and shifts his weight into me. "Eat your gross hot dog so we can go to the next sight you have planned."

I ignore the jab and eat in pure happiness. After we're done, Rowan and I take the subway, which is its own experience.

Where I am completely comfortable, he looks like he's ready to bolt. It's kind of funny.

"You can breathe," I say softly, facing him as we're kind of wedged together right by the door. My hand rests on his chest to balance myself.

On a normal day, this wouldn't be an issue, but I'm still in these freaking heels. I'm totally getting sandals as soon as we stop. There's sure to be someone selling them on the street where we're going next.

"I'm not sure that's a good idea."

I laugh quietly. "You look like a tourist."

"Because I am one."

His eyes find mine and he stares at me, something is different, softer almost. Neither of us smile or speak, it's as though we're saying so much when we say nothing. There is a connection between us, one that I can't understand, but I feel it now.

The train stops and I look up to see it's our stop. "This is us," I say, hating to break the moment.

He nods and places his hand on my back, leading me out. We get up to the street and I inhale, forcing myself to return to the light and fun banter we had. I don't want to think about whatever that was in the subway.

"Okay, I need shoes and we're going to do one of the most iconic things that we can here."

He looks over at the Empire State building. "We're going up top?"

"The observation deck is a must. No matter what."

"I'm trusting the master."

"That's a first," I say as we walk over to where there's a vendor.

"You can get shoes on the street?" Rowan asks in disbelief.

"You can get anything here." I wink and then grab a pair of the slip-on sneakers for twelve bucks.

I hook my heels in my fingers and we walk over to the ticket booth where I'm able to get admission because the New York Gods are looking out for me.

"Did you do all this stuff as a kid?" Rowan asks as we wait in the ridiculous line to get through security.

"I did. My dad worked in the Financial District, but he would always come meet his girlies for lunch once a week. I used to love coming to the Fashion District and shopping."

He purses his lips. "You? Shopping?"

"I know, you would've thought it was my sister, but no, she hated shopping. She wanted to meet Daddy by his work. She loved the stock exchange where I wanted to have armfuls of bags and walk like a fashionista."

It's funny how different we became after we lost our parents. Aurora was so much like Dad. She loved the hustle and bustle of the market and she wanted to study business like him. My goals were to

229

be my mother. She had it made. Married a man she loved who happened to be rich and got to spend all her time with Aurora and me. It was all I wanted—to be a mom.

Now I'm constantly worried about business and I have no real plans to ever get married and have kids. I really wouldn't want that burden now, since I'll be homeless if I don't get the contract.

But I don't want to think about that part now.

"And you're wearing street shoes now, look at how you've turned out."

I laugh. "I think I'm okay. I'm staying in some swanky hotel in the penthouse."

"That's true."

We move through the security line and into the museum area. It's so funny how all these years have passed and it's exactly as I remembered. The photos of the building being built and all the history right here.

Rowan takes my hand, lacing our fingers together as we walk, almost like it's the most natural thing in the world.

A part of me wants to pull away because I can't have feelings for him. He's Rowan Whitlock. He's off limits because of my sister and because he literally is my competition. Talk about sleeping with the enemy.

But the other part, the one that longs to have someone in my corner grips tighter. My heart sometimes isn't in my command, like right now. I've had the most fun I think I've had in years. Walking around, laughing, talking, and smiling with him. The only times I ever feel at peace are when I'm with him, and isn't that the worst thing ever?

We take the elevator up to the first deck and step out. It's got amazing views of the city and we're at that part where it's dark, but not pitch black. The sky still has hints of lighter blues.

"Let's go up top before the sun sets," I say, bringing him back to the elevator to take us up to the top deck.

We get outside, to where so many iconic movie scenes have happened, and we walk around.

I find an open spot at the railing, looking through the fence at the world below. The car lights are like tiny specks, reminding me of that Lite Bright I had as a kid where you stuck the colored pegs in and the light behind it made a beautiful picture.

The wind whips my hair around my face, and I shiver a little from the cold. There's warmth at my back and Rowan's arms cage me in.

"This is something else, Charlotte," Rowan says softly against my ear.

"It is. I love the history here."

His cheek is against mine, staring out at the horizon. "What about the future?"

I turn my head a little. "What future?"

"Yours. What would you have your future look like? If you could write it."

You.

That thought rockets through me, terrifying me because it can never be him. I close my eyes, fighting back the tears that threaten to come at the unfairness of my reality.

Somehow I keep my voice even as I speak. "I'll have a bigger farm than now, thanks to my new contract. Since you'll probably go under, I figure that will be where I expand first."

His deep laugh vibrates through me. "Sure, we'll go with that. What else? What about a family?"

"Maybe someday."

"Don't you want your daughter to stand here one day, looking out at the same skyline as you are, and remember how her mother talked about its beauty?"

Those words break me. I turn so we're just a breath apart. Rowan's blue eyes so close I can see the hints of green that play at the center. "I've learned to give up the dreams that I'll never have."

"Why the hell won't you meet a guy who will give you that?"

"Because everyone that I love leaves. My parents, my grandparents, my sister, everyone. It's not their fault, I get that, well, other than Aurora. Neither my parents or grandparents chose to leave me willingly, but look at my life. I'm alone. I have meaningless relationships so that I won't get attached. I've only really dated one guy who chose to walk away. I'm not sure a man or a family is in the cards."

Other than you. Other than the fact that there is a part of me that opened up to you, against me wanting to. Against my damn permission you seeped into my heart. Damn you.

Still Rowan doesn't move, he's so close. I want him to kiss me so damn much it's a physical ache in my chest.

He closes his eyes, exhaling slowly, and then presses his forehead to mine.

This moment, it's one of those that a girl dreams of. Being on top of the Empire State building with a guy who is unbelievably sexy and happens to be a dream in bed, and it's just utterly romantic.

"Rowan . . ."

I'm not sure what I want to say, but he shakes his head ever so slightly.

"I want you more than I've ever wanted anything, Charlotte, but I will never be the guy you want."

But he's wrong because he is the guy I want and I can have him again, can't I?

"I think you're wrong. I do want you. We can have just this one night. One more time where we can pretend all the reasons it's a bad idea don't exist."

He exhales deeply. "God, I wish we could, but if I have you one more time, I won't ever want to stop. I have to go cold turkey because if we do it tonight, I'll be tempted to do it tomorrow, no matter what promises we make each other. Every night I'll find a way to you because, I could fall for you if I let myself."

"Cold turkey, huh?" I try to make a joke, gripping his suit jacket in my hands, holding on because I know I have to let go.

I've already fallen for him.

"It's the only way."

I lift my head, staring into his eyes. "We'll always have the cabin."

His hands move to my face, gently cupping my cheeks. "We'll always have this night in New York too."

By some miracle I hold back my tears, hating that he's right and I'm the one who said how we needed to stop. "We should go."

"We should."

However, we stand here, holding on to one another for a minute, maybe a hundred because time ceases for me.

Then, much too soon, Rowan steps back, his hands fall away, and the loneliness I hadn't felt in weeks returns like an ice-cold breeze that I'll never warm from again.

twenty-four

ROWAN

Pulling away from her feels wrong, but I know that whatever bullshit she says, she wants a life I will never give her.

She wants kids and a family.

I want no damn part of that. Not after all the shit I've seen with my mom. I know better. I've seen the scars, bruises, and heartache that comes with thinking we deserve things like a happily ever after.

Life isn't a fairy tale. It's ugly, raw, and disappointing.

Charlotte's eyes fill with tears and it fucking kills me because I know what I'm saying is hurting her. She turns, straightens her back, and then forces a smile. "Let's head back to the hotel. I'm exhausted and we have an early morning tomorrow."

If only we could stay up here forever, but that's ridiculous because we don't even like each other.

Although, if I'm actually honest with myself, that's completely untrue.

I like her much more than I thought was ever possible. I like everything about her, even when she's pushing my buttons, maybe even more so then.

"Yeah, both of us have our meetings and then we drive back," I say, as though she doesn't already know that.

Don't I look like a dumbass.

"Why don't we take a cab back?" Charlotte suggests.

"Sure, that's great."

We head down, back to the ground where the world feels different. Up there, it was . . . I don't know, like I could fool myself easier.

Charlotte hails a cab and we climb in. This is all going to end tomorrow, and apparently, I'm a fucking idiot unable to stop myself from making bad choices, so I pull her to me, my arm around her, forcing her head to rest on my chest.

Neither of us feels the need to say a word, and it's probably for the best. We both know what the right thing is, so why bother saying something we'd regret or something neither of us wants to admit?

Against all odds, I have feelings for Charlotte Sullivan.

Ones I've never had before.

Ones I should be leaping out of the moving cab to avoid, but instead, I'm holding her because I fucking need to.

I never thought I'd be happy for traffic and yet here I am. The longer this lasts, the longer I get to keep her, even though she's not mine to have.

"Rowan?"

"Hmm?"

"If we weren't Charlotte and Rowan, if you hadn't been with my sister and we weren't fighting for the same contract, would this end differently? Would we be going back to that big penthouse as . . . more?"

I wish it was that simple.

I lean my head against hers, breathing her in, hating the truth because her sister and the contract aren't what's stopping us from being together. My past and the way I watched my family break apart is. "I'd walk away from the contract tomorrow if that was the only thing in our way. If I wasn't a man who didn't want a family or a marriage or anything even close to it, that's what would make it different."

"Not even for the right girl?"

236

"Are you that girl, Charlotte? Do you think you're able to change how I feel about love and family?" She stiffens, and I hate myself for the way that sounds. "If there was anyone that could do it, it would be you."

The cab stops in front of our hotel. Immediately the door opens, the valet being far too good at his job. He helps Charlotte out while I pay the cabbie, the question and comments still lingering between us. When we get up to our room, the mood feels somber.

As she starts to walk toward the bedroom, I grab her wrist.

Her big green eyes stare up at me. "I'm not that girl."

The way she says it tells me that not only does she not believe that but also that she's saying it to protect herself.

"It's probably better we realize this now, before things get out of control."

"You mean before I fall in love with you and you break my heart?" she asks.

I don't say anything because I'm not really sure what to say.

She exhales deeply, forces a smile, and pulls her wrist from my grip. "Don't worry about that, Rowan. I'm not halfway in love with you. I'm not even a little bit in love with you. I'm well aware of what we were and that it has run its course. The only thing I love is my farm, and it's what I protect, my heart is not in jeopardy of being tangled up with you." Charlotte lifts up on her toes and kisses my cheek. "Good night. Thank you for letting me fall in love with my city all over again. It means a lot to me."

It meant everything to me. Every moment we spent together made my resolve crack deeper, and I need to fill the gaps before I take her to my bed and fill something else.

This woman should not be my undoing, but God help me, she's breaking down my armor. So, it's time to put it back up and get away from her.

I step forward, cupping her cheeks, and I feel her body tense as I bring my lips close to her, but instead of kissing her, I rest them on her forehead, closing my eyes, and I inhale and catch the floral scent of her shampoo. "Thank you for showing me around. I had a great time. Good night, Charlotte."

And then I walk away, go to my separate room in this big ass suite, and stare at the ceiling for hours.

⚷

"I appreciate you staying in the city so we could meet today. Yesterday there was a minor issue that I needed to take care of," Carson explains.

"Not a problem."

Although it was the worst goddamn night of my life. I couldn't sleep, and I was stuck in that room because I knew that if I saw Charlotte again, there'd be no restraint.

The only thing that kept me put was that I knew her reasons for needing space.

She's about to lose everything she loves and cares for if she doesn't get this contract.

He nods once and then leans back in his leather chair. "Kimberly had a lot of good things to say about you and your farm. She feels very strongly that you're the right man for the job. I think she might be right."

"Might?"

Carson laughs and steeples his fingers. "I'm a very intuitive businessman. I usually know the answer immediately, this is the first time in a long time that I'm wavering a bit."

"You really can't go wrong. Charlotte Sullivan is running a great farm," I say and wonder if I'm possessed by an alien.

"I agree, but Kimberly seems to think you're running a better one."

I'm not sure what to say to that. The businessman in me wants to seal the deal. I should. I owe her nothing, but I can't do it. Yes, I would love this contract. It would push my business forward a lot faster, but it's not a make or break for me. It is for her.

For the giant pain in my ass who I can't get out of my damn head.

"There may be a small issue with the certification," I inform him. "I'm not sure when it'll go through, they have questions about a possible pesticide I treated our newest pasture with when I bought it."

"You think this will hold up the certification?" Carson asks.

No, I don't. We used it on the back part of the field that was roped off. It won't be an issue, but that reassurance doesn't come out of my mouth.

"I really don't know."

He nods slowly. "I see. If you were me, would you grant yourself the contract with that question still pending?"

Fuck.

"If I were you?"

Carson tilts his head, waiting for my answer.

"I don't know. You know your business much better than I do. I just wanted to be honest and allow you the opportunity to decide whatever you think is best."

After this, I'm calling a neurologist to ensure I don't have a tumor. If I don't, then clearly, I need an exorcist or a therapist or something to fix my life.

"I admire honesty. I like family businesses, like my own, and I like people who aren't afraid of a challenge." Carson stands, moving toward the window where he looks out at the city. "I need a stable farm to handle the organic line. We're going to be expanding it into schools, hospitals, and colleges. It'll be an entire line made of only organic foods. The restaurant industry already has this, but if I'm going to move forward, I need someone who can produce and also expand." He turns to me. "You understand what I'm saying."

That Charlotte's farm, while already certified, won't be able to keep up with the demand. That means she'll have to sell the farm, losing her family legacy.

"You're sure this is what you want to do?" I ask my sister who had just got done explaining her life plan to the three of us.

The last twenty-four hours have been interesting, to say the least. I drove home from New York, Charlotte chattering nonstop about her meeting with Carson and how she is sure she's going to get the contract.

I had to sit there, knowing that the conversation didn't go that way with me, and that whatever good feeling she has, she shouldn't. If I were a betting man, I'd be sure that in four days I'm going to get the call that the contract is mine, even without the certification.

But maybe I'm wrong. If her meeting went that well, he may have seen something or found out some information I don't have.

"I know that I want to do more than small-town legal stuff. I love the entertainment section and Jacob Arrowood got my foot in the door with Titan Publicity. Catherine runs an amazing company that has a need I can fill," Brynn explains.

"Are you moving to Los Angeles?"

"No, I'm going to stay here. For now, I'm just working on contracts and ensuring the clients have the best terms, but I'm hoping to move into being an agent or a publicist. I'm pretty open."

I really wish she'd told me this any other day than today. My head is clouded with the Charlotte thing and the farm. When I got home, Micah was at the house, waiting to let me know of two issues. One is we lost a calf. We're not sure how or why, but we did. The other is that the homogenizer is broken.

He tried his best to fix it, but he ended up needing to call someone to come out. Which will cost us, and if I have to replace it . . . I don't even want to think about the cost.

Asher releases a long sigh, breaking me from my thoughts. "If this is the direction you want to go, then we all support you."

"Speak for yourself, asshat," I say before turning to my sister. "I need to lay down some rules first."

Brynn crosses her arms over her chest. "I can't wait to hear this."

"First, you can't move away. We tried that shit with Grady and breaking up the band isn't an option."

Grady snorts. "I hope she kills you."

I ignore that. "Second, you can't date some asshole from Hollywood. We already have enough divas in this family, we don't need to add another."

"Who is the diva?" Asher asks.

"All the women in your life."

"Phoebe is not a diva and I sure as fuck don't think you mean Olivia." He gets defensive, and I pretend I didn't hear it. I love them both, but he's delusional if he thinks they're not divas. In the most loving way, of course.

"Moving on." I look at Brynn. "I just don't ever want to see you get hurt again."

She softens at that last bit and sits in the chair across from me. "You can't stop that."

"I can if you stay here. No one wants to piss off the Whitlock brothers."

Brynlee snorts. "Yeah, sure, that's it."

"I'm serious, Brynn, we . . . we need you here."

Brynn and I are the closest in age and I'd like to think in other ways. She's never been afraid to talk to me, probably because I seem like the asshole who is going to screw up first, which is accurate. My sister has been through hell and anyone she meets will have to get through me before they touch her.

I expect one of my brothers to say something against me, but instead, the other two nod in agreement.

"I like this plan," Grady says.

"Same. We keep you here, you do what you want, and no assholes come near you." Asher smiles. "Never thought I'd say this but, good idea, Rowan."

The one thing the three of us still haven't gotten through our heads is Brynlee really doesn't like it when we tell her what to do or even think we have a say in it.

My sister stands, crossing her arms over her chest. Great, now

I've gone and done it. Here comes hurricane Brynn. "You are all unbelievably stupid. I know I've said it before, but this time, it's a collective effort. I will go and do whatever the hell I want—without any of your input—thank you very much. No one is afraid of you idiots, contrary to what delusions you suffer from. If and when I want to date again, I will."

"Are you dating someone?" Grady—apparently, the stupid one in the group—asks.

"It's none of your business."

He at least is smart enough to keep his mouth shut.

Asher stands, coming to his full height, and Brynn looks incredibly small. "What we're trying and clearly failing to say is that we love you. We love having you around. You're the entire reason we all moved to Sugarloaf if you think about it."

Brynn cuts in. "Mom was."

"No, Brynlee, you are. When Mom moved here, we didn't come with her—you did. It wasn't until she died that I came here, and then Rowan. Grady is here for the free babysitting."

He scoffs. "Yeah, because Brynlee never watched Olivia."

My sister sighs heavily. "This is going to go off the rails real quick. I love you all too and I already said I wasn't going to California. You can all calm down, okay?"

Asher pulls her into his arms. "We're all happy for you."

Grady and I flank him, doing what we did to her as a kid and squeeze until she yells at us. Once we let her go, my brothers head to their women and I'm lounging on the couch as Brynn reads some boring document.

She finishes and looks up at me. "So I heard a rumor."

"That's nice."

"It's about you."

I look away from the TV and smirk. "Is it a good one?"

"Depends what you think is good."

"Out with it," I say, tiring of this game.

"I told everyone there was no way it's true, you hate Charlotte, even though you guys seem to be civil enough to ride into New York without anyone being tossed from a moving vehicle."

I laugh. "What makes you think she'd ever be able to toss me?"

"Because my money is on her. Anyway, the rumor is about you and Charlotte."

My stomach drops a little, but I keep my features schooled so as not to give anything away. Not that it's any of my sister's business anyway.

"This should be good," I say flippantly.

"The rumor is that someone saw you both coming out of the storage room at Peakness together—disheveled."

I absolutely can't let this spread. It needs to be put to rest right now. "Yeah, that's totally possible. In the middle of my birthday party where there were a hundred people, I snuck into a closet with . . . Charlotte."

"I know, I said that it's completely ridiculous. Charlotte would never do something as stupid as that," Brynn says and then grabs another stack of papers.

"Wait, what? You defended her?"

Betrayed by my own sister.

Brynn shrugs. "Of course I did. She'd never sleep with you, let alone do it in a closet in a bar on your birthday. Which reminds me, I have to get her a gift."

"For what?"

"Her birthday is tomorrow. I'll have to head to the outlets and see what I can find. That girl doesn't buy herself anything."

Shit. Tomorrow is the sixth. I didn't even think to ask what month her birthday was in. I'm a fucking idiot.

Brynlee watches me and sits there with a smile. "Well, well, maybe the rumors are true."

"Maybe you need to shut up."

"Oh, not a denial."

"Fine. I did not sleep with Charlotte in a closet at my birthday party." Technically, I'm not lying to my sister. I didn't sleep at all.

twenty-five
CHARLOTTE

"Happy birthday to me, Bessy." I pet my oldest and most favorite cow. She was the first calf I got to help be born. My grandfather warned me not to get attached, that they don't live long and we often move them off the farm after their production is done.

But Bessy, she stays.

She's mine and I love her.

Of course the cow doesn't respond because . . . she's a cow.

"I'm another year older, another year alone, and this might be the last one on this farm."

Just saying the words aloud makes me want to sob.

In the next three days we find out.

Carson informed us a decision will be made by the end of the week, so there's that.

My phone rings, and it's a video call from Aurora.

Might as well get this over with.

"Hey," I say, answering.

"Happy birthday, little sister!"

"Thank you."

"Are you doing anything fun?"

CORINNE MICHAELS

I shake my head. "No, Faye is away with her parents and I have a lot of work to do on the farm."

She scoffs. "You're young and single, go do something fun."

So easy for someone without the responsibilities I have, but sure. "Who knows, maybe I will."

"I wish I could be there."

Is it wrong I don't have the same sentiment? Probably, but it is what it is. "You're busy in New York."

Aurora sighs dramatically. "I have a dinner meeting and then I have a date with a new guy."

"What happened to Ryan?"

"He's still around."

I stare at her, my eyes narrowing. "I'm confused."

"Well, I'm just not willing to get my heart trampled on again. I'm being careful and keeping my options open. It works for *others*. So, I figure I might as well try it. Unlike when Rowan did it to me, I'm honest about it."

I can't today. "Can we have one conversation where you don't talk about Rowan? Just one. Today?"

Aurora huffs out her response. "Fine."

I don't want to think about Rowan. I don't want to remember how we stood together on top of the world and I still couldn't have what I wanted. I refuse to dream one more damn night about the way he kisses or smells or makes me feel like I'm beautiful and special. All of that I'm avoiding today, because I don't want to feel that damn ache that won't go away.

We made a choice to stop being stupid.

I'm doing just that.

"Thank you."

"Right." Aurora is clearly pissed. "I have to get going. I just wanted to wish you a happy birthday and tell you I love you."

There is only one person in the world who can piss me off this much and then make me feel like shit about being pissed, and that's my sister. Immediately, I hate that I hurt her and snapped.

"I'm sorry, Aurora," I say, needing to smooth things over

246

because, if I lose the farm, I'm going to need her help. And then I blurt out what I've been holding in for so long. "I'm under a lot of stress. The farm is in trouble."

"What do you mean?"

I tell her everything. How the investment to go fully organic was great, but then we've had a series of issues. Bills that have just been piling up and the truck needing to be fixed, all of it.

I wait for an offer of help. For some elder sister's advice because, surely, she knows a way out of this that maybe I just haven't seen.

"So, you're going to lose our family farm?" Aurora asks with disappointment.

"I'm trying not to."

She tucks her hair behind her ears. "Yes, but you might?"

"Yes, Aurora, I might. I'm doing everything I possibly can to avoid that. If I get this contract, all of this will be fine."

"How did you get this far in debt? How did you not see that you were drowning? This was Mom's farm, Charlotte. It's where she grew up, Granny and Pop always wanted it to stay in the family. You were the one who convinced me to sell my half."

My eyes widen at that one. "Are you kidding? Like, are you kidding me with this?"

"No!"

"Well you should be, Aurora! You ran from this farm. You left to go back to the damn city, and I stayed here! I've been killing myself for the last year to get out of this godforsaken hole I'm in. I've worked nonstop, gone without any luxury or fun, which you continually tell me to do!"

Aurora jumps in. "I didn't know we were about to lose the only thing we have left of Mom!"

Tears that I have withheld fill my vision, making her blurry. "You think this is what I want? That this is at all part of my plan?"

"Well, it's the reality we're facing."

Those hovering tears start to fall. I'm so angry, so hurt, so many emotions that I don't even want to name. I wipe them away and let it go because I am too emotional right now to keep it in anymore. "Oh, now it's we? Where has the 'we' been for the last two years? You're so worried about losing the farm that you haven't come home a single time because of a guy who didn't even like you! Tell me, Aurora, did you even catch him cheating? Because I don't think you did. I think Rowan told you that he didn't want to date you because he didn't want to date *anyone*, and you lost your shit because for the first time the pretty princess didn't get what she wanted. So, you packed your shit and ran."

Aurora gasps. "Wow, that's what you think of me?"

I'm not answering that.

"Tell me the truth. Did Rowan do what you claimed?"

I think we both know the truth. This whole time, for all these years, me and everyone else who believed her have treated him like a piece of shit, and it wasn't true.

"I know what Rowan did," Aurora says, and I want to reach through the phone and slap her.

"He did nothing. You've villainized him, all because he didn't want what *you* did. It's always this way with you. You get what you want or everyone suffers."

Since our parents died, she's done this. She played games to make herself come out as the victim, and I always took her side. I'm done now.

"You are so obsessed with Rowan now. Why? Because he was nice to you? That's what he does. He worms his way into your heart and then breaks it."

I roll my eyes. "I can't do this. I have actual problems to focus on. I hoped that telling you would maybe lead to a civil conversation. One where you'd . . . I don't know . . . help. Instead, you've managed to make me feel worse than I already did. Go have fun on your dinner and date. I'm going to do what I can not to further disappoint you."

I sink down in the stall, my back against the wood wall, and let the tears fall. All of it is too much to hold in anymore. I'm so tired of the weight on my shoulders and carrying it alone. I thought, God, I hoped, my sister would understand and maybe support me like I did her when she left.

Now I just feel worse.

I knew all the reasons I needed to save the farm. It is the last piece of my mom we have left. More than that, it's where I grew up. It's my home and I love this place.

I sniff and more tears fall, then I hear footsteps.

"Charlotte?"

Oh, God. I can't handle Rowan today. I . . . can't.

My breath hitches as I wipe at my tears, knowing that it's going to be no use. My eyes are surely puffy, and I won't be able to hide the fact I was crying like a freaking baby for the last twenty minutes.

"Charlotte?" he calls again.

Bessy, the traitorous cow, walks to the stall, poking her head out.

"Hi, girl, where is your overlord?" Rowan asks, petting her neck. Bessy shifts, forcing me to go to the right to avoid being trampled. "No idea, huh? I figured you'd protect her."

I roll my eyes. Yes, the non-speaking animal isn't telling him. Idiot.

Not that I wasn't just talking to the cow myself, but that's neither here nor there.

Rowan sighs. "I'll go look in the pasture."

Just then, Bessy lifts her tail and I know what's about to come. Oh, hell no. I will take a lot, but having a cow shit on me on my birthday is not on that list. "Bessy!" I yell as I pop up to my feet.

Thwarted by my own cow.

"What the hell are you doing? Hiding from me?" Rowan asks as he sees me appear from the side.

I shake my head. "No, I . . . lost an earring."

Seriously I'm an idiot.

His eyes meet mine, and the teasing look that was there a moment ago disappears. Concern replaces it. In a flash, he opens the stall door and enters, coming right to me. "Are you crying?"

I could lie. I should lie, but instead, I launch myself into his arms. Rowan catches me, holding me to his chest and rubbing my back. The tears I thought were done return with a vengeance.

He's here . . . on my birthday. He's the only one who has ever come.

Rowan holds me tighter. "Hey, don't cry. Don't you know that guys are literally the worst with tears? Especially me."

I snort a laugh—unattractively, I might add. "I just had a fight with my sister. On m-m-my birthday. I'm s-so tired. I'm so tired, Rowan. I can't do this anymore. I'm not enough for anyone! W-why? Why doesn't anyone love me?"

Not that I need to give him more of a reason to hate her, but I need a friend. I need one more than anything today.

"She fought with you today?"

I nod against his chest, still not allowing him to release me. "She s-said I'm going to l-lose my mother's farm. I can't do it. Please, just hold me because I can't lose it-t."

"You're not going to," he assures me. "No matter what."

I jerk back and my puffy eyes widen. "You don't know that."

"I do. I know it because you're the single most stubborn woman I've ever met. There's nothing that will keep you from saving this place. Nothing, Charlotte. You are resilient and smart. You'll do it just to spite me because you know I want your land."

I shake my head and slap his arm. "Ass."

He smirks. "I got you to laugh."

"You did," I say, hating that I needed him to.

"Happy birthday, Charlotte."

"How did you know? Other than me blurting it out before."

"I have my ways." He reaches his hand out to me. "Come with me."

I shouldn't, but my emotions are raw and I've missed him. I place my hand in his and let him lead me out of the barn.

On my back patio sits two chairs and a round table with a box covering what's on it.

"Rowan?"

"Go sit down."

I smile, feeling a little confused, but also excited. It's been so long since I've done anything or been with anyone for my birthday.

He takes the seat opposite of me, leans over, and lifts the box that was hiding the food.

I gasp, my heart pounding so hard against my chest. "You . . . you remembered?"

On the plate is a waffle with ice cream sitting on top.

"You miss your parents, and I know what that feels like. While my mother had shitty taste in men, she was always good to us. Losing her was hard, but I was an adult, you were so young. So, for the rest of today, I will only say yes. If you want something, it's yours. Just for today," he reiterates.

Every dam I had constructed breaks, the flood of emotions rushing forward. Without a word, I rise, knowing there's only one thing I want right now and it's not the waffle.

He looks up at me, my hand brushes the short beard on his perfect face. "Anything?"

"Anything."

"I want my hat back."

He grins, reaches behind his back, and then puts the hat on. "It's mine."

I move closer and straddle him. "Today, you're mine, which means the hat is too."

"God, I love your birthday."

"I think it'll quickly be my favorite too. Take me upstairs and wear the hat."

"Yes, ma'am."

twenty-six
ROWAN

While I didn't plan this, I'd be lying if I said I didn't hope for it.

For a week, I've gone without her, and I'm fucking starved.

I carry her up to her room, her arms looped around my neck. Something feels different this time as I take her to bed. It's not rushed or frantic, it's . . . deeper.

It means something.

When I get into her room, I kick the door closed behind me and place her down slowly. Charlotte looks like a goddess, one I'm not worthy to be in the same room as. Her big green eyes gaze up at me, vulnerability staring at me.

I breathe, trying to get a grip on what I'm feeling, but the only word that keeps reverberating through me is . . . mine.

She's mine.

I fucking want her more than I care about all the reasons we shouldn't. I need her more than I need this damn contract or anything else. She is what matters.

"I've never felt this way, Charlotte," I confess, moving toward her. "I've never wanted anyone the way I want you."

"You want me?"

"Every second of every day."

Her lip trembles and I run my thumb across it. Her eyes close, and she wraps her fingers around my wrist. "I don't hate you, Rowan. I don't hate you at all."

I smile at that. "They say there's a thin line between love and hate, what do you say we figure out what side we're on?"

I already know.

There's no reason in the world I should love this woman. She's frustrating, tempting, exasperating, beautiful, never wrong because she's incapable of believing it's even possible, and yet, I'm falling in love with her.

Fuck.

She lifts her other hand, fisting my shirt and pulling me to her. "That line is blurred. I need you to help me see it better."

"How, sweetheart?"

"Kiss me."

I cup her cheeks, bringing my lips to hers. The moment they touch, I feel like the entire world just aligned again. The last week, it's been tilted, nothing has felt right or fit right, and now, this fucking woman just adjusted it back to what it should've been.

I lift the back of her thigh, pulling her to the middle of the bed, and I cage her in, kissing her with every emotion that's swirling inside me.

"There's no going back, Charlotte. After this, I can't just pretend anymore."

"Neither can I." I kiss her neck, down her shoulder and she sighs.

She leans up, and I pull her shirt up over her head, her lacy bra more alluring than anything I've seen before. With it still on, I lower my head, licking and sucking her nipple through the fabric, feeling it harden beneath my tongue.

"Rowan," Charlotte moans my name.

"Yes, baby. Do you want more?"

"Please."

"I like when you're polite." I slide her bra strap down, running my tongue along the shell of the cup. "I like it when you're rude too."

Charlotte giggles and that sound goes straight to my cock. "I have no problem being rude to you."

"Should we be nice or rude tonight? You are the birthday girl, after all."

She lolls her head to the side and brushes her fingertips down my face. "This time is different for me, is it for you?"

I bring my lips to hers, kissing her softly. "It feels different."

The way her fingers softly thread in my hair makes me want to worship her. It's such a stupid, simple touch, and yet it feels like so much more.

Jesus, I'm turning into a freaking idiot.

"Then I want this time to be different, even if we don't know what it all means."

I sit her up and slowly unhook her bra, tossing it to the ground. "I want you naked, Charlotte. I want to see every perfect inch of you."

"I'm not perfect."

"When I look at you, that's what I see."

Her breath hitches. "Do you mean that?"

I want to kill whoever put these doubts in her mind, and if I was the one who did it, I'll beat my own ass. "Of course I do. You're gorgeous, so goddamn beautiful that it's impossible to look away. I ache for you, sweetheart."

As though neither of us can resist, we both move at the same time, our lips coming together in absolute passion.

I don't need to reassure her with words, I do it with touch. My hand glides down her body, running along her soft skin and loving how she shivers under my touch.

I move my mouth from hers, kissing down the center of her chest, stopping at her breasts to lick and suck her nipples because they're fucking perfect tits.

She bucks her hips and I slide her leggings off. "No underwear?" I ask.

"I had a birthday wish that underwear would've gotten in the way of."

"Was I what you wanted to blow instead of the candles?"

"You totally got me," Charlotte says, her smile growing as I move down, kissing her belly.

"I'm happy to make that wish come true after I make you scream my name while I feast on you." She lies before me naked, and I wish I was a painter so I could have an image of this forever. "Open your legs for me, baby."

She does and I kiss all the way down until I'm at the heart of her. I run my tongue slowly from her opening up to her clit, eliciting a moan from her lips. I continue to draw pleasure from her, circling around the nub, flicking it, and changing the rhythm. Charlotte shifts her hips, her hands threading through my hair, holding me as her orgasm nears.

I don't stop. I keep my pace, wanting her to come, needing to be the one that makes her lose control the way she does to me.

"I can't . . . I need . . ." She pants, her legs tighten around my head as I lick faster and start to finger her. Her pussy milks my finger, the muscles contracting as I keep my pace. "Rowan!" She screams my name and her body locks as her orgasm tears through her.

I don't let up, not until I feel her fully relax, and then I kiss my way back up her body before removing the rest of my clothes and adjusting her until I'm nestled between her legs.

"Charlotte," I say as she fights for breath. Her beautiful eyes find mine, and she smiles. "I'm going to make love to you now."

I've never said those words. Not once have I ever thought of this as more than a fuck. Not this time. Not with her. I have no idea what the hell we're doing. How we're supposed to get through all the obstacles in front of us, but I'll fight until I have nothing left.

Her hand moves to my face, her finger brushing across my lips, then my cheek, then down my nose. "I will never recover from this, will I?"

"I sure as hell hope not because I know I won't."

"I want you inside me. I want you. Just you."

I move a little, pushing inside her, and inch by inch she surrounds me. The two of us never break our connection as I take my time, savoring her heat, wetness, and the way every time I push deeper, I feel something else inside my heart shift.

Charlotte Sullivan, the girl I've spent years despising, wanting to destroy, wishing would disappear from my life because she drove me crazy, is now everything to me.

A tear trickles down her cheek when I'm fully seated. Before I can ask if I hurt her or what's wrong, she speaks. "I've never felt this. I've never been so . . . God, it feels so good, but it's more. I . . . I . . . fuck, I don't hate you."

I close my eyes at the words I've been terrified of my entire life. If a woman ever came close to saying it, I'd already be getting dressed, but not this time. I don't want to run. I don't want to leave. I want to hear them over and over. "Say it again."

"I like you."

"Again," I demand as I pull back and rock forward.

"I like you, damn you."

My hips continue to move, watching as tears move down her cheeks as she says it over and over.

The speed we set with her words drives the two of us forward again. I hold back even though my orgasm is approaching quickly.

"I'm close," I warn.

"Me too."

I reach between us, my thumb pressing against her clit. "Charlotte, look at me." When her eyelids lift, I move a little faster. I want to say words I've never said before, but I can't. Not yet. Not until we figure out what all of this means. "I don't hate you at all. I dream about your smile, your smart mouth, the way you love that horrible city. I fucking live for how you make me crazy. I crave those little noises you make when you sleep." Her muscles contract around me, and I rub harder. "I hate how you make me want to want things that I've never thought about before. Fuck, Charlotte, I don't hate you. I don't hate you at all. Come with me, baby. Come with me."

Her back arches and I feel her orgasm take hold. There's not a chance in hell I can hold back, the two of us find the pinnacle together. Charlotte has just ruined me and saved me at the same time.

We clean up, and I toss on my shorts, head downstairs for the most-definitely melted waffles and ice cream, and bring the soupy mess up to bed. I'm not really sure what the fuck happens now. I've never really dated a woman, let alone loved her.

Hell, I wasn't even sure I could love someone romantically. Love to me always felt like some line of bullshit that people said to explain codependency. My mother loved everyone. She loved and loved to the point that it almost killed her.

It seemed to weaken everyone, make them do dumb shit in the name of love.

Yet, I couldn't stop myself from falling for her. Maybe I am weak. Maybe I'm a complete and total jackass, but I know that I love this maddening woman, even if I'm not ready to say it yet.

I get back upstairs, and Charlotte is in the bed and hopefully still naked under the sheets.

"You know that's completely melted now," she says when she sees my hands full with the plates.

"It is, but you and I are going to have at least some. I didn't make you a cake, so this is the closest you're getting."

She shifts so she's up against the headboard and then takes the plate from me.

"Did you make the waffle?" she asks.

"Do I look like I know how to make waffles?"

Charlotte laughs. "No."

"They're from a box. Now eat because you're going to need sustenance to keep up. I'm going to be very greedy."

"I thought this was my day of yes."

I smirk. "You're going to say yes, and oh God, and Rowan, you're so fucking big, and I've never had anyone make me come so much."

"I'm going to be very chatty."

"If I'm really inventive, I'm sure I can find a way to keep you quiet."

She laughs. "I'm sure you can, but remember, this is my day and you said I can have whatever I want."

I wiggle my brows. "Which is why I'm here. You're welcome."

She leans over and kisses my cheek. "Thank you."

I roll up the waffle and dip it into the melted ice cream. Charlotte does the same and then takes the piece out of my hand and eats that.

"What the hell, you little food thief?" I protest.

"I'm hungry."

"You have a very bad habit of taking food out of my hand and eating it, which you said you wouldn't do."

She grins and leans over to me. "Yet, you still find me irresistible. Anyway, it's my birthday, which overrides any previous agreements."

I laugh and put my plate down, then pull her against my chest. We lie here, her hand resting over my heart.

Charlotte looks up at me. "I wanted this so much. It's been so hard to keep away from you, especially in New York. All I wanted was for you to come to my room and tell me you needed me."

"I needed you, but I didn't want to hurt you. You said you needed us to stop."

"Because I was falling for you."

I nod. "I know."

"So, now what?"

"How the hell would I know?" I ask with a smirk. "I've never done a relationship. Ever."

Charlotte rolls her eyes. "This'll be super fun."

"I'm the gift that keeps on giving."

"Is there a return policy?"

I kiss the top of her head. "Nope."

"A warranty?"

"It's expired, but I'm happy to call you every day to see if you're interested in extending it."

She slaps my chest. "Ass."

I pull her tighter, loving how she fits perfectly. "Only for you, baby."

"Lucky me."

"I think so."

Charlotte sighs, wrapping her arm around my chest. "We're going to have to tell my sister."

That will go over real well. "If you want to be more than some relationship in the dark, then yes."

She doesn't look at me, but I can feel the change in her. I don't know what I'd do if it were my siblings. We're incredibly close, and I would do anything for them. It's part of why I fought against it being more than just sex. Not just because I really never wanted to love another person and lose that control, but also because I didn't want to come between her and Aurora—regardless of my feelings about her.

"I'm going to lose her," she says, her voice cracking. "She'll never forgive me for this."

I shift, forcing her to move so I can look in her eyes. "They always say that love is kind and it's not selfish, but knowing you could lose your sister feels selfish to me."

Charlotte shakes her head. "No. It's not. What's selfish is that she left two years ago and never came back. She didn't come here today, bringing waffles and ice cream. She didn't show up last year because she knew I was alone and needed a hug. She called me today and went off about . . ."

"About?" I prompt.

"It started as you but shifted into how I might lose the house."

That's not going to happen. I don't know what I can do to ensure it doesn't, but she's not going anywhere.

"What did she say?" I ask.

Charlotte sits up, her long brown hair falling to one shoulder. "She started yelling that I let this happen. That this is where our mother was raised and it's all we have left of her. I'm basically an asshole for letting this happen."

That fucking bitch. "Doesn't she realize that you're trying to avoid letting that happen?"

"She didn't really ask."

"Your sister . . ." I hold back because I really can't say what I think of Aurora. "I wish she could see the work you've done."

She moves to me, giving me a sweet kiss. "Today isn't about anyone else, but me, and since it's my day, I don't want to know or talk about *anything* that'll make me sad."

I smile and kiss her again. "Got it."

"Good. I'm going to get dressed and we can saddle the horses, take a ride, and remember how freeing it is."

"Sounds like a plan."

She gets up, and I watch her naked ass move to the bathroom. Then she looks over her shoulder and winks.

My phone pings, and I swipe open the notification, my stomach dropping.

Rowan,

Knight Food Distribution is pleased to offer the contract to Whitlock Farms. Please contact the office tomorrow, and we'll send over the paperwork.

Best,

Carson Knight

twenty-seven

CHARLOTTE

I'm in love.

I'm in love with Rowan Whitlock.

I smile at myself in the mirror, wondering if someone else's face is going to be there because, surely, I'm dreaming. My lips are swollen from his kiss, skin glowing, and if this is a dream, I never want to wake up.

My mind recalls the way I felt when I saw that waffle and ice cream. How thoughtful he was to bring that, and my hat. That damn hat.

Once I'm dressed, I head out, and he's on the bed, head in his hands. "Hey," I say, concerned.

"Hey!" Rowan says quickly with a smile.

"Everything okay?"

He stands, kisses my forehead, and smiles. "Everything is fine."

I'm not sure I believe him, but I don't want to argue on our first day of being officially together. At least, I think we are.

"Rowan?"

"Hmm?"

"Are we together now? Like, dating or a couple?"

One side of his mouth quirks up. "I'd say so. I've never told a woman I don't hate her the way I don't hate you, so, yeah, we're together, Charlotte. You're mine."

That shouldn't make me gooey inside. I've never been turned on by the whole claiming thing, but coming from his deep, throaty voice? I'm totally digging it. I'm pretty sure our not hating each other means we both feel the same way, but . . . it's too soon.

He's never been in a relationship before, it's been years for me, and I have no idea what my future looks like.

"And what about you? Are you mine?" I ask, pressing my body against his.

If I do lose the farm, I don't want to make this any harder than it'll already be. Not that I think us not saying I love you is going to make it any easier, it's just words spoken aloud that we believe are truth.

I need to hide in the dark about this just until I know I got the contract.

"I've never been anyone else's." He kisses my nose.

And now I really am goo. Complete goo. "Who knew you were so romantic?"

"Sure as fuck not me."

We both laugh. "Enough of that, let's go for a ride."

My ranch-helper, as I call him since a ranch hand would be paid, is out in the back pasture, trying to fix the fence with duct tape and glue, because that's all I can afford, so we're able to get the horses without anyone seeing us.

Rowan and I head out, riding the trail between the trees where the creek runs through most of the town. When we get across there, it's just open land. My favorite place to let the horse have his head. Monty was built for speed. I used to love coming out here with my pop and galloping at full speed with him, which we never told Gran about.

"Are you ready to race?" I ask.

"Do I have to let you win?"

I scoff. "I never want a single thing handed to me. You know that."

When he had first offered to step out of the running for Knight Food Distribution, I about lost my shit. I'm the better farm, or at least the one that has exactly what they require, and I don't need charity.

I've proven my worth.

"You know it doesn't make you weak if someone helps you."

I stick my tongue out at him. "Afraid of losing, Whitlock?"

Rowan shakes his head. "You're going to end up being the death of me."

"Probably, but it'll be a fun descent into hell."

"I'm sure it won't," he counters. "Okay, let's race."

"Three, two . . ." I pause, shifting back into my seat so when Monty takes off, I'm in the best position. "One, go!"

I kick the horse and instantly we dart off, I ease up on the reins, allowing him full control. He speeds through the grass and I feel like flying. My smile is uncontrollable as we move, wind whipping through my hair, as my worries drift off with it.

I feel lighter than I have in forever. Nothing can ruin this for me. I'm happy, in love, and I'm going to win the race fair and square.

We keep going, and the edge of the trees starts to near. I grip the reins, preparing to control Monty as we reach the tree line. He's run this with me so many times, he knows what is coming. I hear the hooves behind me, Rowan approaching.

"Come on, boy, let's kick his ass," I say, leaning forward and patting his neck.

Monty speeds up just a bit more, giving us half a head lead. I yell as we easily win and circle him as Rowan comes up behind me.

I smile, victory is so sweet. I look him up and down, my grin not fading but for a different reason.

"Like what you see?"

I quirk my brow. "Easy there, Cowboy, I was admiring the horse, not the rider."

"Sure you weren't. You like riding me too."

"Do I? I can't seem to remember saying that."

Rowan grins. "You don't have to say it, sweetheart, your body tells me otherwise."

I snort. "Full of yourself there."

"I'm happy to make you full of me if you'd prefer."

"Oh Lord." I laugh. "On your day of yes, we'll do whatever you want."

"Good to know," Rowan tosses back. "All right, birthday girl, what's next?"

I can't remember the last time that I've ever felt so free. Even if it's just for today, it's amazing and I'm loving every second of being with him.

"Food?"

"Are you asking or telling me?"

"Telling," I say with a nod.

"Okay, do you want to go out? We can go to the diner or I can call up to Summit Views and see if we can get a table."

My stomach instantly clenches because that would truly be letting our relationship out in the open.

"Do you think we should tell our family and friends about us before we go out on a date?"

Rowan dismounts from his horse, walking to me, his hand rests on my leg. "I don't care what anyone says, Charlotte. I'm with you, and I'm not going anywhere, but . . . yeah, we should. Your sister especially."

"I just don't want her to find out from anyone else."

"I get it."

Although, we all know how this is going to go over. She's going to lose her ever-loving mind.

I rest my hand on his cheek. "Do you know what I want?"

"Me?"

I roll my eyes. "Sure, but I mean next."

"What's that, baby?"

My grin is wide. "To beat you back to the stables." I kick Monty, leaving him behind, loving that I know he'll chase me.

"Favorite color?" I ask Rowan.

We're sitting on the floor, I'm wearing his T-shirt and he's just in his boxers. We've had sex twice more, both our normal, frantic, and incredibly hot ways. He took me in the barn when he finally caught up to me, pushing me into a stall and using a lead rope to tie my hands above my head. Then we had dinner and he decided I should be dessert.

Both were magnificent.

Now a movie is on, and we're ignoring it, playing a series of quick questions.

"Yellow."

"Really?" That surprises me.

"Yeah, it was my mom's favorite. She had yellow everywhere in our house."

I lean forward and give him a quick kiss. "That's cute."

My phone rings, but Rowan snatches it, putting it behind him.

"Hey!" I protest.

"No phones. It's my time with you."

Normally, I'd bite back, saying something about taking a girl's phone away, but it's cute and sweet, and honestly, there's not a person alive I want to talk to right now.

"Fine, but you know Faye is going to call, and if I miss more than two, she'll send a search party."

He glances down at the phone. "It's not Faye."

"Who is it?" I ask.

"Nope. It's my turn to ask the questions. What's your favorite color?"

"Hmm, you know, my favorite color has changed so many times. I loved pink when I was younger, then blue when I got into my teen years. Then I had a crazy teal phase. Now, I'm more of a sage girl. It's neutral but still has color, and it reminds me of being warm."

He shakes his head. "If you say so."

"I do. Next one, favorite food?"

"Can I say you?" Rowan asks.

"I mean, it's not a bad answer."

He wiggles his brows. "You and then tacos."

"Who doesn't love tacos? They're the best."

"Agree, so they're yours?" Rowan asks.

"No, I love dessert. My favorite foods are sweets. I love cake, brownies, pies, cannoli, ice cream, you name it . . . I love it. For my wedding, I didn't dream about the food or the parties or even the guy," I admit. "I dreamed of the cake. I know exactly what I want, how it'll look, the flavors, the icing, it's going to be perfect."

He stares at me like I have two heads. "The cake?"

"I like cake."

"You should like the groom," he says with a brow raised.

"I'm sure I will, just not as much as the cake."

Rowan laughs. "All right then."

I refill my wine glass and then move so I'm next to him, my head resting on his shoulder. This day has been perfect. He made it perfect, and I'll never forget this. If I thought I might have been falling for him before, this solidified it. I'm head over heels in love with Rowan Whitlock.

Loving him will cost me some things, but not loving him would've cost me everything.

So, once we tell my sister and his family, I'm going to tell him how I feel and figure out a plan moving forward.

I hear a rattling noise, but before I can say or do anything, the door opens.

"Charlotte! Happy . . ." The voice trails off as Rowan and I come face to face with my sister. "What the fuck?"

I jump up quickly, realizing that was probably a bad idea since I don't have pants or underwear on. I grab the blanket, pulling it up. "Aurora."

"You're fucking him? You're kidding me, right? Please tell me this is a joke. You're sleeping with my loser ex-boyfriend?"

Rowan stands, his impressive height and size causing Aurora to step back a little. "First, I was never your boyfriend. Second, do not come in here after being out of your sister's life for two years, show up on her birthday, and yell at her."

I put my hand on his arm. "Rowan . . ."

He turns to me. "No, not today. I will not let anyone ruin this day for you."

The tightness in my chest eases just a little.

Aurora laughs. "Get out of my house."

No. He's not leaving. Absolutely not. I step toward my sister. "It's not your house anymore. It's mine, and he's not leaving."

I see the hurt flash across her face. "You're choosing him?"

"Rowan has been here. Rowan makes me happy. Rowan is who took care of me when that drunk guy was trying to get me to sleep with him. Rowan is who carried me in the woods when I hurt my ankle and then helped me for days when we were stuck in the ice storm. It was Rowan who supported me, drove me to New York for a meeting for a contract that he's also competing for. Where were you, Aurora? What exactly in the last two years have you done to make me choose you? Nothing."

"I'm your sister." Her incredulity seeps through the words.

"I know, and I planned to come to New York in a few days and tell you about everything, how it happened, and how I feel about him. This wasn't supposed to be how you found out."

She shakes her head. "I can't believe this. First, I find out we may lose the farm, and now I find out you're hooking up with the man who ruined my life!"

Rowan steps forward. "Enough. We weren't together. We slept with each other for a few months. You said you wanted to date, I said no, and three days later, you were telling everyone I cheated on you, and you witnessed it. With who, Aurora? Who exactly did I fuck that you walked in on? When we weren't even in a damn relationship! No one. It never happened, and instead of being a decent human being and admitting you lied, you doubled down."

Aurora's jaw drops. "You're insane."

"No, sweetheart, that's the truth, and we both know it. However, I let you say whatever you needed to because, apparently, you needed me to be the villain. The thing is, I'm with Charlotte. I care about her. I want to be with her for as long as she's willing to put up with me. I want to take care of her, hold her when she cries, make her smile, and support her. If you can't be happy for her, then you can fuck off, but you won't make her birthday sad. You want to attack me? Go for it, but you'll have to get through me to get to her."

I look up at this man who just defended me like a warrior and tears fill my vision. Not because I'm hurt or worried about my sister but because I've never had anyone go that far for me.

"I said no tears," I say as my lip wobbles.

Rowan turns his body to me, his hands moving to my face. "I'm sorry if I made you cry, baby."

I shake my head. "I'm not sad. You just . . . you . . . no one has ever stood up for me like that."

He huffs out a breath and leans close to me. "I will fight the world and ruin myself in the process to make sure nothing hurts you."

I lift up, not caring that I'm half naked or that my sister who hates my boyfriend is standing here, and kiss him softly.

My phone rings, I drop back and reach for it.

Oh, God, it's Carson.

Rowan's eyes find mine and I smile. "I have to answer this," I say.

He probably thinks it's Faye.

I swipe the screen, ready for my life to be changed. "Hello?"

"Hi, Charlotte, it's Carson Knight."

I turn around so I don't see my sister or Rowan as I hear the news. "It's great to hear from you."

"Listen, I wanted to give you a call and let you know my decision. After a lot of debate, and back and forth, I've decided it's best to go with a larger farm. I think you have a wonderful setup and you'd do great, but maybe for a smaller scaled project. I have a few things down the line and when they come around, I'd like to reach out again."

My heart breaks. Literally. I feel the pain in my chest like I've never felt before. I somehow keep my voice steady. "That would be great. I'd appreciate it."

"Of course, and again, it was nothing personal or anything like that. I genuinely went back and forth a lot more than I've ever done. It was a toss-up until this morning, and I just went with my gut."

"I understand," I say, the defeat loud even though I was close to whispering.

"All right. Good luck to you, and I'll be in touch when the right project comes around. I hope we find a way to work together in the future, Charlotte."

The phone goes dead, and I stand here, staring at the photos in front of me through watery eyes. Gran and Pop on the front porch, his arm around her waist as she holds my mom in her arms. The one to the right, my parents' wedding photo where they are staring into each other's eyes. A photo of my dad climbing the maple tree out front, the one where he carved his daughters' names beneath his and my mother's. Then my sister and I sitting on the front porch swing.

So many memories in this house that will never be passed down.

"Charlotte?" Aurora calls my name, and I swipe at my tears.

I turn to her, shake my head, and look at Rowan. "Congratulations."

"I'm sorry, Charlotte," he says, coming toward me, but I raise my hands. "I'm sorry you didn't get it. I'm sorry the news came now and like this."

"You knew?" I ask, feeling a new wave of pain hit me.

He moves toward me again. "I just found out."

"And you didn't tell me?"

How could he keep this from me?

"I got the email, and it's your birthday. I didn't want to ruin it."

I take two steps back. Everything and everyone in my life sucks. Today was finally looking up. I had this wonderful man come and be so kind and tell me he loves me. It was all I wanted and now this.

271

Instead of joy and laughter, it's yelling and despair. I can't deal with all of this. I'm going to lose my mind.

"I'd say the day is ruined, wouldn't you?"

"It wasn't supposed to be. I'm so fucking sorry."

I bet he is. As angry as I am at him for not telling me, I'm just too broken to care. However, he needs to leave. I can't look at him, not when I know I'm going to lose everything.

My lip trembles as I stare into the blue eyes I love so damn much. "Right now, my heart is breaking, and as much as I want you to comfort me, I need to talk to Aurora. Please, please, I'm begging you, I need . . . to be with my sister."

Rowan sighs heavily as he runs his hand down his beautiful face. His eyes find mine. "Okay. I'm coming back tomorrow, and we'll figure this out."

There's nothing to figure out, but I nod because if I speak, it'll be sobs that escape instead of words.

He tosses his clothes on—well, not his shirt since I have that—and heads to the back door. Rowan pauses, looking at me for a moment. "I'll fix this."

"You can't."

Rowan walks back to me, both hands cradling my face. "I'll be back tomorrow."

I grip both wrists, pulling them down. "I'll let you know when it's a good time."

He searches my eyes, and I'm sure he can see my heartache. It's not his fault that Carson picked him, I know this, but it feels like he did this. It feels like he took something from me, even though he had no say in it.

It's best he goes home and allows me to process it.

Without another word, he leans into me, pressing his lips to my forehead, and then walks out the door, and I sink to the floor and sob.

My sister comes over, resting her hand on my shoulder. "Now what?"

I look up at her, my tears falling. "I don't know. I don't know how to fix this, Aurora. I can't save the farm."

She jerks back a little. "I wasn't talking about the farm."

What? "Then . . ." It dawns on me, she's worried about Rowan. "Don't even," I warn her.

She gets to her feet, throwing her arms up. "He's a pig! A fucking piece of shit!"

"He's not," I defend.

After she walked in, I felt such relief, in a way, that she knew the truth. I hated carrying this secret around, and I knew it would be bad. At the same time, I didn't care. My sister showed up here, without a word, after making me cry this morning. Rowan was who soothed my pain and always manages to make me feel better.

She waves her hand. "You're clearly under the influence of something. Did he drug you? Are you drunk?"

"No, Aurora, I'm none of those. He's been here for me every day. While you hate him, I don't."

"Clearly, since you're fucking him! How could you, Char? How could you, with him of all the men in the world?"

I hate that question and the hurt in her voice. I hurt her. I'm hurting her and that part isn't okay with me. However, I've gotten to know him, and the things she said he was—he isn't. Rowan didn't cheat on her. I believe that in every part of my soul. After knowing what I do about his family life, there isn't a chance he'd do that to a woman.

That leaves me with the most likely possibility, which is that he was never with Aurora in that way or she made it up. Considering her flair for the dramatics, my money is on the last one.

"Once and for all, tell me the truth. Did you ever walk in on him cheating on you?"

Her mouth opens and shuts before she sits on the couch. "Does it matter?"

"To me it does," I explain.

"Do you love him?"

273

I nod. I'm not ready to say the words aloud, and when I do, I want it to be Rowan that hears them first.

"It was complicated," she says, her gaze not meeting mine. "I was angry. I still am. He broke my heart. You know that, don't you?"

"I do, but that doesn't answer the question, Aurora. Did you lie about the cheating?"

She owes me the truth. For years I've believed her, championed her, and it's time to know once and for all if I was being stupid.

"We weren't really together, and I didn't catch him. I saw him talking to some girl after he told me that he wanted to end whatever we were doing because he was worried I wanted more than he did. I was so pissed. Then, to see him with her? It was a slap in my face."

I exhale through my nose, really hating my sister's selfishness. "You lied to me. You made me think he was this horrible person. All the while you made it your mission to tell people that not only did he cheat but that you walked in on him. Why would you be so damn mean? Don't you see how incredibly cruel that is?"

My sister doesn't apologize or explain more. She turns her eyes to find mine and shakes her head. "I was angry."

"I don't care! That's not an excuse to try to ruin someone."

"You wouldn't because he picked you. He didn't sleep with you for months only to decide you weren't worth it. No, sister, he fell for you, so you wouldn't get it."

"Say whatever you want, Aurora. Right now, I don't really want to see you. You lied, you tried to destroy him, all for what? Your petty anger? Your ridiculous idea that you *deserved* something more than he was willing to give you? I won't let you paint me as the bitch here, you are. You did this. You pushed me and made me think I was doing something so wrong with someone who hurt you. God! You're such a selfish asshole. I wanted to tell you myself about Rowan, not have you find out this way," I admit with regret. My sister deserved to have me sit with her and talk, not walk in on us. My heart aches for her, even though I'm angry in some way at how she acted.

"Then why didn't you?"

"Because I knew you'd act like this. Always the victim. Always making me feel stupid and horrible. Always doing the things that make you happy. What about me? What about the years I've suffered, trying to shoulder it all? Instead of you coming to me with kindness and love, you made me think I did something wrong. You didn't offer to help or be a friend. You chastised me. So, I didn't come to you because I couldn't trust you."

For the first time in forever, I see hurt and a bit of regret in my sister's eyes. Good. Maybe she'll finally see the damage she's done to someone else in service of herself. Aurora picks up her purse, puts it over her shoulder and stops when she gets to the door. "I'm going back to the city now. I'm really sorry your birthday has been ruined. I'm sorry that I'm not the person you want me to be, but I do love you."

"You're my sister," I say, not sure what it even means. Do I forgive her? No, not really. Do I think she owes Rowan a very long apology? Absolutely. While I don't doubt she loves me, I think she has a really twisted view on how love is.

She sighs heavily. "When we lost Mom and Dad, I searched so much for a love like theirs. They had it all, didn't they? One day I hope we find a love like theirs."

A part of me wonders if I haven't found it, but then I remember how today went. He didn't tell me about the contract. All day I would've gone around, thinking that all was well, only to learn it was a lie.

"I hope so too."

Aurora looks at the photos on the wall and then to me. "I want you to be happy, Charlotte, and if Rowan is the guy that does that, then no matter what anyone says, you should be with him. It's just going to take time for me to be okay with it."

"It's going to take some time for me to forgive you for all of this too."

"I believe that. Just know that you have a place to land if this all falls to shit. I will never turn you away, contrary to what you think of me. I do love you, Charlotte. You're my sister and I'm sorry I'm not the sister you wish I was. Like I said, if you can't find a way to save Mom's farm, come live with me and I'll try to be a better person."

I nod, because no matter what, Aurora is my sister and wouldn't let me be homeless. She's a lot of things but I don't think she'd purposely let me suffer.

With that, she blows me a kiss and walks out the door, leaving me feeling more alone than ever before.

twenty-eight
ROWAN

"Wait, you're actually with Charlotte?" Grady asks. My sister and future sisters-in-law are doing some girl date thing where they're spending money on candles or some shit. The guys are all sitting around the fire.

"Yes."

Asher snorts. "Didn't see this coming. You're like a walking cliché."

"Says the man who is marrying his daughter's nanny in a few months. Yeah, I'm the cliché."

"Got you there," Grady says with a smirk.

"I'm just saying she's the girl next door, literally, and the one you'd never date. Although, to be fair, I didn't think you'd ever date in general," Asher explains.

I shrug because it doesn't matter what she is out of all the labels, she's the woman I want. The one I'm falling in love with and the one I might lose.

"She's all that and more."

Grady looks at Asher, eyes wide, and then stares at me. "You love her?"

"I don't know. I've never been in love, so I have no clue what it feels like."

"Do you think about her all the time?" Asher asks.

"Yes."

"Do you feel like if you could just see her, it would make everything better?" Grady questions.

"I do."

Asher speaks this time. "Does it feel like nothing makes sense anymore?"

I nod. "She's got me completely twisted."

"But, at the same time, the world makes perfect sense because of her," Grady says with a laugh.

Asher smirks. "Would you lay down your life for her?"

"In a fucking heartbeat."

"Then, brother"—Grady lifts his beer in salute—"welcome to the club, it's miserable here, but none of us have any desire to leave."

"So what you're saying is that this sucks and I'm going to be miserable?"

Asher shrugs. "Pretty much. You're going to live in a perpetual state of anxiety. First, she's going to do the opposite of what you think she'll do, trust me. Second, you feel like half your heart is missing from your chest and you can do nothing to protect it. If she hurts, you're going to want to kill the person who did it to her. If she's in a bad mood, you're going to want to kill the person who put her in that mood because you're now reaping the benefits of said mood. You'll worry when she isn't around, and you'll sometimes wish she wasn't around because she's a bit unglued. It's wonderful."

Sounds it. I drain my beer and grab a new one out of the pack. "I don't know how long this will last anyway," I say, feeling frustrated by the current situation.

"Why is that?" Grady asks. "You started officially dating yesterday? Even Asher didn't fuck up a relationship that quickly."

Asher flips him off.

I go over the series of events from yesterday. Both of my brothers listen, nodding when I explain my decision not to tell her about the email and enjoy her day. I wish I'd known it was Carson calling, I would've held the fucking phone.

After I'm done, both Grady and Asher are leaning forward, elbows resting on their knees. "Well," Asher starts. "I'm not sure what to say. On one hand this contract is great for you, but it's clearly going to destroy your relationship."

"I know."

Grady clears his throat. "What are you thinking?"

"I'm going to tell Carson I can't do it. I'm not even certified organic yet and that was part of the deal," I explain. "She deserved it."

"Clearly, Carson didn't think so," Grady says and then raises a hand when he sees my face. "Easy, killer. I'm saying that there had to be a reason. Maybe he saw the farm in disrepair and didn't want to chance it."

Sure, that could be it, but that contract would've saved her farm and she could've hired back the people she needed to get it out of its current state.

Asher clasps my shoulder. "You're going to give it up for her?"

As much as it pains me, I can't accept it. "I'd give up my farm for her."

"She's going to be pissed."

I look to Asher. "I know. She's going to hate me either way."

And that's the rub. If I keep it, she'll lose her farm and probably move with her sister to New York. If I give it up, she's going to feel like she doesn't deserve it or it was charity. Lord knows Charlotte is prideful.

Grady sighs heavily. "Look, Carson is a smart man and picked you for a reason. There's nothing that says that if you walk away from the deal it'll go to her. It's something to consider."

He's right. I have no guarantees. Which means I'm going to lose her right after I got her.

"Well, for now, all I can do is wait for her to tell me she wants to see me."

"That's how you left it?" Asher asks.

"Yeah, she said she'd let me know when it was a good time."

Asher's face scrunches. "Fuck that, it's woman code for she's upset, and you need to go over there before she decides you're a loser and it's over before it began."

Grady shifts forward. "Yeah, dude, yes means no, and no means fuck off, and then don't even get me started on when she says maybe. Maybe is a whole other world. You need to outsmart her." He taps his forehead. "Think strategically and outthink her before she can think."

What the fuck does that mean?

"I don't think Charlotte plays games like that."

They both laugh.

"Oh, young one, you have so much to learn," Asher says.

"You've each been in like one relationship." I turn to Grady. "Two for you, but neither of you are all that experienced with women."

"It's your funeral." Grady lifts one shoulder and drains his beer. "I would get your dumb ass up and over to her house."

Asher nods, pointing in the direction of her house. "Go! Don't walk, run."

I'm not sure if they're fucking with me, but something in my brother's face has me wondering if maybe he's right. If I give her time to think about all the reasons this is the end, then there will be no going back.

I stand and hand my beer to Asher. "You're not being a prick?"

"Row, I'm trying to help you. I don't want to see you go back to your misery and lonely life with the cows," Ash says. "I want you to be happy, and if Charlotte means what you say she does, then you'll stop talking to us and go fix this."

I never thought Asher or Grady would be encouraging this, but I don't want to stand here and debate whether they're right or wrong. I want to be with her, to find a way to fight together and both have what we want.

So, I turn and head to her house.

The entire walk, I do nothing but go over possible responses to what I'm sure will be her brush-off. Charlotte doesn't want or take help. She's strong and needs to do it all on her own, no matter how stupid it is.

When I get to her front steps, I find her sitting on her porch swing, mug in hand, blanket wrapped around her. She looks over at me, wipes under her eyes, and then looks back out. "I won't see this view for much longer. I want to soak up as much time as I can."

I make my way toward the swing. "You're giving up?"

She scoffs. "I'm being realistic."

"I never thought you were a quitter."

"Fuck off, Rowan."

"Let me help," I plead with her. "We can merge our farms, it'll allow me to expand, you'll keep your house, and we can be a team."

Charlotte's eyes lift, and the green irises flash with some emotion I can't decipher. "What?"

Anger it seems. Okay, exactly like I thought. "I need help. I'm growing, and this contract is going to set me back. I need land, help, equipment, all the things that, if we worked together, we'd be able to accomplish. You're certified, and I'm held up again, so if we work together, we can make this profitable for both of us."

Maybe if I appeal to her more realistic side and that she'd be helping me, it'll go my way.

"You're kidding, right? Your solution to this is to merge the farms?"

"Tell me your objections."

She gets to her feet. "My objections? I don't even know where to start. How about for one, until about three weeks ago, we hated each other. Second, I don't need you to come in and fix my life for me. You got the contract because your farm is better. Mine is completely a shambles."

"Well, us merging would fix that," I toss back.

"No it wouldn't. It would destroy everything. I'd have, what? The part of my farm where the house is and maybe an acre around it while you get the rest? You'd own my cattle, my falling-down barns, and all the broken equipment. I'm a burden, Rowan, and I'm not going to let you come in here on your white horse like I need saving."

She's so fucking stubborn. "Fine. Then I'm going to turn the contract down."

Charlotte turns, her jaw clenched. "The hell you will."

"The hell I won't."

"I won't take it if he comes to me."

I raise one brow. "Sure you won't."

"Don't!" she warns, pointing her finger at me. "Don't you dare do that. If I'm going to lose this farm, then I'll do it the way Pop would've been proud of. It'll be on my own back."

I laugh because she's ridiculous. "Stupid. Completely stupid. I knew your pop and he wouldn't have wanted you to go down in a blaze of glory. He would've wanted you to fight, and if that meant taking a deal with the devil, which I'll play in this scenario, then that's what he'd have done. Do you really think that, in all his years, he didn't have to make the same choices?"

Charlotte crosses her arms over her chest. "You don't know anything."

"The fuck I don't! My family bought part of your farm when my grandparents owned it. And guess what? My grandparents sold it back when they got into trouble. It's what people do here, Charlotte. They step up and help people out."

It's her turn to laugh. "Where were you and all your help last year? What neighborly thing did I mistake that happened?"

"I didn't know you were in trouble."

She shakes her head. "It wouldn't have mattered, Rowan. We weren't friends and we sure as hell weren't whatever this is."

The softening of her voice calls me. I walk to her, pulling her into my arms. "I won't let you go without a fight."

"You can't win this battle."

"You can," I say, pushing her hair back behind her ear. "You can let me in, let me help. I need you to be here, Charlotte. I need you."

Her forehead drops to my chest, and I pray this means she'll take me up on my offer.

I feel her muscles tense a second before she straightens. "I need time."

"Time for what?"

"Time to get my shit together. Time to think about what the next step is. Aurora wants me to move to New York. She has a two-bedroom apartment, and I can easily find work there. This farm, it was a dream. A silly dream that young girls have and it's clearly one I meant to live. I need to accept whatever my new life will be. I can't do that with you ... making me want the dream."

I knew this was going to be a possible argument, but it still pisses me off. "So, that's it? You won't fight for whatever we could be, either."

Charlotte turns her gaze toward the open field. "You have no idea what I want to do. Fight? I want to burn the world down. The first time I find someone I want to be with, and I can't have him."

"You can! Jesus Christ, Charlotte. I'm here, asking you to let me stand beside you and help!"

"You can't!" she yells, throwing her arms up. "I have to do this, Rowan. I have to sell this place, deal with the consequences, and. figure out the next step. You can't be the reason behind whatever choice I make. You want me to give in and let you fix this, then what? How do we go forward with me always in your debt? What if something happens to you? Because something always happens, so please don't try to tell me I'm ridiculous," Charlotte says, moving around the porch. "A drunk driver, cancer, lies about a semi-boyfriend—whatever the reason is, things happen. This is why I rely on myself. This is why it's so much easier to just be the sole person who is at fault. I lost this farm. I lost the contract that would've saved it. I lost it all and I need some freaking time to think about how I go on."

I stay silent, weighing my response because we both know the time isn't going to be anything but a wedge that drives us apart. "I've never been in a relationship. I have far less experience than anyone else, but even I know that time apart isn't what we need. Things happen, you're right. My father left my mother, and she went on to marry more losers and then died. Olivia was born deaf because of a complication, Brynn suffered because we didn't protect her. All of those things happen, but the only reason any of us made it through was by relying on someone who loves us. You can choose to fight alone, that's fine, but I'm asking you to let me stand beside you so when you're fucking exhausted, you can lean on me."

There's nothing more I can say. She's hurting, I get it, but I will be there and help her if she lets me.

Which she won't.

"You say that, and I believe you mean it. I really do. You just don't get it. I need to figure out how I'm going to do all the things I need to or whatever my next step is."

"What things?" I ask. "The only thing I'm asking is that you let me in, Charlotte."

"What things?" Her voice raises. "What things? All the fucking things, Rowan. The things I haven't had time to do because I had to go to New York or got stuck in the woods or was desperate for you that I neglected the farm to spend the night wrapped up in your arms where the world wasn't horrible." She lifts her hand and starts to list things off. "I have to mend the fence in the back field because the cows got out again, but I don't have help. The roof on the barn is one wind gust away from blowing off, but I don't have the funds to repair it or the ability to do it alone. I need to get my truck fixed. There's a gear on the bucket milker that keeps popping off, no idea where it's coming from, but that's another two grand I don't have. I need to plow the hay field, but my fucking hay bailer is busted, so I can't. What things you ask? All of that and a million more I can't even name. So, if you care about me, at all, even a little bit as much as I care about you. Give me a few days. Let me wrap my head around this . . . hellhole I'm entering on my own."

Every fucking part of me wants to argue this more. If I thought for a moment it would work, I'd do it. I'd talk until my voice was gone and then I'd sign it. However, Charlotte's instinct is to retreat into herself when shit goes wrong.

She's said it before, people leave, and she's guaranteeing I'm just like everyone else.

As much as it kills me, I know I need to walk away and prove that I'm not going anywhere.

So, I go to her, tip her chin up, and kiss her lips before walking away without another word.

twenty-nine

CHARLOTTE

My head is pounding, but that's what crying yourself to sleep will do to you. There's a loud banging and I can't tell if it's coming from outside or in my head.

Lovely.

I roll over, the sun is just starting to peek through the windows, so I roll back over, tossing the pillow over my head.

"Go away!" I yell but it's clearly muffled.

The banging starts up again, and I groan, knowing I need to go figure out what the hell is causing it. Not to mention, it's time to get my shit together. The cows need to be milked, fed, and cared for, no matter what state my life is in.

Once dressed, I make coffee, mix in some of my protein shake because breakfast ain't happening, and walk out.

When I do, the banging is louder, and I gasp.

Up on the roof of the barn are Rowan and two other guys.

"Rowan?" I ask because maybe it's not him.

He looks down from over the side. "Did I wake you?"

"No, I was up."

"Good. Do whatever you need to do. Pretend I'm not here."

Yeah, that's not going to happen. "Why are you here?"

He moves up on the roof and bangs in a nail. "I like the view."

"You don't like heights," I remind him.

"Says you."

"Says you!"

His grin is wide. "Go to work, Charlotte."

"Get off my roof, Rowan."

He puts the hammer down and sits, watching me. "Are you ready to let me in and help you?"

My chest tightens, and I bite my tongue. My immediate reaction is to tell him to go the hell away and I can do this on my own. I always do. It's who I am and what I've had to learn to do. It's years and years of disappointment and heartache built into my chest.

"I just need some time," I say, and he nods.

"I'll be here when you're ready."

Then Rowan turns back to his knees, picks up his hammer and doesn't look at me again while my self-loathing goes even higher.

Seriously, what is wrong with me?

***

"You need time for what? The man was on your roof," Faye says as she tosses popcorn in her mouth. She returned home yesterday, came by to bring me a gift, and ended up listening to me drone on and on about the mess I'm in.

"My head is a mess. The last thing I want to do is say something stupid and lose him for good. I just . . . I need to think. To get my stupid emotions in check."

She shrugs. "I mean, mature and all, I guess. How long do you think Rowan is willing to deal with your need for space?"

"I don't know."

"Why didn't you tell me you needed money?"

I grab a cookie and sigh. "Because you'd give it to me, and I don't want that. I never want to be in debt to the people I love."

"Did you ever think it's not a debt to those people? That it's someone who loves you and wants to help? If it was me, would you offer and help?"

"Of course I would."

She slaps my arm. "Well, dumb-dumb, why the hell do you think I wouldn't?"

"Faye, you don't have a job. I love you and you're the most giving human in the world, but, like . . . how?"

"I have money, Charlotte. I know you think me being a beauty ambassador isn't a thing, but I make a lot of money. I have contracts with all these brands that not only pay me but also send me stuff. It's a pretty sweet gig."

I knew she was doing a lot, but she's never mentioned the ins and outs. "I should've come to you," I admit.

"Yeah, but even more, let's say I couldn't afford to help you, I'm still your best friend. I would've shouldered some of your stress and been someone you could cry to."

I take her hand, squeezing once. "I'm sorry."

"You should be."

We both laugh. "I don't know what I do now."

"Is it too late to save it? I'll give you the money," Faye says, squeezing my hand back. "I'll help without question."

She's incredibly sweet to offer, and it's not pride that stops me from saying yes, it's really not. It's more that I worry that, if I take her up on this, in a few months, I'll be right back in this same position. My farm hasn't been profitable in years. I've struggled since I took it over, and without that contract, it would be like putting a Band-Aid on a stab wound.

"I love you for it, but I really do need time to think through my options. I love this farm, so much, but I don't love farming, if that makes sense."

"It does. It's hard to do something you don't love all the time and you live this."

I do. I live here, trying so damn hard to save it because of my mother. I want her home, her family, to live on. I just wish I didn't suck so much at the dairy side of things. This isn't what I dreamed of, in so many ways. My goals were to be married and be a mother, to raise a family, not cows.

"One way or another, it'll work out," I say, praying it does.

"Okay. I'm here if you need it. I'm just curious, but what did Rowan suggest?"

I exhale, feeling a mix of love and anger. "He offered to merge the farms. I'm guessing that I'd keep my house and land around it, but the dairy farm would sort of fall under him."

"And you . . . are . . . a complete and total asshole, why wouldn't you take that and run?"

My head jerks back at that response. "What?"

"He literally would allow you to keep what matters most, the damn house, and you get to still do your cow crap, but not have to constantly worry about the money. So, yeah, are you just . . . a fucking dumbass for fun?"

"It's not just the house, Faye. This farm, the land, the cows, the whole thing has been in my family for generations."

"And? You just said you don't love it!"

"I don't, but it's part of what I was supposed to save."

She huffs, clearly irritated with me. "Why are you working so hard to save something, the cow part, you hate? Seriously, Charlotte, it makes no sense. Look, if you and Rowan work out and you get married, the farms would merge anyway. Just merge them now and write the ending of the story."

Oh, Jesus. "Getting a little ahead of yourself there. We haven't even officially been together for forty-eight hours yet!"

"So, every love story has a beginning."

I roll my eyes. "Well, our beginning was hate-filled fucking, so . . ."

"All the better." Faye smiles and leans back. "I guess I can understand a little."

I truly don't believe she does, but I'm not going to argue with her because I'm exhausted. "Good."

"I mean, even incredibly intelligent people like yourself can be stupid sometimes. I guess this is your turn."

I grab a handful of popcorn and toss it in her face, which starts a small food fight and a lot of laughing.

❦

I grab the roll of fence wire and my bucket with all the tools I need and walk out to the area where the hole is. I need to fix this so I can let the cows roam out in this field since they've pretty much cleaned out the pasture they're in. I need them to eat more of this so I'm not spending as much on grain.

The walk out feels peaceful. Last night, I went through all the expenses again, where the most debt is, and tried to squeeze a dime out of a penny.

It was . . . frustrating.

I think I can make the house payment if I sell off some of my cows. I just can't do it any other way, and if I'm going to lose the farm anyway, I might as well start thinning the herd anyway.

I posted in the group I'm in and got two offers in ten minutes, which is amazing, and they offered to come today, which is the immediate cash infusion I desperately need.

I arrive at where the first hole in the fence is and look around. What the hell?

Where is the hole?

I swear it was the ninth fence post from the east.

I count again, looking at the posts in the immediate area to see if I miscounted.

Nope. No hole.

I flagged it. I remember it was the post by the elm tree.

But it's not there, and there's no gap in the fence.

Okay.

There were two more on the back. I can see the colored ribbon flapping in the wind. Maybe I'm not completely crazy.

The first one marked, again, is fixed. It's clear this was mended because I can see where the wire is bonded to the existing one.

"Son of a bitch," I say because, really, there's only one explanation.

When I go to the next spot in the fence, I find the same repair.

Does he want to make me cry? I think so.

I'm headed back to my place, ready to confront Rowan when I notice something very big and red is on my hayfield.

Oh God. I can't handle this. I need that hay.

I drop my bucket and wire and run toward the field, needing to see who the hell is running equipment on my land. When I get there, I see that half the field is cut, the hay laying in the neat rows.

Waving my arms and yelling, I move toward the plow, careful not to get too close to whoever the hell is out here so I don't get run over, and then I see his perfect fucking face.

Rowan is plowing the field.

He stops when he sees me, turning the machine off and opening his door to the tractor. "Charlotte?"

I exhale through my nose and go closer so he can hear me. "You're plowing my field?"

"I'd rather plow you, but you need time."

He looks rather proud of himself for that comment. "Cute."

"I'm not trying to be cute, just honest."

"This is literally the opposite of giving me time," I say back to him. "You're here every day fixing something. I'm going to assume you did the fence."

Rowan shakes his head. "That was not, in fact, me. Do you have another boyfriend I don't know about?"

I fight back my smile. "I do not."

"Good, I'd hate to have to kick someone's ass and injure myself. I'm a very busy guy."

"Yes, it seems so."

He shifts forward out of the cab of the tractor, his eyes focused on me. "Are you ready to let me in and help you?"

"You seem to be doing that without me being ready."

His lips purse, and he nods. "I have a lot of work to do today, I'd love to stay and talk, but idle hands and all that shit. I'll see you around."

He closes the door, fires up the tractor, and goes back to it.

I want to go to him, tell him that I'm so damn in love with him, but he's already halfway down the field, and I'm an idiot.

I wrap my arms around my chest, watching him get to the end, and decide that I need to do something to show him how much I appreciate this, even if I'm too stupid to just say it.

thirty

ROWAN

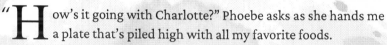

"How's it going with Charlotte?" Phoebe asks as she hands me a plate that's piled high with all my favorite foods.

"It's Charlotte, I expect next month she'll finally get her head out of her ass." I'm clearly aggravated. I know she's got issues, we all do, but I miss her.

Really, that's the heart of it.

I fucking miss her.

Once I finished fixing the roof, the fence, and plowing, I went back to where my ATV was and found a batch of cookies waiting for me on the seat.

I thought it was a peace offering, that she was ready to talk to me and come up with a solution, but she wasn't home and didn't answer the phone.

"You know," Addison cuts in. "I know you may not want to hear this, but sometimes, we have to make the wrong choice to know what the right one is."

Phoebe nods. "Preach, sister."

"Amen!" Brynlee adds on.

Oh, for fuck's sake. "So, you make bad choices just to make the right one? What the hell kind of logic is that?"

"It's girl logic."

"Oh, so no logic. Are you all this ridiculous?"

Phoebe tosses a roll at my head. "Now you've done it," Asher mumbles.

I turn to my brothers, who are both silent for the first time in their lives, both with shit-eating grins on their faces. "Some help?"

"Not a chance." Asher shoves a forkful into his mouth.

Brynn stares at me, a brow raised. "You and Charlotte's relationship is the equivalent of a newborn. Maybe you should be understanding. She can't trust you yet, Row. You're the asshole who bought land out from under her feet last year, and now you've gotten the contract she needed. Her sister is a . . . well, I don't have nice things to say, and you're a bit of a dick." She pauses. "Said with love."

I know she's right. I've not exactly proven myself to be this trustworthy and kind guy. I've done the right thing, like taking care of her when she was drunk or injured, but every man should do that. It's doing the right thing when no one is looking, that's the mark of a man.

I've always strived to be a man my mother would be proud of. One that my sister would look at with respect. Most of all, one that Olivia would see as a role model.

"It's not about the time, I get she needs that. I really do. She's gun-shy, and rightfully so, but I've shown up to prove I'll be there for her."

Phoebe clears her throat. "As a woman who has been in Charlotte's shoes, who had a man promise things and completely abandon me, I get why she wants space. I tried to leave Asher for the same reason."

My brother shifts. "Didn't work."

"No, because you didn't let me take it. You were there. You proved you'd always be there. You loved me when I didn't think I was deserving." Then Phoebe looks to me. "She wants and needs space, but she also needs to know you're always there, standing ready. You're doing that, Rowan. You're fixing things for her." She clutches her hands to her chest. "Sigh."

"Dreamy sigh," Addison says.

"Good thing then that farm is falling apart. It means there's no shortage of things to fix."

And I already know I'll be back there in the morning.

⚷

"Did you eat a muffin?" Micah asks before shoving one in his mouth.

"No, I'm working." My hands are covered in grease as I search for why the hell this tractor isn't running. "Which you should be helping."

"She's not my girlfriend."

I put the ratchet down and wipe my forehead. "Well, considering you work for me, you get to do things for my girlfriend. Isn't it a great day to be me? I think so."

"Well, boss, I had to go to Donny's at o' dark thirty and play let's make a deal to get Charlotte's truck done by today."

"And you did good," I note before going back to the damn tractor.

I can fix a lot of shit, but this one has me stumped. There's nothing wrong that I can find. It fires up, runs for about three minutes, and then just dies. I've already replaced the battery and the alternator. Everything else looks to be fine.

"Still nothing?" Micah asks through the food in his mouth.

"Stop eating muffins and get in here. You're better at mechanics than I am."

This morning, when we arrived, there was a basket of muffins, orange juice, cups, plates, and coffee.

Instead of going to her to figure out why the hell we had breakfast waiting, I'm giving her the space she asked for—at least for another hour and then I'm storming the house.

"Looks like a loose plug there." Micah points to the plug I just loosened.

"No shit, asshat. I pulled that out to check behind it."

"Well, that's loose. I helped."

I huff, stand, wipe my hand, and toss the rag to the floor. "Since you're such a pro at getting Donny to do what we want, why don't you go down there, get the truck, and bring him back with you. That way, he can fix the fucking tractor."

"I'll see what I can do, boss." He salutes me and leaves.

I need to find better help.

I stand up, looking at the mess, wondering what part of my brain thought I could fix a tractor and then I know exactly what part, the one that misses Charlotte. The part that wants for her to finally come to me, tell me that she trusts me to help her. Not fix it, but fucking help. I've realized that when you love someone, there is no mountain too high to climb to make them feel loved.

"Hey there, Cowboy." I hear her voice from behind me.

I turn, and I swear, I'm every fucking cliché that has ever lived. She literally takes my breath away.

She's not dressed in anything special, just jeans and a half-untucked T-shirt. She has a baseball hat on with her hair coming out the back opening, and she has a cup of coffee in her hand.

"Is that for me?"

"Maybe."

"Maybe?"

Charlotte shrugs. "It could be. Do you want it?"

"Not at this moment," I say.

She lifts the mug and takes a sip. "Are you sure? It's really good coffee."

I could give two flying fucks about the coffee. I want her. I want her so much I'm having to stay perfectly still so I don't maul her.

"I'm not really interested in the coffee."

"No?" Charlotte asks, all innocence in those green eyes.

"No."

"Shame. I spent about ten minutes preparing the perfect blend.

I took a dark and a medium roast, blended them together, and then added the right balance of cream and sugar." She tsks. "It's sort of perfect."

Her standing here right now is perfect. I don't give a damn about the coffee. I take a step, breaking my control, the need to be even an inch closer to her too great to resist.

"Why are you here?" I ask.

Her long lashes flutter, and then she lowers the mug. "This is my land, at least for another few months, if I'm lucky. I think the question, Cowboy, is why are you here?"

"For you."

I'm not playing games. I'm not going to keep doing this dance with her. I'm here for her, and if she'll let me, I'll always be here for her.

"I knew that."

"Then why did you ask?"

She moves toward me, placing the coffee on the stool as she passes it. "Because I don't trust myself sometimes. I push people away and fight against what I want because I am so fucking tired of being hurt."

The ache in her voice causes my chest to tighten. "I'm not trying to hurt you."

"I know that more than anything else."

She's here for me.

She's here because she finally knows that I fucking love her. We may not have said those words to each other, but words are just that.

I could tell her I love her, or I could tell her I hate her, but in the end, she sees the truth.

I'm here.

Right here.

Right now.

I'm standing in her garage, neglecting my own farm, doing everything humanly possible to be the man, the person, in her life who has put her first.

We both move closer, but I never drop my eyes from hers.

No matter what I think the truth is, I want to hear it from her, that she's done keeping me at an arm's length. That she is ready to open herself up without my having to break the doors down. My voice is low, praying the answer isn't the same as it's been the last few times I've asked.

"Are you ready to let me in and help you?"

thirty-one

CHARLOTTE

I have never been more afraid and also eager to answer a question. I hoped it would come, and I've been ready to tell him how I feel, to give him my heart because he stole it from me weeks ago anyway.

Tears fill my vision, and I close the distance between us, my hand resting on his hard chest. "I need you. So, yes, you're already my whole damn heart. You're the only person I want or need."

His eyes close, and he rests his forehead to mine. "Thank fucking God." I smile through my tears as his arms wrap around me, pulling me to his chest. "I will do anything for you, Charlotte."

"I know. I'm so sorry it took me a few days to believe it. I was just so scared that you'd think I wasn't worth it. I never should have doubted you." I pull back, needing to see him as I say what's in my heart. "I love you, Rowan. I have never loved anyone like I do you and I was terrified. I needed time to sort it out and figure out how I live with having to lose you. I can't. I can't do it."

"I wouldn't let you."

I sniffle a little and then let out a laugh. "You would bully me into getting your way."

"I'd buy your farm. I'd buy all of Sugarloaf if it meant you would stay with me."

"This is crazy, you know that?" I say, shaking my head in disbe-lief. "We didn't even like each other."

He smiles at the echo of words we've used so many times. "I like you now. No, that's a lie. I love you. I love your crazy, ridiculous, maddening ass so much that I took apart a tractor and now have to pay Donny to fix it."

I duck my head, fighting back a laugh. "I wanted to come to you days ago."

"Yeah?"

"When you fixed my fence and then plowed the field. I was going to chase you down and beg you to love me."

Rowan brushes his thumb against my cheek. "You wouldn't have had to beg at all, sweetheart, you pretty much own me."

"That sounds terrifying," I joke.

"It is. You're a fucking mess."

I laugh and then sigh, staring up into his beautiful eyes. "Now what?"

"What do you want, Charlotte?"

That's a loaded question. I want a lot of things, one of them involves a whole lot of naked time. "I don't know how to answer that."

"Honestly," Rowan says before kissing me softly.

I like that. I like how he feels against my lips. I like how he kisses me, touches me, shows up when no one else in my life has. I like it all, and I really never want to know another way of life.

"You."

"You have me."

I lift up on my toes, kissing him this time. "In my bed."

"That will absolutely be happening, but I meant with the farm, love."

I really don't know what I want because nothing has ever felt possible. Faye, again, offered to pay off the debts and I would just re-pay her, but that felt like a really bad idea. She's my best friend in the world, and I don't want to owe her anything. I want to just enjoy the love, laughter, and sisterhood that we've built.

The bank basically laughed at me.

The only thing in the last few days I was able to get some good news on was my truck. Donny said he was able to work on it and he'd have it to me today. He said he found some kind of program through a historical foundation to repair it at no further cost than I've paid already.

Which makes me wonder . . .

"Did you pay for my truck to be fixed?"

Rowan tilts his head. "Yes."

"Rowan . . ."

"Charlotte, don't start when you're finally being nice to me again. Listen, Donny owed me a favor, so I called it in. You needed the damn truck to work so you weren't walking or begging for a damn ride all the tim—"

"I wasn't going to chastise you!" I cut him off before he can go further. "I was going to say thank you."

I mean, at some point I was. I probably would've started off with the complaining. I am who I am.

"Sure you weren't."

"Anyway," I say, not wanting to argue. "Thank you."

"You're welcome." Rowan kisses the tip of my nose. "Now, thoughts on the property. I have some ideas."

That's scary. "Ideas?"

"I told you, I can buy some of the farmland and we can become partners. You'd keep the house, and I'd make sure the land around it is protected. I have another idea that might be a little less terrifying for you."

"Let's go inside and talk about it," I suggest.

Rowan takes my hand in his, grabs the coffee that was on the stool, tosses it back without even tasting it, and then grins at me. "You were right, it was good coffee."

I roll my eyes and then pull him toward the house.

When we get inside, I pour myself a cup, trying to recreate that perfect cup I made for him, and then sit at the table next to him.

"All right, what's your less terrifying idea?"

"You sublet the pasture to me."

"What?" I ask, confused how that would work.

"I'm planning to increase my cattle, which I've already done a little."

"You have?" I ask. It's been a few days and half of the time he's been here fixing things. "What have you increased?"

He shrugs, ignoring the question, and then gets to his feet, moving around the kitchen. "I figured with the need for more land and the ability to work the fields into a better rotation, you could just let me pay you for use of certain parts of the fields. That way, I don't have to buy the land, and you don't lose any. You'll have a steady influx of cash, which should help you get back on your feet."

I'm stunned. Which isn't something I usually feel because I always have a comeback at the ready. But there's nothing in my brain at the moment. "You . . ." I shake my head, hoping for the answer to come out. "But . . . you just . . ."

"Am brilliant, I know. Also, I have a big dick, a fabulous ass, and some people have been known to comment on my shining personality."

"Sure to all that, but, Rowan, that's . . . crazy! You have no assurances that I still won't sell the farm at some point or lose it, even with this influx of cash."

He lifts one shoulder. "If you lose it all, we get married and buy it back."

I nearly choke. "I'm sorry, *what?*" Now I'm out of the chair and feeling like I shouldn't have gotten up because surely the world is tilting.

"I'm hoping it never happens, the loss of the farm part, I mean."

I blink several times. "Okay, but you want to get married?"

"I'm not ruling it out."

Ruling it out? What the actual hell is going on? Rowan Whitlock, the man who hasn't ever dated a woman, went from being the asshole next door who I wanted to beat with his own arms, to my boyfriend, and now he's talking about marriage? I can't.

"We'll get back to that in a minute. I'm going to need rules about this leasing of the land." I focus on that because at least my brain can think rationally about it.

"Like what?"

"Things to protect us both. A contract that spells it out and makes sense."

Rowan leans against the counter, arms crossed. "I'm listening."

"Right. So, for your protection, we need to make sure that if anything happens, you don't get screwed here."

"I'm actually hoping to get screwed."

I ignore that. "As I was saying, what if in the contract it gives you first right of refusal?"

Rowan nods his head first. "That's fair."

"We have clear terms and rotations in it."

"Fine."

Okay, this is going way too easy. "Last one is that if you don't buy the land, then when I sell the house, you get part of the profits to compensate for the loss of the field."

He pushes off the counter. "No."

"No?"

With measured steps, he moves closer. "No, because if you're in trouble, the money isn't enough, or you can't manage, you're going to tell me before it gets bad. You're going to trust me to be your partner in this. You're not going to shoulder all the goddamn burdens on your own anymore, Charlotte."

He stops before me, and I tilt my head back to look up. "I'm not?"

"No."

"Because you'll be here?" I ask, knowing that he's already shown me the truth.

"I'm not going anywhere, sweetheart."

My stomach does a little flip. "Why do you have new cows?" I ask because he sidestepped the question before.

"I'm expanding."

"Okay, *where* did you get the new cows from?"

"You."

I close my eyes, my heart pounding with both love and hate for him. "I should've known."

When I look back up at him, he doesn't seem all that concerned with my take on that. Each cow sold so quickly, it had to be someone local. I didn't ask many questions about who bought them, mostly because at that point, I didn't care, but Sawyer explained to my ranch-helper that the buyer is on a great farm, and he felt it was a good sell.

I just assumed it was someone he was working for.

Stupid me.

"I'm not going to apologize," Rowan says as he brushes his knuckles down my cheek.

"I didn't think you would."

"Do you know why?" he asks.

"Because men don't know how?"

He laughs once. "Funny. No, I won't because you needed me, and I could do it. That's what a relationship is. It's giving and taking. It's being strong when the other person is weak. It's putting the other person's needs above your own, which is why I said I would've walked away from Carson's contract."

I shake my head. "I didn't want that."

"I know, but God, baby, I wanted to give it to you. I wanted to see you smile and be happy."

He makes me happy. My fingers tangle with his. "You did that. Every day you showed up."

"I'll always show up for you, Charlotte." He leans down, pressing his lips ever-so-slightly to mine. "Now, do we have a deal?"

I sigh heavily, still feeling weighted down by all of this. He's giving me so much, and I will forever be grateful. I also can't be stupid and walk away from this.

"We have a deal."

Rowan grins. "Seal it with a kiss?"

Only him. I fight back a smile and lift up on my toes, wrapping my arms around his neck, running my fingers through his thick, brown hair. "I love you."

"I love you. Now kiss me so I can take you to bed and make this deal official."

Our mouths touch, and he clutches me against him. The kiss is sweet, slow, and full of promises and love. His lips part, and I slide my tongue into his mouth, loving the taste of that perfect cup of coffee, only made better mixed with him.

Rowan breaks the kiss, squats down, and lifts me, forcing my legs to wrap around him. "Rowan!"

"Shut up and kiss me again."

I do, holding on to him as he moves us through the kitchen.

"Ouch!" I yell as he knocks me into a wall. When he does it for a second time, I pull my lips from his. "I think you should focus on walking and not giving me a concussion," I suggest.

"Fine."

He moves his head to the side and then climbs the stairs faster than I do on my own, let alone carrying someone.

We enter my bedroom, and he kicks the door shut with his foot before tossing me—yes, tossing me—onto the bed.

He pulls off his shirt, staring at me. "Take off your clothes unless you want me to rip them off."

I pull my hat off, throw it to the side, and then I pull my shirt over my head. "Lose the pants," I tell him.

The two of us get undressed, and then, like two planets colliding, we move to each other. He kisses me like a man crazed. Our hands are grasping for one another, his one hand is holding the back of my head, mine is grabbing his ass. The two of us are messy and amazing and I love it.

His kiss is demanding, and I open to him, letting him kiss me so deeply I feel it in the tips of my toes.

He moves his mouth from mine and down the column of my throat, nipping at the spot where my neck meets my shoulder. I moan as his tongue soothes the spot.

"You're so beautiful," he says, kissing down the slope of my shoulder. "So perfect and so fucking mine."

I am his. I can't even deny it. I love this man in a way I never thought possible, let alone even existed.

"You're mine too," I say, moving my hands up his big arms and to his face. "All mine."

He kisses me again, robbing the breath from my lungs, but at the same time filling me up.

He climbs onto the bed and then hooks his hands under my knees, dropping me onto my back.

"It's been days I've had to go without you," he says, his eyes soft.

"I know, baby."

"Days that I didn't get to kiss you."

"I know, baby."

He rubs his nose against mine. "Days I haven't gotten to touch you, feel your skin against mine, taste you, or feel how good it is when I'm deep inside you."

"You're here now," I remind him.

"I'm going to make love to you now, sweetheart, because after I do, I'm going to fuck you so hard you can't walk without thinking of how big my cock is."

I grin. "Sounds like a plan to me."

Rowan kisses me softly before moving down my body, his tongue makes a swirl around my nipple before he takes it in his mouth, sucking harder. My fingers dig into the back of his head, moaning when he moves to the other breast.

"That's it, baby, let me hear how much you like it," Rowan encourages.

He toys with me before moving down farther, kissing my belly and then pushing my knees apart. He settles between my legs, his eyes finding mine before he brings his tongue to my clit, sliding it up and down.

"Yes," I moan, keeping my eyes on him. "You feel so good."

Again, he makes the same motion. I watch him lick and suck until it becomes too much and my head drops back.

Rowan stops.

"Eyes, baby. I want your eyes. Watch me love you. Watch me make you come."

I work hard to do as he says but the pleasure is too much. I climb higher, fighting so hard to keep my focus on him. My heart is pounding, every muscle in my body starts to tense.

"I can't," I confess. "I can't, God, I can't."

He extends his hand, grabbing mine and squeezing, his tongue still swirling around my aching clit.

My orgasm is coming, it's like a train barreling forward and I can't stop it. It's too fast, too hard, too unwilling to slow.

"Rowan!" I scream his name, my head falling back, my arms giving out as my orgasm crashes through me. Wave after wave until I feel as though I'm drowning under the never-ending pleasure.

When I open my eyes, Rowan is already on top of me, his cock nudging against my entrance.

"Open your legs, love, I want to be inside you."

I want it too. I need him to make me whole again. "Make love to me, Rowan."

He adjusts the angle a little and enters me, inch by inch. The two of us groan at the same time, letting the moment speak for itself.

I can't explain what I'm feeling other than everything. All at once. It's the most beautiful moment I've ever shared with another, and I never want it to end.

Neither of us moves for a breathtaking moment. We just stay, him fully seated inside me with his eyes on mine, but then he moves, and we make love until the two of us collapse.

thirty-two
ROWAN

"Stop fidgeting," I say as we're standing outside of Grady's house.

"If you didn't want me to be nervous, maybe you shouldn't have spent the last hour telling me how funny it was going to be when your siblings harass me."

That's probably true, but would've been a whole lot less fun. "They'll only do it if you appear nervous."

She rips her hand out of mine. "Well, I am nervous, asshole."

"You know my siblings."

Charlotte huffs. "Yes, but not as someone who isn't dreaming of ways to make you cry. They don't know this . . . Charlotte."

I lean in and kiss her just to irritate her. "I like this Charlotte."

"Well, I don't like you."

"So, just like old times," I say with a grin.

The door opens after the second knock, and Grady looks frantic as he's got one of his kids upside down in his arms and the other on his back. "Untle Rowan!" Elodie yells from where she's dangling with her hair brushing the floor.

"Elodie, you're upside down."

"I know!" She giggles.

Grady swings her back and forth. "A little help?"

Not likely. "Good luck." I slap his chest, take Charlotte's hand, and pull her inside.

"Hi, Grady!" she calls and I keep tugging her away.

"Thanks, jackass!"

"That's a bad word, Daddy!" Jett chides and I laugh knowing he's about to get scolded from his kids.

We walk into the kitchen to find Addison is cooking, Phoebe is making something at the island, and Asher is holding Sienna.

Before I can look for Olivia, the wind is knocked out of me as she barrels into me, giving me a bear hug.

Charlotte giggles and I extricate myself from her. Signing and speaking at the same time. "You almost crushed the family jewels, kid."

Her eyes narrow. *"Family jewels?"*

Asher sighs dramatically. "Great, now you're going to have to explain your balls to my kid."

I smile at her. *"Ask your dad about it, he'll tell you. Olivia, you remember Charlotte?"*

Charlotte waves.

Olivia looks at Charlotte, then me, and lifts her hands. *"Please translate."*

"Sure, I'll translate."

Her eyes narrow. *"Correctly."*

"Of course." I sign and then clear my throat.

Olivia moves her hands, and I actually do say what she's saying. *"I'm so glad you're here, and thank you for seeing that Uncle Rowan isn't always stupid."*

Everyone in the kitchen laughs, and I tap my niece's nose. *"Hey now."*

"I said always."

That she did. *"What else do you want to say?"*

Again I repeat what she signs. *"I hope you'll come fishing with us. We have a lot of fun."*

Charlotte smiles wide. "I love fishing."

Olivia looks to Phoebe and signs. *"See, girls like fishing too."*

Phoebe signs back. *"Not this girl."*

Asher looks up at his fiancée. "One day, love. One day, you'll come over to the dark side."

"Not likely."

Elodie and Jett run in, grabbing Olivia's hands and pulling her into the living room. Grady enters, mumbling something about kids and calling the doctor to inquire about a vasectomy.

His fiancée scoffs and then comes around the kitchen island, standing in front of Charlotte. "I'm so glad you're here. Thank you for coming to our madhouse of a dinner. Normally we have this weekly dinner at Brynn's house, but she's in California for a meeting, so I drew the short straw. Which means toys galore and children randomly yelling."

"I love it, and I'm just happy you guys invited me."

Phoebe speaks this time. "You're always invited. Truth be told, we like you more than Rowan anyway."

I roll my eyes. "Please, we all know you wanted me and had to settle for Asher."

"Yes, that's it."

I wrap my arm around Charlotte's shoulder. "I'm sorry, Phoebs, I'm taken."

She clutches her hands to her chest. "What ever shall I do? How do I go on in this world?" Then she grabs Asher's arms. "You'll save me, won't you?"

My brother, who's forever the stick in the mud, huffs. "I can't with you people."

"There's always one party pooper, and it seems you're it, big brother."

Asher stands, kisses Phoebe's temple, and flips us off. "I'll take the baby and go hang out with the cool people in this house—the kids."

Addison claps her hands. "That's the idea, all you boys go, leave us to get the food done without you distracting us." She shoos us. "Go, take care of the kids."

I slap Charlotte's ass and then give her a kiss. "Behave and don't tell them anything. They're the worst gossips."

"Please, we're angels," Phoebe lies.

I love Addy and Phoebe, don't get me wrong, but with the help of my sister, Brynn, they're lethal. Good thing they love me, so hopefully their talk will be encouraging Charlotte to continue to see my amazing qualities and not run for the hills.

Grady and I follow Asher, settling on the couch, and Asher puts the football game on.

"Seems she caved." Grady says as Elodie climbs on his lap.

"She saw the error of her ways."

Asher snorts. "More like she realized she loves you more than she hates the idea of accepting your help."

"Either reason is fine with me. She and I are in a good place."

Grady nods once. "Good. I like Charlotte. She challenges you, and God knows you need someone who can put up with your shit."

She does more than that. Charlotte is the first woman who has ever made me want more. To think about a future like my brothers have. I didn't get it before, Asher going from this eternal bachelor, even as a single dad, to being so deeply in love with Phoebe he'd give everything up.

It made no sense and I really saw him as weak.

I turn to him. "Phoebe made you see life differently?"

As though he understands where my mind is, he smiles. "She made me see life at all."

"Olivia didn't?"

He looks to his eldest daughter. "Olivia taught me what it was like to love someone so much you'd give your life for them. She brought me true happiness in a way I didn't know before I was a father, but there was a hole. A part of me that wasn't really living. Sure, I had Liv and I had my job, but . . . it's not the same. When Phoebe came into my world, it was like someone turned on every light in the house. I could see before, but it wasn't bright."

"I get it," I tell him. "I always thought that Mom was so stupid for the shit she did. Like, if I loved anyone the way she did, I'd be fucked in the head."

Grady laughs once. "You are fucked in the head, but Mom wasn't that way because she fell in love. It was because of who she fell in love with. She was searching for a love that wasn't healthy or real."

I'm not really sure what that means, but considering neither of my brothers or Brynlee have tried to dissuade me from dating Charlotte, they don't see any red flags.

"I was always so afraid of being like her. To fall for someone, fuck my life up, and be left with nothing," I admit.

Asher leans back. "We all have the same fears, Row. Each one of us dealt with some crazy shit as kids. Mom getting hit, Brynn with her father, not to mention the shit that happened later on. It's why Brynn won't date either. It kills me to see her so afraid when she has more love to give than the three of us combined."

I hate it too. My sister deserves to be worshiped by someone. To see how fucking special she is, because we all do.

"One day, she'll get there," I say, willing it to be true.

"She will in her own time, just like the three of us did. It just takes the right person to come along and make you rethink everything."

I hear Charlotte laugh in the kitchen, and I settle back, thanking God we got stuck in the woods together.

***

"You look beautiful," I tell Charlotte as she exits the house as we go on our first public date.

She's wearing a black skirt and a one-shoulder sweater. Her dark brown hair falls in waves down her back, and I love that she doesn't need to wear makeup. She's just beautiful without trying.

"Thank you."

Charlotte gives me a quick kiss, and then I extend my hand, guiding her to the truck. Like the gentleman I am, I help her up, which allows me to put my hand on her ass before closing the door and going around to my side.

She pulls at her skirt, shifting against the leather seats. "I hate your truck."

I shrug. "I love it."

"I know. You get to pretend you weren't copping a feel when you oh-so-gallantly put me in the passenger seat."

"Perks of my life, sweetheart."

She rolls her eyes. "You're lucky I love you."

"You're lucky I love you, but sure, I'm lucky too."

Charlotte ignores me, fixing her hair in the mirror. "Where are we going?"

"On a date."

Her gaze cuts to me. "Clearly."

"You asked," I tease.

Tonight we're going on a real date. A date where we will officially show the town of Sugarloaf that we do, in fact, like each other. We keep the fighting for the bedroom.

Charlotte wanted to sort of show up at the diner for lunch and let it happen. I thought we needed a little more. So, while my beautiful girlfriend thinks we're going to dinner at Sugarlips Diner, she's actually about to get a rather different surprise.

Which I'll pay for later.

We pull in and she sighs heavily. "What the hell is going on in the diner? This place is packed!"

"It's a Friday night."

She ducks her head, trying to get a better angle at the crowd inside. "Yeah, but it's never like *this*."

"I don't see that many more people than usual."

Charlotte jerks her head back. "What? It's like every damn citizen of the town."

She's not incorrect. "I figured it's better to get it over with in one fell swoop. You can thank me later."

"I'm going to kill you."

"I expect nothing less."

She opens the truck door, not waiting for me to help her down, and jumps from the running board. I wince as she slams the door, wondering if she didn't break the damn hinges, and rush around to catch her as she's making her way toward the road.

My arm wraps around her waist. "Oh, no you don't."

"Put me down."

"You're being ridiculous."

"Me?" she yells and then squirms out of my grasp before turning to face me. "I told you I wanted to do this slow."

"Give me one reason. Why?"

"Because!"

That's really a great answer. "Listen, I don't see why the hell it matters if we tell everyone today or in small batches. The whole town has probably already figured it out since my truck is parked at your house or yours is at mine every night. Not to mention my brothers, their women, and my sister know, and none of them are known for keeping secrets. Your sister knows, and if she has a single friend in this town, you know she's bitched about it. And . . ." I pause for dramatic effect. "Faye knows. Therefore, everyone knows because Joey knows."

Charlotte lets out a long sigh, seeming to take my very well-thought-out speech to heart. "I don't care." She starts walking.

"You're a stubborn pain in my ass."

She stops, turning to face me with her eyes narrowed. "I'm a stubborn pain? You have some balls, buddy."

"I'm still waiting for your answer about why we should've done this slowly."

"I don't have one," Charlotte admits.

I laugh under my breath. "So, you just dug in because . . .?"

"Because I like to win."

I move to her and rest my hands on her hips. "I think you've won already."

"How so?"

"You won me."

"I want a refund."

I smile. "I already told you there aren't any."

"Then an exchange," Charlotte says back, the anger leaving her eyes.

"Nope."

She sighs. "So I have to keep you?"

"You do."

I tug her so her chest is to mine. "Fine. If I must."

"Kiss me."

Charlotte, unable to ever resist biting back where she can, turns her head. "No."

God, I love this woman. I love that she makes me crazy at the same time she makes me smile. I spent so much time hating her, thinking how ridiculous she was, and now I wish I could go back in time.

She's not ridiculous, she's beautiful, funny, sweet, loyal, and mine.

I lean in and kiss her cheek. "Kiss me," I say again.

Her cheek tips up as she attempts to hide her smile. "You don't deserve my kisses."

"Fine. Marry me," I say, surprising us both.

Charlotte's eyes go wide. "Excuse me? Did you just tell me to marry you?"

"I did."

"Please tell me you're kidding. You're kidding, right?"

I could lie and say I was doing it just to get her to flinch and kiss me, but after I say it, I realize I'm really not kidding. I love Charlotte. I want to be with her and be her partner in everything. Since I've never been into the dating life, this really isn't such a huge stretch for me to want to marry the first woman I've loved and wanted a life with.

"I'm not kidding."

"Rowan, stop. We can't get engaged!"

"Why?"

Charlotte sputters. "Because. We can't! We're like a whole four days old."

"We've been together for months if you want to get technical."

She tries to take a step back, but I don't let her go. "Okay, sure, but I'm not . . . I can't answer this now."

"Is it a no?" I ask.

"No."

"No to which part?"

"No, it's not a no. It's a . . . you're a crazy person and we need to take a second here. I love you. I want to be with you. I need to think before we get engaged on the street outside of the diner."

"You want more romance, got it."

Her shoulders shake with laughter before she turns to face me, her arms moving to my shoulders. "I'm never going to be bored with you, am I?"

"Nope."

"You know, I have to admit something," Charlotte says, her hands brushing the hair at the back of my neck.

"What's that?"

"I lied."

Now this is interesting. "About what?"

"Not wanting to kiss you." Charlotte moves closer, giving me a sweet kiss. "I hate that I always want to kiss you."

That's one thing I do not hate. "I like that you can't resist me."

"Yeah, it works in your favor since you like kissing me too."

"I do. Now, how about we go inside and give the town something to talk about? Unless you want to add on our engagement."

This time when she presses her lips to mine, it's not soft or sweet—it's hot and heavy. She slides her tongue against mine, moaning into my mouth.

Very quickly, the kiss gets away from me, and I'm clutching her hips, pulling them against my aching cock. I'm hard, and I no longer want to go in the fucking diner. I want to take her in my truck, let her ride me, fog up every window, and make her scream.

Right when I pull back to say we should do exactly that, she pats my chest. "I'm ready to go now. Come on, lover boy."

I stand here, my jaw slack, as Charlotte walks into the diner without turning back.

thirty-three
CHARLOTTE

"And what does your sister think, darling?" Mrs. Cooke asks as she and her posse of old biddies sit in rapt attention.

"Aurora . . . well, you can imagine."

My sister hasn't spoken to me in two weeks. I called her after Rowan proposed a way to save the farm, and rather than being happy that I found a way to save our mother's farm, she ranted about how stupid I was to trust him.

Needless to say, Aurora and I won't be speaking until she grows up and stops this bullshit. She admitted that Rowan never cheated on her, and yet, she's still being a bitch.

"Always a hothead, that girl," Mrs. Symonds says with a nod. "I used to tell your gran that she needed to get that girl's expectations under control, but you can't stop the rain from falling once it starts."

Mrs. Cooke rolls her eyes. "You can't stop it even before then, you ninny."

"You know what I meant, you old hag," she tosses back at her.

These two are like bickering siblings most days. "Well," I jump in. "I hope one day Aurora can just be happy for me, but if not, then that's her choice."

I used to feel like the two years of her being away couldn't hurt more than anything else. I see how wrong I was. This hurts so much more.

"She'll come around, honey." Mrs. Symonds pats my hand. "Sometimes, we just need to give people time to see their decisions are wrong."

"She would know," Mrs. Cooke says while jabbing her with her elbow. "Lord knows she makes a lot of them."

I laugh softly, and then I feel a hand wrap around my arm. "Here you are." I turn to see Brynlee.

"Hey."

"Sorry, ladies, I need to grab Charlotte and bring her back to Rowan. He is too afraid to come over here and be cornered by you."

You'd think that would upset them, but instead, they seem proud. "Smart boy," Mrs. Cooke says.

We walk away to where Faye is literally bouncing up and down. "Oh my God. Oh my God. I can't."

"Can't what?"

I'm starting to worry. Is she excited? Nervous? Upset? I just can't tell and she's not using her words.

Brynn takes Faye's hands in hers. "Easy, Faye."

She shakes her head. "Right. Okay. So." She inhales deeply, and then on her exhale, she rambles whatever has her so keyed up. "I used that balm thing you gave me with the cute little sprig on it. I got this stupid pimple on my chin, and well, I can't have a pimple when I need to do a sponsored ad for that big makeup deal I just got. So, I was like, hey, Charlotte gave me that weird nature shit and said it worked. I opened it, put it on, and went to bed. When I woke up, it was, like, gone. The zit was flat and gone. I swear, it was insane."

I nod slowly. "Okay . . ."

"I posted this." She shoves her phone into my hand with Instagram already open, and there is a video of her basically saying everything she just said to me. She talks about its magical properties and then she shows a bruise on her leg before she rubs the salve over it, promising to report back. On and on Faye talks about how great it smells and how they need this product for breakouts.

I blink when I see the number of views. "Faye?" My voice is shaking as badly as my hands are.

"Where is this you're sending them to?"

She grins. "As your bestie, before I posted this, I made you an Instagram account, and a website for your new business, it was meant to be a surprise."

"You have?" I ask, feeling stunned. "Why would you do this?"

"You told me you love this, Charlotte. You love making these, don't you?"

I do. I talked to her about it a few days ago, actually. I told her how I've been making them more and was going to do a few craft shows next week. Rowan made space for me in the barn the other day to stack my boxes. He bought me a special double boiler too so I can do things a little faster.

It's fun. I'm enjoying the simplicity of it, and I think each batch is a little better as I keep tweaking.

"Yes, but . . ."

"Well, you mentioned a name, I thought the least we could do was get a cute logo after you joked about it."

"A name? I was tossing weird ones out because you told me to!"

She grins. "Yes, well, I liked one."

I look back at the screen, reading the name aloud. "Rosemary and Vine Apothecary."

Brynn nudges me. "Okay, that is a really cute name."

It is. I love it.

"After I had the name made and the website went up, it sort of spiraled," Faye explains. "You know how I am. I get a little excited and, again, I wanted to do this for your birthday. We all love and support you, Char. Rowan and I thought you'd be happy."

Rowan knew? I feel a mix of things, and I'm trying to focus on the good ones. I'm scared because I'm not exactly tech savvy and don't know much about selling goods like this. I'm also touched beyond belief that they did this and have so much faith in something I really didn't think would be anything other than a fun hobby.

"I am happy!" I say, feeling like I can smile after the shock and fear have run out a little. "I'm so overwhelmed, Faye. You guys . . . I mean, I didn't really plan anything."

"Well, plan all the things!" Faye says, pulling me in for a hug. "Listen, I'm going to get a little ahead of myself because I am who I am. I was talking to Brynn earlier and Mrs. Cooke owns that little store over on Main Street, which would be kind of the perfect place to open a store. I'm just saying . . ."

Yeah, I'm not even going there right now. Not a chance. "Can we take a second to let me even absorb part one of this?"

Brynn laughs. "I'm sure I can negotiate a great rate if you decide you want it. Just know that."

"Okay."

Rowan comes over, a smile on his lips as he walks right to me, ignoring his sister and my best friend, pulling me to him. "Hi."

"Hi."

"Did Faye tell you how famous you are?"

I laugh a little. "She did. How long have you known this?"

"About five minutes longer than you. I knew the other stuff but not that she went viral," he admits.

I exhale, my hands resting on his solid chest. "I'm a bit over-whelmed."

Not to mention I'm still reeling from his insane proposal that I don't even think he was serious about anyway.

"I'll overwhelm you later."

I snort laugh and then turn to Faye. "So, you have over two million views, what does that mean?"

"It means"—Faye hooks her arm in mine, pulling me away from Rowan—"you have many orders and are going to need to get to work. Because you, my friend, are about to have a very good start on your new business."

"How many more orders came in, love?" Rowan asks as I'm canning the newest batch.

When Faye said a good start, she wasn't even close. It's an unbelievable start. A start I can't even process because we have nowhere near enough product to fulfill orders.

"I can't look," I admit while trying not to spill a drop of this liquid gold.

He walks over, kisses my temple. "I'm proud of you, baby."

I smile. "Thank you."

Rowan not only believes in me but also he's gone above and beyond. He bought another double boiler for me so I can have two batches going, had Brynlee set me up with all the business paperwork I needed so I can ... do taxes. However, the best thing he does is come over every night, after working all day, to help me tie little ribbons with sprigs of pine.

It's ... my whole fucking heart.

He shows up.

He is always here. He hasn't failed me once.

Rowan hasn't had to tell me all the things he wants to do for me, he just does them. For the first time in my life, I feel like I can actually rely on someone, no matter what.

It's fucking terrifying.

"Are you still working on adding new products?" Rowan asks as he heaves over the one hundred and twenty orders we were able to fill today.

"I spent about an hour on the eye cream, but I don't love it. Faye thinks I should try to work on something that will be more marketable like a wrinkle something. As though I have a fucking clue what to do with that."

He sits beside me, tossing his legs up on the table. "You used a lot of weird shit when we were in the woods. Maybe one of those will work."

"Maybe. I thought about the ash remedies we used. I don't know, all of this feels so crazy, you know?"

His deep chuckle rumbles in the space. "Sweetheart, the fact that you're melting pine sap and beeswax is a little off, but whatever other shit you're adding is working. So, if you want to use ash, go for it, I'm sure it'll make a lovely lipstick or some crap."

"There's an idea!"

Rowan helps me set up the next batch since we have over four thousand orders to fill. That in and of itself is absolutely mind blowing. Since it went viral, I've learned a lot about pricing and value as well. We've upped the price of the salve, and there hasn't even been a tiny slow down. Faye has also taken a bunch of product and distributed it to other influencers. It's been . . . amazing.

"I think I need to hire someone to help," I say to Rowan as we sit at the table that's now housing all the business supplies.

"I told you that a few weeks ago."

"Yeah, I guess I just couldn't wrap my mind around it."

"Well, hire someone, get this thing going."

I nod. "I have another idea." This has been floating around my head the last few days, and the more I think about it, the more I feel like it's the right decision.

"What's that?"

Letting out a long, deep sigh, I straighten myself and lay it out. "I think we should merge the farms."

That seems to stun him. "You do?"

"I hate the dairy farm part. The cows, the chores, the never-ending issues, all of it. I love this farm. This place is where I grew up, where my home is, and that's what I was fighting to save, but you, you're good at the dairy part of it all. You've built a thriving farm, got that contract, already bought a bunch of my cows, and need more land. We can become partners, the way you originally wanted to do it, and we can live here, if that's okay with you since you live in a tiny ass cabin."

Rowan studies me, his eyes not moving from mine. "Partners?"

"Yeah, we'll merge. That way, you'll get my certification for the organic label and can take over the business part of it, and I can do this or . . . I don't know, but we'll be a team."

The light in his eyes brightens a bit. "We are a team, and if you're sure, I think it's by far the best idea. It gives us both what we want."

I grin, feeling light. "I can't believe this is all happening. Like one day I'm a failing dairy farmer and now I'm a thriving business-woman who wasn't meant to be a businesswoman. I'm in love with an amazing man, and now we're going to live together. It's . . . kind of perfect. Other than the fact that I basically lost everything and can't seem to keep a business afloat."

"You don't see yourself, do you?"

I stay quiet, not really sure how to answer that.

Rowan leans forward, resting his elbows on his knees. "You're so smart. So damn capable. You kept this farm afloat when you had everything trying to beat you back. You don't ever back down from a fight. You're resourceful, unwilling to bend to anyone's whim. No matter what obstacle comes at you, you're able to pivot. How can you not see just how fucking amazing you are? This business you started is going to be more than you dreamed of simply because you're behind it and I'm right beside you, love."

My heart pounds, and I feel more love in my body than I've ever felt before. "Marry me," I say, knowing that I want him here for the rest of my life. I want him with me.

"What?"

"Marry me. I love you. I want you to be my husband, my part-ner, my heart and soul."

He smiles, sinking down in front of me. "Marry me, Charlotte."

"You know you stole my line?"

He reaches forward, cupping my face in his hands. "It's only fair since you stole my heart." Then, he releases me, reaches into his jeans, and pulls out a ring.

My heart drops, and I stare at him. "What? Where? How?"

"I bought this ring the day of your birthday. I knew that day there was no other woman in the world for me. I may have asked you the other day in the most unromantic way, but it's only because I didn't want to go another day without you knowing how I feel. I want you to be beside me when I wake up, be in my arms when we fall asleep, and next to me so you can drive me absolutely crazy when you're awake. So, this is me, on my knees before you, in the way I should've asked before. Marry me, Charlotte."

My lips touch his and I breathe this beautiful man in. "Yes. I'll marry you."

He grabs the back of my head, holding me to him. "I'm going to make you question your life choices every day."

I laugh. "Promises, promises."

"I promise that I will love you until the day I die."

I kiss him again. "That's a promise I can live with."

epilogue
ROWAN

"What time will Brynn be here?" I ask, as I'm scrubbing the sweat and dirt smell off me. Today was a fucktastic day. If there was one thing wrong, there were a hundred.

And on all of the days that I could have things go wrong, today wasn't one of them. So, I spent hours fixing a machine that broke. I had to reinforce the fence that ten cows found a way through, which was fun, and listen to Charlotte bitch about my shit still being in boxes.

As though I have time to unpack.

"Probably twenty minutes."

"Can you grab me a pair of jeans and a shirt that don't look like I rolled in manure?" I ask, rinsing my hair.

Instead of my beautiful fiancée doing that, she opens the shower curtain and climbs in—naked.

"Sure," she responds and starts to exit, but I grab her wrist.

"I like this better."

"Do you?"

"I most certainly do." I pull her to me, her tits pressed against my chest.

"We don't have time," Charlotte says, but I see her eyes think otherwise.

"Then why would you get in my shower, sweetheart?"

She shrugs a little. "I need to rinse off."

"How about I wash you?"

Charlotte grins. "You have exactly five minutes."

"I can do a lot in five minutes," I reply.

"Maybe less."

"I only need two minutes if I'm efficient," I say, pushing her back against the tile wall.

She laughs a little, and then the laughter fades when my thumb grazes her clit. "Efficiency is what I like most about you."

I bet it is. I kiss where her neck meets her shoulder, biting playfully there, then kiss down her body. Once I'm on my knees, I hook one leg over my shoulder, exposing her to me. "I'm going to make you like a whole lot more than that."

I lick at her, not teasing, not even giving her a second to breathe. My goal is to make her come quick and hard so that I can fuck her the same way. The two of us are competitive in every way and I have no doubts she's going to make me work for every ounce of pleasure. I use my hand to keep her open to me, moving my tongue in quick circles and varying the pressure.

Charlotte moans, her hips rolling, so I suck harder.

She's getting closer, I feel the way her body undulates, as though she has no control. I push harder, then move my hand so one finger is near her ass and my thumb can push inside her cunt.

"Rowan," she pants as I start to play with both holes, not knowing how far she'll let me push this, but time is of the essence, so I use all my tricks.

She doesn't shove me away or protest, so I enter her in both places, all the while fucking her with my tongue. Charlotte's hands move to my hair, holding me there as her body trembles. I move my thumb inside her, then my finger in her ass, alternating them while my tongue laps at her. Without warning, she screams, and as her body starts to sink down, I move to catch her.

"Good girl, now face the wall, hands there." I arrange her while she's still panting and unable to speak. "Stay there," I command.

She turns her head, her dark, wet hair moving around her, and I adjust her hips, driving in without preamble.

"Fuck!" she screams.

"God, you're so tight!" I say at the same time.

Then I fuck her. My hips shift, pushing in and out, and the sound of wet skin hitting wet skin echoes in the small bathroom.

I use my one hand, grabbing her hair and pulling her head back as I dominate her. "That's it, baby, you like when I fuck you hard."

She whimpers. "Yes."

"You like when I take control?" I ask, feeling feral as I slam into her.

"Yes!"

"Do you want me to fuck this pussy hard so you feel it all day?"

"Please," Charlotte groans.

I slap her ass hard and jerk my hips. The way she tightens around me is too much. I move my hand to cover hers, the diamond ring rests against my palm. "Mine," I say.

"Yours."

"Mine!" I say louder, needing her to hear it. I know it's caveman, but God, she brings it out of me. And, even though I'm claiming her, she's claimed every part of me right back.

That thought sends me over the edge, and I pump my hips faster, my orgasm coming at a speed that can't be slowed.

Two more deep thrusts, and I yell her name as I come so hard my knees buckle. I crumple against her back, her body being the only thing holding me.

It takes me a moment before I can get control of myself and stand, pulling out of her and then turning her to kiss her tenderly.

Charlotte's arms wrap around me, the two of us shaken by the intense sex. She pulls back a little to look at me. "You did pretty good for two minutes."

I smile, kissing her nose. "You bring out the best in me."

"Well, at least someone does because, before me, you were pretty pathetic."

"Says you."

"And the town, babe."

I roll my eyes. "You're worth changing for, then."

Charlotte kisses me. "We better hurry up before your sister finds us like this."

I shudder. That's one way to kill the mood. "Go get ready and please pick out my outfit so I don't have to hear your shit about what I'm wearing."

Seriously, what is it with women and griping about what I wear? Jeans and a T-shirt are appropriate for every occasion. Or, at least, they were before I fell in love with Charlotte. Now I'm dressing up to go to dinner? I'm a damn farmer. A cowboy. A rough-and-tumble dude. I don't need slacks.

"Sure thing." She gets out of the shower, and I finish two minutes later.

When I enter our bedroom, I nearly kick the box on the ground that wasn't there when I went in. It's a subtle jab to get that box put away, most likely. She's laid out clothes on the bed for me. Sure enough, it's dress pants and a button-up. I'm going to look ridiculous wearing this.

However, it's our wedding rehearsal and they've all informed me that I need to dress for the occasion. Never mind tomorrow I'll be in a damn tux.

Whatever. It's not worth the fight. Especially not after the shower we just had.

Charlotte yells from downstairs. "Brynn is here!"

Of course she is. "I'll be down in a minute!"

I head downstairs after I'm dressed, prepared for both women in the house to chastise me because I'm wearing jeans and not the damn pants Charlotte picked out.

When I get to the kitchen, my fiancée looks up at me and rolls her eyes. "I should've known."

"I'm comfortable being the rancher." I look to my sister, who is dressed up. "Besides, Brynn looks like she's about to try out for a movie. Didn't know we were going so dressy."

"I'm not dressy, I look like someone who cares."

I grin. "I care about after the wedding."

She nearly gags. "Gross. You guys ready to go?"

"Yup."

We head over to Addison's house, where the barn we're using is. It's been completely cleaned out, thanks to my brothers and I. Addison has never used it for farming, which made it the perfect location. Grady and I laid a wooden floor, Asher worked on hanging lights up top, and Olivia supervised, letting us know when something wasn't clean enough.

She's really lucky I love her so much.

When we get inside, I hear Charlotte gasp. Since the last time I was here, it seems the girls got to work. They put tons of drapes or gauze-type stuff all around, and it went from being a decent looking barn, to somewhere someone would actually want to get married.

"This is stunning," Charlotte says, moving deeper in.

"You're happy?" I ask, never really knowing with this woman.

"I love it. The floor is amazing, you guys did so good."

I preen. Damn right I did. "For you, baby, there's nothing I wouldn't lay for you."

She laughs. "Half romantic, half dirty."

"Me in a nutshell."

Charlotte moves toward me, placing her hands on my chest. "And all mine."

"Not yet," I say, stepping back. "I still have time to change my mind. You might want to consider that."

"Right. It's you I'm worried about?" she scoffs.

"Oh my god, you two, can you stop for two minutes?" Brynn asks with exasperation. "We have to get through the ceremony and practice the changing of the room again. Can we proceed?"

I glare at my rather annoying sister. "Fine."

She rolls her eyes, turns to Olivia, signs something that I can't catch and then my niece walks over.

"What did your aunt say?" I ask aloud and sign.

"She said it is my job to watch you."

I laugh once. "And she sent you?"

"I am not afraid of you."

No, she's not. In fact, it's usually the other way around. I look over Olivia's head to see Brynn who grins.

"Do all the women in my life have to manage me?"

Olivia shrugs and Charlotte nods. "Pretty much. You're kind of a mess."

"All right everyone," Addison says loudly. "We're going to run through the ceremony once and then we're going to work—as a team—to get the barn from wedding to reception in under thirty minutes. Okay?"

Everyone mutters various replies and we take our places.

I stand at the front of the aisle, hands clasped in front of me as our faux ceremony begins. My brothers are beside me as one by one, the girls make their way down. First is my sister, who smiles at me as she passes to the left, then Phoebe and last is Faye.

The barn doors open wide and Charlotte is there.

She's wearing a short white dress, holding a handful of fake flowers as she walks towards me. While it's not our actual ceremony, the joy that fills me is beyond words.

I love this woman.

I have never felt such a longing for another person in my entire life.

She's the reason I breathe and why seasons change. She's why I have hope for the future and can let go of the past.

Charlotte is what gives my life meaning and I feel so goddamn lucky that we are where we are today.

She reaches me, smiles at me softly and since it's not our wedding day and I can do this, I take her face in my hands. "I love you, Charlotte Sullivan," I say before I kiss her with all the love inside of me.

Which takes a while, because I have a lot of it for her.

Do you love the Whitlock Family?

Read the series
Forbidden Hearts (Age Gap/Single Dad)
Broken Dreams (Fake Dating/Single Parents)
Preorder: Forgotten Desires (Marriage of Convenience/Single Dad)

I wasn't ready to let Rowan and Charlotte go just yet. Swipe to the next page for access to an EXCLUSIVE Bonus Scene!

Dear Reader,

I hope you enjoyed Tempting Promises! I had a hard time saying goodbye to Rowan & Charlotte. I wanted to give just a little more of a glimpse into their lives, so ... I wrote a super fun scene.

Since giving you a link would be a pain in the ... you know what ... I have an easy QR code you can scan, sign up, and you'll get and email giving you access! Or you can always type in the URL!

https://geni.us/TP_Signup

If you'd like to just keep up with my sales and new releases, you can follow me on BookBub or sign up for text alerts!
BookBub: https://www.bookbub.com/authors/corinne-michaels

Join my Facebook group!
https://www.facebook.com/groups/corinnemichaelsbooks

books by corinne michaels

Want a downloadable reading order?

https://geni.us/CM_ReadingGuide

The Salvation Series

Beloved

Beholden

Consolation

Conviction

Defenseless

Evermore: A 1001 Dark Night Novella

Indefinite

Infinite

The Hennington Brothers

Say You'll Stay

Say You Want Me

Say I'm Yours

Say You Won't Let Go: A Return to Me/Masters and Mercenaries Novella

Second Time Around Series

We Own Tonight

One Last Time

Not Until You

If I Only Knew

The Arrowood Brothers

Come Back for Me

Fight for Me

The One for Me

Stay for Me

Destined for Me: An Arrowood/Hennington Brothers Crossover Novella

Willow Creek Valley Series

Return to Us

Could Have Been Us

A Moment for Us

A Chance for Us

Rose Canyon Series

Help Me Remember

Give Me Love

Keep This Promise

Whitlock Family Series

Forbidden Hearts

Broken Dreams

Tempting Promises

Forgotten Desires

Co-Written with Melanie Harlow

Hold You Close

Imperfect Match

Standalone Novels

You Loved Me Once

acknowledgments

My husband and children. I love you all so much. Your love and support is why I get to even have an acknowledgment section.

My assistant, Christy Peckham, you always have my back and I can't imagine working with anyone else. I love your face.

Melanie Harlow, you have no idea how much I cherish our friendship. You are truly one of my best friends in the world and I don't know what I would do without you.

My publicist, Nina Grinstead, you're stuck with me forever at this point. You are more than a publicist, you're a friend, a cheer-leader, a shoulder to lean on, and so much more.

The entire team at Valentine PR who support me, rally behind me, and keep me smiling.

Nancy Smay, my editor for taking such great care with my story. My cover designer who deals with my craziness, Sommer Stein. My proofreaders: Julia, and Michele.

Samaiya, thank you for drawing that lock so perfectly!

Every influencer who picked this book up, made a post, video, phoned a friend ... whatever it was. Thank you for making the book world a better place.

about the author

Corinne Michaels is a *New York Times, USA Today, and Wall Street Journal* bestselling author of romance novels. Her stories are chock full of emotion, humor, and unrelenting love, and she enjoys putting her characters through intense heartbreak before finding a way to heal them through their struggles.

Corinne is a former Navy wife and happily married to the man of her dreams. She began her writing career after spending months away from her husband while he was deployed—reading and writing were her escape from the loneliness. Corinne now lives in Virginia with her husband and is the emotional, witty, sarcastic, and fun-loving mom of two beautiful children.